Replete

D. T. Hopmann

A SellSharp Book

ISBN-13: 978-1466470507

ISBN-10: 146647050X

Wealth is a camel.

Ethics is the needle's eye.

1

A Wanted Man

He had been a friend of mine back in school. Well, not a friend so much as a classmate. Borgie, as we called him, was a true genius, the one other PhD candidate I honestly felt was smarter than I was. We were both pursuing the new and amorphous field of emergent systems, and, although we shared and debated countless thoughts and theories, our competition for recognition and accomplishment had prevented deeper social bonding. But that was years ago.

Now he was dead.

I had gone into the office to get in a half-morning of work before leaving for a major presentation the Institute was giving that afternoon, and I was sitting in on a project review when Nicki tapped the window of the conference room door. I was actually glad to be interrupted. The project being reviewed was going well with only minor issues to discuss, but damned if we weren't going to discuss them for the full allotted 90 minutes anyway. Grabbing my notebook and coffee mug—I had no intention of returning—I slipped out quietly and faced my nearly too efficient administrator in the hallway.

"Did I take you from something important?" she asked. Her eyes signaled she had something serious to tell me.

"No, not at all. They're following the universal gas law in there–expanding the meeting to fill the time available."

"I'm afraid I just received some news. The gentleman you asked me to get on the phone, Mr. Borgman? His office informs me he died last evening."

"Oh no! What happened?"

"They had no details, Roger. They could only say he died sometime after work yesterday."

Life was full of coincidences, I supposed, but this one did make an impression. Only that morning Nicki had given me an unopened envelope that had arrived by mail with the word "personal" in hand-printed block letters on both sides, and no return address. When I opened it all I found was a business card, one that frankly looked as if it had been produced on a home computer. On the front was a large, square, busy-looking logo and Borgie's name. No contact information, just the name. On the back were two handwritten words: "You're it." It was the first contact we had had in years, and, naturally, had prompted my attempt to reach him.

"I'm sorry to hear it; Borgie was a gifted man. See if you can get any details, and find where to send a card and flowers, would you?"

"Of course," she replied, then she turned about sharply and quick-stepped back to our office, arms clutching her notebook with a grip as tight as the bun in her hair.

No, I thought, he and I hadn't been close friends, but ours was a small community and the loss of a mind like Borgie's was tragic.

Half an hour later I found myself driving to the airport with the radio tuned to a twenty-four hour news station. I normally left it off, preferring that rare bit of solitude a car ride can afford, but I was following a breaking news story. Senator Vincent Wyecroft, known best for his recent bill to ensure ethics and transparency in the corporate boardroom, had just announced his plan to withdraw from the upcoming race at the state convention the following week. The move surprised even his closest friends and advisors. Our state's favorite son, Sen. Wyecroft was enormously popular, and his reelection to a third term had seemed a foregone conclusion.

The announcement came on the heels of a near-tragedy for the senator and his wife. Their six year old son, a severely autistic child, had gone missing during a family outing two days before and wasn't found until late the next day in a wooded park not far away. Thankfully the boy was fine, though unable to explain what had happened, and the entire state rejoiced at his safe return. Even so, the senator and his wife were noticeably shaken during the just-aired press conference. The man whose words could sway the US Senate was barely able to stammer through a written statement.

The same media commentators who had expressed such heartfelt relief the night before were now swarming over Wyecroft's withdrawal, dissecting his motivations and divining all sorts of ramifications that only the self-proclaimed inside elite could foretell. They also implied, some less subtly than others, that the senator's pronounced trauma may be an overreaction to an event that, after all, had ended well enough. I withheld judgment on that; only the family knew what they had endured over the past three days.

The pundits did all agree on one thing: the likely reaction within Wyecroft's party, lending it the same certainty they had given his re-election only the day before. With Wyecroft out, we were told, the party's most viable alternative was State Senator Ron Hanover. Hanover had enjoyed a rapid rise to state-level prominence. By reputation he wasn't a scholarly type, but he was apparently a savvy politician. He had a strong family name in business, he was openly ambitious, and he was reportedly backed by powerful behind-the-scenes political operatives. Some said he was pro-elite, believing that the ability to accumulate massive wealth was integral to the American Dream. I had no issue with success, although I had serious doubts that ultra-success could be achieved ethically. I had remembered hearing questions about Hanover when it came to ethics; rumors, mostly. In any case, Hanover was new enough that he was not burdened by a long voting record, making him a difficult target for any competitor. For many this made him an ideal candidate for Wyecroft's seat, but those people tended to think only as far as winning the election. They would worry about actual performance in office later.

By the time I turned into the airport parking ramp the news anchor was interviewing fellow reporters in that incestuous way such stories progress between actual events. The number of opinions would now grow by the square of the number of reporters involved, as each fought for a larger slice of air time.

Reporters and commentators lived for stories like this. They relished any chance, however transient, to pass themselves off as knowledgeable. To them it was a career opportunity. To me it was the loss of a good public servant in exchange for a vacuous politician.

I walked across the parking ramp through early-summer heat, followed by a blast of chilled air as I entered the terminal. I carried only a satchel that held my small computer and a growing bulge of miscellanea I kept resolving to clean out when I had time. It was a day trip for me, making me feel almost conspicuous as the one person in the entire airport without a black rectangular bag click-clicking along in tow. That made the security screening go quickly, though, and I was soon dawdling in one of the concourse shops, passing time to avoid the tedium of the gate. That was where Jerry caught up with me, a friend and the only one on this trip that I knew well on a personal level. I was glad to see him; Jerry was a good traveling companion. We shared many interests and had a long enough history that we could talk and joke with each other about both work and personal lives.

"So how has Ms. Morgen-Holz been treating you, eh?" He said it with that leering grin of his, a grin that would make livestock nervous.

"Better than I deserve," was my standard response, leaving him to imagine the rest. Cynthia's name was actually Holt, but Jerry enjoyed twisting it and attaching it to my name (Morgan) after he found that the German phrase "morgen holz" translates into "morning wood." I had to agree she was inspiring to look at. On a professional level Cynthia was smart, articulate and an asset to the Institute. On a more primitive level she was a very attractive woman, almost aggressively so. Cynthia had that moneyed look that came from coiffed hair, pressed suit and tasteful accessories. She cultivated that look with care, and it clearly worked to her advantage in business meetings, where men seemed eager to please her and women were grudgingly impressed by her ability to control a room. She was surprisingly effective, but I wasn't worried about being manipulated. Cynthia had sought me out for diversion and status and perhaps carnal interest, and I suppose I had a similar purpose for being with her.

What I didn't tell Jerry was that Cynthia and I had decided to part ways just a few nights before. The relationship was physically fulfilling, but we both knew our intimacy was purely tactile. I had thought I needed someone like that, a casual relationship that helped fill gaps in my personal life, and I had found I was wrong. Cynthia was a friend and our relationship provided a form of release, but she was not the long-term partner I needed. For whatever reason, that partner had eluded me.

"Yeah, well, you don't deserve all that much," was his wry retort. As he spoke he nudged my arm and nodded toward a blonde that had caught his attention from across the concourse. Jerry was a true hound. "So what's this I'm hearing about the new recruiter Ariel promised to contract for us? I'm desperate for someone to help find some qualified system modelers, and now I hear you scared her off yesterday. Besides, she wasn't bad…"

“Well, it wasn’t me as much as Ariel who rejected her.” Ariel Ming was our COO and general manager, a buffer between corner-office politicians and those who actually got work done. “The woman kept referring to our staff as ‘human capital.’ And by the way, I agree with Ariel; our people aren’t rank and file chair fillers, and anyone finding candidates for us needs to understand that.” I was being polite. Most employees found the term “human capital” degrading.

Jerry dropped his complaint and we made our way toward the crowded gate with the idle chat that always seems to accompany business travel—office politics, weather, and travel tales. It was a long trek, taking us to the far end of the glass-enclosed concourse on a series of moving walkways. We seemed to be swimming upstream against waves of travelers who ran the full spectrum from jaded road warrior at one end to cranky children and exasperated parents on the other, and it was with limited success that Jerry kept his bawdier comments contained as his volume competed with the echoing public address system.

When we reached the gate the other four members of our expedition were already waiting. Three, like Jerry, worked full-time on the project that had precipitated this trip. The fourth was Dale Crest, our VP of Business Development. The three were newer to the Institute and fell quiet on my arrival. Even Dale showed deference; such was my position at the office. A little of that deference to the boss was okay; it always helped that people actually listened when I spoke. At the same time, it had a way of making my work day seem cold, and I sometimes found myself wishing for a more congenial balance between respect and camaraderie. In any case, the conversation quickly mutated into an *ad hoc* business meeting, and we spent the few minutes before boarding in review of our game plan. We were traveling to make a major presentation to a major customer, and while we each knew our role it never hurt to reinforce our strategies, especially for the two more junior members of our group.

The six of us were seated separately on the flight, giving me a chance to relax while the others, I hoped, reviewed their materials. I already knew mine by heart. Although my title at the Institute was "Sr. Principal Researcher," I was lucky if even half my time was spent in actual research. The rest was spent in meetings and in presentations like the one that afternoon. It was a necessary evil; as a recognized guru in an esoteric field I was often called upon to explain our work to customers or investors or the academic community. None of that was in my job description, but the Institute ran on money and reputation and, as I had learned years earlier, the business of science is mostly business.

As I sat in the cramped plane, staring at the seat in front of me and half-hearing the drone of pre-flight instructions, I felt a brief wave of mental weariness. It had been over two years since I'd taken any real time off, and the long hours had begun to affect both my work and demeanor. Nicki had spent a month dropping hints, and finally even threatened to make the arrangements herself before I finally committed to a vacation. In fact, I would be leaving in just over twenty-four hours for an incredible full-week getaway. Already I was mentally stepping back, shrugging off the office pressures and taking an objective look at my career and my priorities. I had few complaints, really. My time at the Institute was much as I had expected. I couldn't imagine a better place for me to work in my field, and that's a statement few could make. Thinking about it, though, reminded me of my academic days, and that in turn had me reaching for my wallet to retrieve Borgie's cryptic card. What had happened to him? Why had he contacted me now, why a card instead of email, and what had he meant by his note? I turned the card over and looked at the note again, tapping the card against my fingertips. "You're it." But what was "it?"

Once back on the ground the team climbed into an airport limo we hired for the ride to the auditorium. I could feel myself rising to the occasion, shaking off my fatigue and taking one last opportunity to advise the team.

"Okay, this will be a pretty good-sized audience, but don't let that throw you," I said. Actually, I believed it to be the largest the Institute had yet to draw, but I didn't want to say that aloud. "These people paid a lot of money for this system and they are already thrilled with the results. Just give them what you prepared, and remember: you're not here to sell, you're here to explain. Believe me, you're going to be treated like geniuses and heroes."

I got nods back from each of them, but few words. Looking around the limo reminded me of a paratrooper scene from an old war movie, the pre-jump jitters producing wide eyes and closed mouths. I smiled inwardly. They'd do fine.

While I didn't share their nerves, I did expect this presentation to be different. In recent years we had begun attracting large-scale projects, and unveiling our results had drawn progressively larger audiences. In this case the Institute had just completed a large contract for the state's Department of Transportation to develop a sophisticated highway planning tool based on emergent system analysis. The contract had been a huge success, spawning several papers we presented in academic, government and industry venues. This particular event was hosted by our state DOT and would be attended by DOT brass from several other states who, I predicted, would soon clamor to become customers. Before that, though, they would need a basic understanding of the concepts we employed, and as the subject matter expert I was to present my stock introduction to the Institute and its work.

Our drive to the auditorium was "slow and go" at best, a live reminder of the crying need for traffic improvement, but we arrived nearly on schedule. By the time people began filling seats we had checked the projection and sound systems and were ready for the event to proceed. At the appointed hour, the DOT's program manager made brief opening remarks and introductions, after which I walked on stage to warm applause. Touching a button on the podium lit up the large screen behind me, giving the audience an animation of a pinscreen depicting waves and shapes and finally morphing into the logo of the Institute for Emergent System Analysis (IESA). Beneath it appeared the bureaucratic-sounding project title "Emergent Behavior Projection and Analysis for Traffic Planning and Control." House lights dimmed, the audience fell quiet, then as a video clip of flocking birds appeared I launched into my over-simplified primer.

"There is something fascinating about a flock of birds," I began. "We often marvel at it and wonder how these simple creatures perform such intricate moves and tight formations. They fly *en masse*, flowing and undulating as they gather up their evening meals. Sometimes, while watching these displays, we realize we don't really see the birds anymore. Instead we see a flock, a thing unto itself with purpose and behavior and a life of its own. If we are aware of individual birds at all, we marvel at how they can fly at high speed through sharp twists and turns, and yet they don't collide and they don't drift off by themselves.

"We see similar things in other groups. Schools of fish. Herds of animals... Generations have watched these things, and generations have asked the same question: 'How are they coordinated?' Is it ultrasonics? Telepathy? We're pretty sure they're not texting each other." I paused a beat for an audible smile. "And just who choreographs those incredible maneuvers?"

The bird clip faded, and the screen now showed a simplified definition of emergent systems.

"Today we know there is no specific choreographer within these groups. Instead each individual is acting on its own, following a set of simple rules that are hard-wired in their brains. Rules like 'pursue food,' 'don't fly too close to your neighbors,' and 'stay with the flock' and so on. These few rules—in this case only three primary rules and a dozen secondary—cause birds to form a group entity with its own purpose and movement. The flock has *emerged* from a number of individuals following a simple set of rules."

The screen now showed an animated graphic depicting the emergence process.

"The study of emergent behaviors, and the rules that underlie them, has helped us understand much about animals. But the most complex emergent systems have to do with human behaviors."

A bulleted list appeared behind me.

"Why is our behavior so complex? Because *we* are complex. The wide range of choices humans can make, the large number of underlying rules we follow, the specialization of roles within human groups, differentiation between individual capabilities and our extensive use of tools and information all make human emergent behavior thousands of times more complex than any other."

A second list appeared.

"But consider what we would learn if we *could* model human behaviors. Imagine how we could fine-tune our laws, manage the economy, perhaps control communicable disease and so much more. Well, thanks to significant breakthroughs in modeling technology, the Institute has proven that many very complex human behaviors can, in fact, be modeled and studied and even predicted with a useful degree of accuracy."

The IESA mission statement came onscreen, followed by a tree chart of the disciplines involved in our work.

"IESA has adopted a dual mission to exploit this new capability. The first mission is basic research to expand our understanding of emergent systems. The second is applied research, studying how we can use that understanding to improve the human condition. In order to pursue these missions, the Institute has developed world-class capabilities in sociology, physics, psychology, biology, math, engineering, economics and much more so that a new, broader capability in emergent studies will, well, emerge.

"Now, under contract to the DOT, we've studied traffic behavior on the state's highway system. The goal was to build a tool that predicts how proposed changes in highway design effect overall system efficiency *before* any money is spent. Today I am proud to say we've achieved that goal. We have produced a new traffic simulation tool that optimizes traffic behavior while minimizing both the cost and inconvenience of highway projects. In other words, by modeling proposed changes—like adding a lane or tweaking our rules of the road—the DOT can now predict the impact of these projects and select those with the greatest economic advantage, the most 'bang for the buck.' The system was tested by comparing the results of several recent projects to simulated projections, and in each case it accurately predicted the project's impact on traffic flow throughout the road system.

"The results are dramatic. After reviewing our initial simulations of currently proposed projects, the state is projecting savings of over twenty-five million dollars in the first year alone." Pause for applause. "Now here to describe the system and tell us how those savings will be realized is our project team leader, Janice Gannon. Janice?"

Fade back to the IESA logo and project title as I exited stage left. It was short and painfully superficial to anyone in our field, but to our audience it was empowering. It was magic.

He found me there in the wings, just as the core of our presentation was getting underway. I remember that first impression vividly. He was tall, thin but not athletic, older but not old, and in the shadows of the off-stage recesses he had a dark, almost foreboding appearance. His eyes were intent and assessing, and he spoke in the precise, carefully worded sentences of one who was accustomed to being listened to.

"You are Roger Morgan, yes?" he asked, as if he didn't already know.

"I am," I replied. "Are you with the Department of Transportation?"

"No, no I am not. My name is John Carstairs. I wonder, are you involved in this portion of the presentation or might you have a few moments to talk?"

"I have until the question and answer period at the end. How can I help you?"

"Perhaps we can step over here." His gesture indicated a short backstage hallway and he ushered me to a small alcove where we could talk without hushed voices.

"Mr. Morgan, I understand you are an expert in the study of emergent behaviors in human bio-systems."

"Yes, that's my field." He was confirming the obvious, and I couldn't tell where this was heading.

"Tell me, does your work apply to all forms of human behavior?"

"Many, but not all. It applies to group behavior, not individual, and then only when the individuals within the group have some freedom to make decisions on their own. The more defined the rules and the greater the individual freedoms within those rules, the easier the simulation becomes. The highway system study was a perfect candidate for us."

"Yes, I see. And has that program been your primary focus?"

"Actually, as principal researcher I am an advisor on this and most other studies we do, but I have another project I lead myself."

"May I ask what that is?"

"Of course, it's no secret. We're studying some of the emergent behaviors associated with a limited free market economy. It's a powerful area of study; a lot of promise."

"Yes, I've seen your articles. Very impressive work."

He had seen my articles? Then why did he ask? I was always happy to chat about emergence and the Institute, but there wasn't a lot of time before I was expected back on stage and this conversation wasn't making any progress.

"Mr. Carstairs, just what is your interest in the Institute?"

"Actually, I am more interested in you, Dr. Morgan. Tell me, have you ever considered taking on a private consulting project? As a side job, of course; a bit of moonlighting."

"Not seriously, no. It would be impossible to do my kind of research without using the Institute's tools, and even with those tools I don't know where I'd find the time. This isn't exactly a nine-to-five job with free evenings and weekends."

"Of course. I understand completely. But the project we have in mind may be quite simple. All the pieces are complete; they just need to be put together into a finished system analysis. It may take only a few days, and it would pay very well."

Oh, how I wished I had a dollar for every time someone wanted just a few days of my time! Half the people I met, after hearing a few sentences about my work, had an idea for a project they thought would be terribly interesting. The good news, I supposed, was that my work sparked imagination. The bad news was that I had to listen to, and politely reject, a constant flow of superficial ideas. My gut response was to turn down John Carstairs completely, but this man was somehow different. He was serious, he had done his homework, and he obviously had a specific purpose for approaching me.

"If you would like to propose something to the Institute I'm sure we could take a look..."

"I'm afraid there isn't a lot of time for us to negotiate a contract and wait for the Institute to allocate resources. We really need your guidance as soon as we can get it."

"Well, I will be out of the office for a week beginning Monday," I said, alluding to my long-overdue vacation. "Maybe I could take a look right after that, if you still have the need. But I honestly can't promise any results—I don't even know what we're talking about here."

"I understand, of course, but I'm afraid that would be a week and a half from now, at least. Is there any way I could entice you to look at it sooner?"

"I'm afraid my plans are already firm," I told him.

A fleeting look crossed his face, and he glanced at the wall for a moment before re-engaging me. "I see. In that case, here is my card. I ask that you please contact me if there is any earlier opportunity."

We exchanged business cards and I glanced at his before inserting it in my wallet next to Borgie's. It said simply "Mr. John Carstairs, Consultant" along with his contact information, the mark of a freelance contractor of some sort.

"Then I may see you in a couple weeks," I said as I stood. "Meanwhile I should get back to the stage."

"Of course. I appreciate your time."

He gave me a look as we shook hands, an assessing look that peered through my eyes into my head. Then he turned and left.

By the time I returned to the wings the enigmatic Mr. Carstairs was out of sight, and I soon rejoined my colleagues on stage for a lively question and answer period. The DOT was almost giddy about their new and powerful toy. That was money in the bank for the

Institute. For the project team, of course, it was a quick pat on the back followed by a chance to do it all over again on the next contract in our growing queue. For me, though, it was the last major duty before my first full week of vacation in years. My mind had already begun shedding the burdens of the office, and John Carstairs was all but forgotten as I left the auditorium.

Our presentation a success, we celebrated with a reception for our team and key players from the DOT. Dale, our marketing VP, had chosen an exclusive chop house, treating our team and key members of our audience to a venue they rarely experienced. To the left as we entered was a low-lit room with dark paneling and a long, curved bar where I found they served scotch in every price range imaginable. The stuffy, men's club décor belied the congenial mood of the room; it was lively and full of talk and laughter. Next to this was a large dining room where they served hedonistic cuts of meat while their well-trained staff did everything possible to promote pleasant indulgence. Their reputation was well-deserved, both for quality and for outrageous price, and I was glad the check was on the marketing department's budget.

As expected, the bar chat started with the shiny new tool we had just delivered with numerous segues to those inevitable bright ideas for future research. I usually found these functions pleasant—even interesting. They were often the best opportunity to learn more about the customer's interests, and, as in this case, a chance to meet potential customers. This time, though, I felt disengaged. I tried to blame it on my peripheral role on the project, but, frankly, my upcoming vacation was claiming a larger mindshare than these people were getting. Thankfully, I didn't need to suffer long. I left for the airport as the rest of the party was being seated for dinner, having scheduled an evening flight home so I could be ready for my trip. I also needed just a couple of hours in the office the next morning to get things settled before leaving—my hectic schedule manifested itself in tangles of office clutter that would be nearly impossible to unravel after a week's absence. Besides, straightening up my desk would go a long way toward keeping Nicki happy.

It was late evening when I arrived at my apartment door. The eighth floor was quiet by that time, and as I put my key in the lock the quiet swoosh of the elevator closing behind me seemed to signal the end of a long day. It hadn't been particularly stressful, as these things go, but the sheer size of the DOT event combined with the rigor of a one-day round trip had me feeling drained. It was with these thoughts that I entered my apartment, only to be surprised by lights and the smell of food.

"Hello, Roger, welcome home." It was Cynthia, and she gave me a mischievous look as she handed me a glass of one of the better wines in my small collection. "How was your trip?"

"I guess I forgot to get my key back, didn't I?" We touched our glasses in silent toast while I managed a smile.

"Yes, well, I thought you might like a little something special before you leave on your adventure." She gave a sly smile as she said this, and I fully understood her intent. I must admit it was enticing.

"And you brought food?"

"Beef sirloin tips in a merlot sauce, pasta and some steamed vegetables. I talked Justin's into letting me have take-out." Justin's was a favorite haunt, and I appreciated her thoughtfulness. Cynthia could be a caring person when she set aside that ambitious "passion with a purpose" flirtation of hers. In moments the surprise and, frankly, the frustration at her presence gave way, and I gave her a hug and kissed her cheek.

Actually, her visit gave me a second wind. I hadn't eaten, after all, and we discussed the DOT presentation between mouthfuls of delicious food. We hadn't spoken privately for several days—since the night we had decided to move on—and our conversation passed through several layers of office gossip and project updates in a futile attempt to avoid a rehash of that decision. By the time she touched on that topic I found it wasn't uncomfortable for her at all. In fact, it was almost like listening to one of her project plans. Cynthia acted as though our breakup were a simple change of tactic in her overall socio-political office strategy, an almost clinical reaction on her part. I supposed I would have preferred the topic to feel just a little awkward for her.

Eventually, though, the conversation moved on to more current events. "I spoke with Nicki today," Cynthia said. "I understand you lost a friend."

"Yes, yes I did. Leonard Borgman. 'Borgie.' You've heard me speak of him."

"I remember the name, I think. Who was he again?"

"Classmate when I was going for my doctorate. True genius. We used to debate for hours in the grad lounge at school. Others used to sit there just to listen to our debates." The memory made me smile, but only for a moment. "But to be honest, the guy had something of a dark side."

"What was that?"

"Well, to me emergent system analysis is an incredibly powerful tool for optimizing systems—getting the most efficiency with the fewest rules and constraints. In the process we modify group behavior, but it's indirect and we do it to get that efficiency. Everyone benefits." I paused for a moment, remembering some of the more contentious moments with Borgie. "Borgie, though, saw emergent system analysis as a way of manipulating a group. He argued that any time we made a change to a system it was to influence behavior, and that the ability to influence behavior was a source of power and control. True, I suppose, but there's a difference between influence and exploitation. Anyway, that was the biggest issue separating us."

"Do you think he may have been right? I mean, is it really possible to exploit emergent systems?"

"It's possible, sure. A good simulation could help someone design a better way of selling a product, for example. But it would take Institute-scale resources to do anything significant."

I saw Cynthia's brow furrow for a moment as she pondered the implications. It was about time; she had been at the Institute long enough to know all this anyway. Cynthia loved political power, and for a moment I thought she might be intrigued by the potential I described, but then she changed the topic.

"So, Roger, had you spoken with Borgie lately? What kind of things was he working on?"

"No, I hadn't spoken with him for some time. I read a paper of his last fall, that's about it."

"He wasn't sharing his work with you, just as a sounding board?" Her eyes were looking directly into mine as she asked.

What a strange question. "No, I've had no real contact with him at all, really," I said. My mind flashed on the business card for a moment, but that wasn't real contact. It seemed more like bait. Cynthia again watched my face as I answered, as if she needed to be sure of my response, then she simply moved on to another topic.

"So you're set on taking this little adventure of yours?" She asked in a way that made my trip seem like an adolescent flight of fancy. "What are you going to do there for a week all by yourself?"

In fact I had very nearly canceled the trip when we decided to part ways. I knew being there alone would feel awkward at times, especially in the restaurants, but the tickets were non-refundable and with my fiscally conservative upbringing, I hated waste. There was plenty to do in DC, with museums and monuments and so much more. Besides, I did need a good break, and it would give me a time to work on my pet project, a system study I had been working on just for personal edification. I would be fine.

"Oh, just some relaxing and a little exploring. I've earned a break, Cynth. Maybe I'll bring back a suitcase full of those little highball stir-sticks you collect."

"Thank you, but it wouldn't be the same," she smiled. "Those sticks are for keeping track of my own consumption, Roger. It's no fun to see someone else's."

"Got it. Okay, maybe a t-shirt then."

She gave me a dour look—I knew t-shirts weren't exactly Cynthia's style. Then she asked, "By the way, I may have to do a bid for a new project next week. Is it okay for me to call if I have a quick question or two?"

"Well, sure, I guess," I said, but I hoped the non-verbal side of my response was more discouraging. I really, really wanted this to be a vacation.

"Don't worry; I won't be pestering you, Roger. Only in an emergency."

Then she took her remaining wine in one hand and my right elbow in the other and led me to the couch. The view from my condo was spectacular at night, with city lights forming a vast array striped with lines of streetlights, the flow of head- and taillights giving life to an ethereal display. Cynthia pushed a button on the remote, and soft music formed an audible backdrop as we made ourselves comfortable on that couch, the same couch where we had first made love nearly nine months before. I was being seduced, and it was flattering, but I had no intention of slipping back into a relationship with her, if that was indeed her intent. Still, a moment of gentle caress confirmed that we could still be close if and when desired.

2

FREEDOM

Cynthia hadn't stayed the night, but she had still caused me to wake later than planned. After hurrying through a shower and breakfast I double-checked my luggage and added the last minute toiletries I had left out for morning use. I tried not to over-pack; they would have stores in DC if I was desperate for anything. A note and generous gratuity left on my counter ensured my twice-weekly housekeeper would take care of plants and any extra mess left behind, and I whisked myself out the door with a growing sense of adventure and expectation. Only a brief morning appearance at the Institute stood between me and nine whole days of living just for me.

First I spent a half-hour straightening up my office and delegating items from my "urgent" stack to Nicki either for dispatch or to remind me about upon my return. That wasn't nearly enough time, as Nicki made a point to tell me, but it was progress and I think she appreciated the effort. It was one of those moments when I wasn't certain who worked for whom.

I did have to attend one meeting that morning, only because it was for my own project, and if its schedule slipped during my vacation it would be me burning midnight oil to catch up. Even so, the meeting reminded me of a last hour high school class, with a ponderous wall clock that would pause indefinitely between minuscule steps toward an end-of-the-day bell. I had to force myself to actually hear the status updates and to hand out meaningful assignments and expectations for the week of my absence.

"We have the business-to-business and business-to-consumer scenarios pretty well modeled," said Jacob, the lead system architect. "What we still need to define are the economic drains—areas where generated wealth can simply disappear. That's really your sweet spot, Roger, so I'm not sure how much progress we can make before you get back."

I sighed internally. Jacob was already building excuses.

"Look, there are only three mechanisms you need to worry about for next week, Jake," and I moved to the white board to write out the list. "First is the inefficiency of outsourcing. You already have that one nearly complete. Second is trade imbalance, especially oil. Third is illicit trade—drugs, knock-offs, pirated software and the like. You'll need to patch in some standard consumer dynamics models from the system library and modify them to reflect the material costs, addictive behaviors and so on. You've done that all before, and there are good people on your team. There should be no problem. We really need those done when I return." Jacob was good; he just lacked the confidence to act independently, probably as a result of working in my shadow since joining the Institute. Maybe my vacation was a good thing on multiple levels.

"Okay, I'll try to have it ready for you to test when you get back."

"Actually, you need to get it done and have Sharon test it *before* I get back. It's not done if it doesn't work, Jake, and we don't know it works until it's tested, right?" I'd told Jacob numerous times before that "I'll try" just means "I'll fail."

"It'll work." I had pushed the right button and had finally gotten the commitment I wanted. Jacob was timid at times, but he took a lot of pride in his work.

"Great. Have the test results on the server a week from Monday then. Anybody have anything else? No? Make it a good week, everybody. I'll see you in ten days."

Nicki caught me in the hall on the way back to my office. "Roger, I got the address and ordered a card and flowers for your friend," she began. "I charged them to your credit card. His remains have been shipped to his home town."

"I see. Thank you, Nicki."

"There's more, though, Roger." Her demeanor softened ever so slightly as she told me. "Mr. Borgman didn't die from natural causes or an accident."

"No…you mean he was killed?"

"They said it may have been a robbery that went bad, but they're not certain yet. I'm sorry, Roger."

"Thanks, Nicki. How tragic. I don't know if he had a family of his own, but I did meet his folks once. Nice people. We haven't been in touch for so long now, but still, what a shock."

"One more thing, Roger. A Mr. Carstairs is here. He's with Ariel now, and she's looking for you."

Oh, oh. Carstairs was likely begging Ariel for some of my time, and I felt a severe case of "vacationus interruptus" coming on. "Nicki, this is a man I met yesterday at the DOT conference and he has some project he wants me to look at right away. I'm going to sneak out before they find me. Run interference for me, will you? Ariel can find someone else to help him out if it's that urgent."

Nicki smiled. "Of course, Roger. Have a great time!"

"You're the best, Nick. A week from Monday."

"A week from Monday," she confirmed, handing me my computer bag and the journal I hoped to read on the plane.

As I moved quietly to the back stairwell I saw Cynthia standing at the far end of the hallway. I was about to wave goodbye; then I saw she was talking with Ariel and the tenacious Carstairs, so I turned away and padded quickly down the steps. Ah, Cynthia, ever the politician. She could probably smell a well-funded project and was already baiting her hooks. Well, maybe she would satisfy Carstairs in my absence. As for me, I was well on my way back to the airport before Ariel knew I had escaped.

I was free.

DC is impressive from the air. Even more so at night, I thought. The flight into Reagan National Airport brushed the southwestern edge of the District, giving me a glittering aerial view of streets and buildings outlined in lights. The capitol mall was just visible, surrounded by monuments, museums and the seats of democracy. It truly was America's front yard, and as I peered out the small window of the plane I looked forward to walking its length and exploring its sights. I tried to think of how often I had been to the district without having a real chance to explore all the area has to offer. This time would be different. Being alone on a vacation was unusual, yes, but at the same time it gave me a feeling of incredible freedom. None of those "I don't know, what do you want to do" negotiations; I could choose my itinerary and go, or I could simply stay put if I wanted. I would be alone, but I didn't expect to be lonely.

The airport taxi line was short as Reagan National spilled the last of the day's arriving passengers into the warm evening. The brunt of the day's heat had passed, but the residual humidity held me like a steaming blanket until I made it through the queue and into a cool cab. No matter. Weather is just a style of dress, as a former boss had told me. Of course, he grew up in northern climes where one could always add a layer for warmth. In heat one can only undress so far.

I checked my messages while en route to the hotel. I was surprised to find several messages from the office, although they clearly knew I was on vacation. Jerry needed a file he couldn't find, Jake had a technical question... The last one was from Cynthia, just hoping I made it to the airport okay and wishing me bon voyage.

When I arrived at my hotel I knew I had made an excellent choice. Given Cynthia's tastes and my desire for a hassle-free vacation, I had chosen a high-end hotel just blocks from the white house. I supposed their typical guest was a diplomat or other VIP, but it was perfect for my needs—close to the White House meant walking distance to the mall, the capitol, and museums. Many of the crown jewels of our American heritage would be accessible by foot.

"Good evening, sir. Are you checking in?" the desk clerk asked. Her nametag, peeking out occasionally from behind a long curl of dark hair, gave her name as "Valerie."

"Yes. Morgan," I replied, handing her my credit card.

The keyboard clicked for a moment. "Yes, here you are: two guests, non-smoking and leaving on the twenty-third. Is that correct?"

"Yes, but it will just be me now." I hadn't updated my reservation.

"No problem, sir. One moment."

I looked around the lobby while she again tapped on the keyboard, already feeling very much like a tourist and imagining the faces of political power that frequented that very room. When she spoke again she gave me the room price. I tried not to blanch, reminding myself of the great location and amenities, but I'm sure she noticed.

"Just a moment, please," she said and clicked her mouse. "I'm sorry, I gave you the rack rate—list price. Who did you say you are with?" She gave me a conspiratorial smile.

"The Institute for Emergent System Analysis. Oh, and I am a member of the awards club as well." I should have let Nicki make the reservations; she wouldn't have forgotten that important detail.

"Ah, that will make a difference. Just a moment, please." Before turning to her computer, though, she made a short phone call.

"Yes, ma'am, I believe it will be about three minutes," she told the other party, then came back to the business at hand.

She typed and waited and typed and waited before she finally smiled up at me again. "Here is the corrected rate, sir. Will you please sign here?"

The revised rate was a pleasant surprise, relative to the first one, anyway. I credited her for the generosity, but I knew the hotel was trading a little revenue now for good public relations and customer loyalty in the long run. Everybody wins.

"The elevator is just past the lounge on your right. Enjoy your stay!"

I towed my bag past the quiet and comfortable-looking lounge, promising myself I'd go back for a nightcap after getting squared away in my room, then stepped into the open elevator car. When I got to my floor, I was surprised to find a woman standing at my door, jamming her key card in and out of the lock and looking flustered.

"Can I help you?"

"Thank you, but I doubt it," she said still glaring at the lock. "I'll have to go get another key."

"Let me try this one," I said, and slid my key card into the lock. The light on the lock turned green, the door opened easily, and a fascinating pair of brown eyes peered around a shock of auburn hair in wonder.

"How did you do that?"

"Simple. I used my key," I smiled at her. "I think you have a wrong room here."

She inspected the little key envelope from her purse and gave a sigh of embarrassment. "I'm so sorry. I have the room above you. Thank you so much for your help!"

"It happens," I smiled again. It would be hard not to smile into those eyes. "Have a good evening."

I re-opened my door, turned to get my bag, and tried not to be too obvious as I watched her walk back toward the elevator. "I've been traveling with Jerry way too much," I thought to myself, and closed the door behind me with that smile still intact.

When I got to the lounge there were more people than I had seen earlier, relegating me to a seat near the far end of the bar. I settled in, ordered a scotch and water and turned to survey the room. The lounge was tastefully appointed, in keeping with the hotel's prominence, but informal enough to provide a relaxing venue. The low tables were small and round and lit by a single candle in a red vase. The chairs were well-cushioned, and the service was friendly. A small party was laughing aloud in one corner, but overall the room was quiet enough for casual conversation. I people-watched for a short while, but by the time I was halfway through my drink I had turned my back to the room. I was jotting thoughts for the next day's itinerary on a bar napkin when I heard a voice behind me.

"Hello again," said the woman with the brown eyes. "Lisa, this is the man whose room I was breaking into," she informed her companion. Lisa was attractive like her friend, but with blond hair and lighter complexion. Her bright eyes and quick smile portrayed a playful personality that had already attracted the attention of others at the bar.

"Well hello," Lisa said. Then her tone turned mock-serious. "And don't worry about Amber. She not a stalker, she's just addled. I really shouldn't let her wander off by herself like that."

"Ha! I'll remember that. I'm Roger, by the way. So, you're Lisa, and—Amber, is it?"

The fluster I'd seen in the hallway upstairs had been replaced by a confident charm. She was about to reply when the bartender interrupted.

"Something to drink, ladies?"

"White wine for her and a kir for me, no lemon," said Amber. Then, turning back to me she said, "Yes, I'm Amber. Happy to meet you. And I did eventually find my room. Above yours, just where it's supposed to be. I'll try not to stomp around too loudly."

Her words had what I supposed was the desired effect, creating an enticing mental image of her above me. I grinned, but before I had formed a safe reply the bartender came back with their drinks. We chatted for a moment more, with them asking what brought me to DC and me responding with a word about vacation, but when they didn't invite me to their table I stopped. I hadn't gone there to prowl, although they had planted an interesting thought or two in my head.

"Have a nice evening, Roger," Amber said as she handed a bill to thc bartender. Lisa also smiled a pleasant "nice to meet you," and they walked away leaving me with a great first impression of DC as a tourist destination.

3

HIDDEN

The first full day of my vacation began slowly as I allowed myself to sleep late and adjust to eastern time. When I did get up it was nearly eight-thirty, so I decided to forgo breakfast and get my in-room office set up before visiting the first on my list of sites. I could grab a bite while out on the mall easily enough, I reasoned, and I wanted to ensure I had the right connectivity and all the software I was going to need to work on my project in case I returned too late in the day to resolve any glitches. The room was small—smaller than I had expected for such a high-end hotel—but there was a good sized table with convenient power, and they provided wireless internet that, fortunately, worked just fine with the VPN (virtual private network) I used to access the Institute's behavioral simulation server. I tried a few simple tasks and found I could work nearly as easily as I did from my home office, the biggest difference being the small size of my notebook's screen. No problem, I reasoned; it was only for a week.

That accomplished, I headed out to see and experience the very core of America, and in that spirit I had selected the National Archive as my first stop. I had seen it once before, many years earlier. At that time I was surprised and, frankly, disappointed with its condition. There were two majestic murals in the main hall, one depicting the signers of the Declaration of Independence and the other the signers of the US Constitution. Back then both were in serious disrepair. Faded and wrinkled, the murals had torn and peeled away from the wall in several places, and they were covered with the grime of years on display. This time I knew it would be different. Thanks to a recent major restoration, the murals were once again vibrant depictions of those important events.

The Archive's main attractions—the Declaration of Independence and the Constitution—were encased along the far wall. A line of tourists slowly shuffled past under the watchful eyes of security guards. The documents were not as fortunate as the murals, although they were preserved as carefully as possible. The old iron-gall ink was barely distinguishable from the yellowed parchment background. It was okay, though. The documents were just media. It was the words and the ideas they expressed that were important, and those were well preserved.

The Archives were inspirational, but having seen what there was to see in the main viewing room, I made my way back out to Constitution Avenue and began the short walk to the National Museum of Natural History, one of the large buildings lining the mall that belonged to the Smithsonian. It was late Saturday morning, and as it was a picture-perfect summer day the streets were lined with vendors and the walks thick with tourists. The crowd was a social anthropologist's dream, an open air exhibit of the human species in its vacation state. In a block one could hear a dozen domestic accents and an equal number of foreign languages, all from people with cameras and sunglasses who were just beginning to sense how badly their feet would feel by the end of the day. I had to smile. I was no different; I was here to gawk like the rest of them. Rather than actually doing something ourselves, vacations often meant looking at what others had done before us.

My route to the museum's front entrance took me through the Sculpture Garden where a dozen or so modern works stood among carefully labeled plants. The collection included a giant typewriter eraser (a typewriter eraser?), a steel rectangle weathering in the elements and a gaudily painted aluminum house, items and shapes that, honestly, did little for me on any aesthetic level. I admired those with the artistic talent I so obviously lacked; still, I couldn't help but think there might be more appropriate works for such a prominent venue.

Once through the sculpture garden I was on the mall proper, a long green space with gravel walks that stretched from the capital building to the Lincoln Memorial. The twinkling night view from my airplane window had given it an ethereal look, a magical place of knowledge and inspiration and reverent memories. Up close and in daylight, it was another thing entirely. "America's front yard," for all its prominence in location and import, looked more than a little shabby. The grass was rutted and worn in many spots, with no visible attempt at repair. Several sections of the gravel walk were lined with cheap lathe and wire fencing that looked like it had been erected for some long ago event and left to weather and sag in the elements. In some areas, security from errant vehicles driving on the mall was provided by "jersey barriers," those long concrete blocks with a triangular cross-section used during highway repair. A series of short concrete pillars would be both attractive and functional, but I supposed they would have cost a bit more. Still, a few dollars worth of national pride would certainly be well-placed on the mall, and I vowed to write my congressman about it when I returned home.

As those idle thoughts drifted through my mind I felt my phone buzzing with a call from Nicki. It was curious. She rarely called me outside business hours, and never on a Saturday.

"Roger, I am so sorry to bother you on your vacation. Do you have a moment to talk?"

"Sure, Nicki, what's up?" I replied, and walked to the shade of a large tree outside the museum.

"There was a break-in at the Institute last night, Roger. Apparently someone got past the security system and the people on the Operations floor (our 24/7 computer facility). I'm afraid they were in our offices, but it doesn't appear they were anywhere else. Nobody noticed until this morning."

"Our offices? Yours and mine? What did they take?"

"They took nothing, as far as I could tell. Ariel called me in to check it out. Some drawers were left open and there were papers all over, but I couldn't tell if anything was missing. Of course, Ariel had to call the FBI."

"FBI?" That took me by surprise. "Why the FBI?"

"Whoever did this got into the confidential files on your government contracts—you know the ones—

and Ariel had to follow the protocol. The FBI went through your entire office, including my desk, even the trash. There may be more to it, though. They asked Ariel and me about Mr. Borgman and some work that you may have been helping him do. I had to tell them that you were trying to reach Mr. Borgman the other day. Had you been working with him? I don't have any project files for that at all."

"No, no I wasn't. I have no idea what it's about, Nick, but you did the right thing. Did they describe the project at all?"

"That's all I have. But, Roger, they were quite serious about this, and Ariel is very concerned. I thought you might want to call her."

"Good thought, Nicki, I'll do that. Let me know if you hear anything else, okay?"

"Of course, Roger. I assume everything else is going well?"

"I've barely gotten started, really; just the National Archives so far. Have a good weekend, Nick, and thanks for the call."

I stood under that tree a few minutes longer, surveying the mall as I tried to make sense of Nicki's call. There was obviously more behind this than simply tossing my office, something that linked me to Borgie. This was the third time Borgie's name had come up in as many days, none of them good. Something was happening, something very serious, but I had nowhere near enough information to figure out what it was. After reviewing it again, though, I realized I wasn't going to solve this little mystery while standing on the mall. Besides, the problem seemed worlds away. It was Saturday, I was on vacation, and I was sweating outside under a tree, just yards from the steps of a nice cool museum. I decided I would call Ariel when I got back to the hotel.

The National Museum of Natural History, one of several large edifices on the mall, is a stone building capped by a large dome. Its main entrance was atop two wide flights of steps and behind six tall columns supporting a broad triangular pediment, completing the institutional effect. Home to the Hope Diamond and scores of exhibits ranging from geology to mineralogy to plant, animal and human development, the museum traced the progress of nature itself. Only a small fraction of their collection was on exhibit at any time; even so, I was warned it could easily take days to fully absorb the displays.

I climbed the stairs and passed through the security checkpoint to get my first full look at the rotunda beneath the dome. The room was surrounded by stone walls with columns and balconies that gave one the feeling of being outdoors, a feeling reinforced by a large, stuffed bull African elephant dominating the center of the room. Incredibly lifelike, the elephant calmly tolerated the noisy flow of tourists and constant flicker of cameras. Yet through this sensory noise one face caught my eye, a face that watched anxiously as I crossed the few steps to her side of the display. She wore tourist casual, comprised of a nicely fitted white cotton top under a loose light-blue short-sleeved shirt, designer jeans that she made look good, and a small, leather bag on a strap over her shoulder to complete the ensemble. The look was good—more than good, I thought—but there was something very wrong.

"Roger, I'm so glad to find you," Amber said. Her voice had an urgent tone, and her eyes were puffy and red. She had been crying. Before I could say anything, she pulled me aside, away from the stream of tourists flowing through the rotunda.

"Good to see you, too, Amber. Is everything okay?"

"No! No, not at all," she said, and cast nervous glances around the rotunda. "Is there someplace we can talk?"

"Uh…yes, sure," I responded, looking around the room for ideas. I had no idea what type of help she required, but with me being male and she being decidedly not, a natural testosterone-induced protective instinct took control. Then I noticed the sign above a staircase. "There's a cafeteria downstairs where we can sit and talk."

"That's good, let's go," she said, and we soon found ourselves on the lower level walking between two large gift shops and into the cafeteria. Given the crowd upstairs and on the street I worried it would be some time before we found a table, but a little luck and Amber's sharp eyes had us seated in no time with a tray of food that looked better than a high-traffic tourist venue might suggest. Amber had no interest in eating, and as soon as we were settled she put her elbows on the edge of the table and leaned in to speak without raising her voice.

"Roger, something awful has happened. It's Lisa—you remember the woman who was with me last night?" Her eyes were welling up with tears as I nodded in response. "It's horrible. She was killed, Roger. I think—I know—she was murdered!"

"What?" I had barely met Lisa, but I was shocked nonetheless. "How did she die? Have you gone to the police?"

"She was hit by a car. The police think it was just a random hit and run, but I know it was no accident. I'm afraid to talk to them, though. I can't. I can't risk it."

Amber was crying now, an amalgam of grief and fear. I glanced nervously around the room, aware that we were probably making a spectacle, and took a beat to digest the situation. Before I could find out what this was about—and why she sought me out to tell about it—I had to calm her down.

"Amber. *Amber!* Please, talk to me. You need to catch your breath and tell me what is happening."

She took a deep breath, but it was another moment before she regained enough composure to speak again. "I'm sorry. Roger, it's all happening too fast. Lisa's dead and I'm in danger. And, Roger, I think you are too!"

Not to seem unsympathetic, but it was that last part that really got my attention. "Me? What do you mean? I haven't done anything!"

"No, you don't understand. They think you have something they want!"

"This isn't making sense. Who are 'they' and what do they think I have?"

It was another moment—several, actually—before she was able to start over. "Yes, you're right," she said. "I'm sorry. Lisa was my best...my only close friend in DC. She lived in my apartment building. We were going to be roommates after her current lease expired."

"Okay, but..." I was completely at a loss. "Amber, I'm just a guy here on vacation."

Amber looked at me squarely. "I know who you are, Roger. You're the senior principal researcher at the Institute for Emergent System Analysis. The question is why you are *really* here. I hate to be blunt, Roger, but I really need to know!"

"I don't understand. How do you know about me? Who are you?"

She produced a laminated ID card on a long lanyard, the kind office employees hang around their necks. On it were her picture and some agency initials I didn't recognize. "Amber Meadows. I'm with Inter-Agency Resources, Roger, and I work, that is, I worked, with Leonard Borgman."

My jaw dropped at hearing Borgie's name again. "I'm completely lost here. What does 'inter-agency' mean? Is it FBI?"

"No, not FBI. Not CIA, either, or NSA or any other letters you would be more familiar with. The IAR is a resource pool that supplies all those other agencies with specialized capabilities they can't afford to have full-time."

"Like what kind of resources?"

"Like emergent system analysts, for example. No one agency can justify keeping them full-time, so the IAR maintains a group that gets lent out when there's a need. Now, Roger, please. Tell me what you're working on with Borgman."

I had no idea what was behind this, but it appeared Borgie had gotten into something that would have been better left alone. "I knew Borgie—that's what we all called him—back in my post-grad days. We were both doctoral candidates, both working on emerging systems. He was a genius. I admired his talents, but we didn't see eye-to-eye."

"Why was that?"

"Emergent system analysis is a great tool for understanding and optimizing a group behavior. That's what we call 'didactic analysis.' But Borgie saw it differently. He saw it as a tool for manipulating behavior—influencing, even controlling rather than optimizing. That's called 'hegemonic analysis,' and most people in our field have serious ethical concerns about it. Borgie didn't, though. His ego made him believe he would never go down the wrong path with it. Anyway, we've had no real contact since school. We were both trying to get the same job when we graduated. I got the job, and he was pretty unhappy about it, so we never kept in touch. I have seen some articles he wrote and I read a paper he presented a couple of years ago, but that's about it until this week."

"This week?"

"He tried to contact me a couple of days ago, first time since school, but when my assistant tried to place a call back to him she was told he had died. I never got a chance to speak with him. Amber, what the hell is going on?"

She gave me a penetrating, almost pleading look before responding.

"You weren't working on something with him?"

"No."

"He didn't keep in touch with you?"

"No."

"He didn't send you any of his work?"

"No! Now what is this all about?"

The cafeteria had an ornate décor that matched the museum's theme, with images of artifacts and reconstructed scenes from antiquity. The room had the resounding acoustics of hard floors and walls, and it was alive with people who brushed by our table and created a loud din as the lunch crowd thickened. Yet all that faded out of sight and hearing as I watched Amber prepare her response to my question, deciding how, and probably how much, to tell me. She was clearly ad-libbing her way through uncharted waters. But now the pause after my question had grown long enough to harden into silence, and I wanted answers before that happened. I decided to approach it again, more slowly this time.

"How did you find me here?"

"Last night in the lounge I saw the itinerary you were writing on a bar napkin and took a chance that you'd stick to it this morning."

"Clever. Why didn't you ask me about this last night?"

"Last night we were only watching. We wanted to see what you were going to do here in DC, see what it had to do with Borgman."

"Why?"

"Borgman was working on a personal project. That's okay—in fact, they encourage it rather than let people go idle between assignments. But he was being very secretive about it, covering his tracks, hiding the software code he developed, that kind of thing."

"What kind of project?"

"It was a behavioral simulation, I guess, but no one knew what it did. He never ran a complete simulation. For the past several months he had been developing and testing small parts of the whole. Only in the past couple weeks had he started assembling them all into a complete system. Without knowing how to knit all the fragments together no one could tell what he was trying to do."

"Okay, so what does this have to do with me?"

"Last week, just before Borgman was killed, he had a loud argument with someone on the phone. I could hear him from my desk. One of the things he said was 'there is only one other person alive who could make this simulation work.' Then he said your name."

I went almost dizzy as this sunk in. Somewhere, right there in DC, were people who believed I had something or knew something they would kill for.

"Okay," I said. "Okay. This is a problem."

I poked at my food without appetite while Amber watched me process her story. Borgie, stealth project, Lisa… I was staring at a huge jigsaw puzzle with a small piece of blue sky in my hand, not knowing where to start. Somehow I was being drawn into a cloak-and-dagger world and feeling way, way out of my depths. Hell, I was just a guy on vacation! A few more moments passed before I could even begin looking at the situation rationally. When I did, I realized all I had so far were questions.

"Amber, am I some kind of suspect?"

"I'm not a cop, Roger, I just work at the IAR."

"Doing what?"

"That's the problem. I lead a group in Information Technology, including the software archives for the IAR. You know the work: making sure everyone has the current versions of code through the development phase, keeping copies of earlier versions...the usual stuff." There was a new expression of worry on her face as she told me this, and I understood why.

"You mean you know where all the pieces of Borgie's code are?"

"Yes, I do." Her eyes glanced around the room as she admitted it. "Borgman was archiving his work under a series of fake project names. I have all the pieces he submitted, I think, but I don't have the file that tells how they all get put together."

"Amber!"

"I know! But, Roger, they think you might have it, or at least some knowledge of it. That's why they searched your office."

She knew about my office being ransacked? This was completely surreal. Clearly I was in as much danger as Amber, but in order to find who was behind this and why, we would need to know the purpose behind Borgie's code. It took several moments for me to regain self control, and when I did it came out in a statement that surprised even me.

"Okay. Yeah, you're going to need my help," I said matter-of-factly.

We soon found ourselves walking back to my hotel on the logic that any help I could lend would require my computer and the custom software suite on its disk. At Amber's insistence we took a circuitous route through two of the large office complexes just north of the mall, approaching the hotel from the opposite side. Amber seemed to be comforted by having someone to share the situation. I had to admit I liked Amber's company as well, despite the circumstances. I certainly wasn't looking for a short-term vacation relationship, yet I enjoyed watching her. In fact, I enjoyed it more than I had liked watching Cynthia, which was saying a lot, and that thought led to a mental comparison of the two. Amber was attractive from within; Cynthia's beauty was more external, something she applied as needed. Amber seemed open and guileless; Cynthia's looks were a tool in her political arsenal. I found myself sensing in Amber many good qualities I had been unable to sense in Cynthia.

By the time I made that silent observation we were standing together in the hotel elevator. I realized I was staring, and that Amber was returning my gaze with a bemused look. I had just dropped my eyes like an embarrassed schoolboy when the elevator door opened, but, as I shifted my weight to step out, Amber shoved me backward, out of sight of the hallway, and gestured for me to remain still as she backed into the other corner of the elevator. Her eyes were wide with warning, and she quickly pressed the "close door" button followed by the button for the next floor. It wasn't until the door was closed and the car had started to rise that she could explain herself.

"They're breaking into your room!"

"What? Who?"

"The FBI." The elevator door opened again, to the floor above mine. "Come on!"

"FBI? What? Where are we going?"

"My room. Right above yours, remember? We can't leave now; they'd see us!"

As we walked toward her room I had a revelation. "Hold on. Last night when you were at my door—you weren't lost, were you?"

"No…no, I was just leaving your room when I saw you coming. Lisa gave me a bug to plant in your room."

"What? You bugged my room?" Invasion of privacy was a serious matter to me.

"It was Lisa's idea. She had access to the equipment, but we didn't know which room was yours until you checked in, so it was a last-minute job. That's why you caught me."

Amber's room was identical to mine, right down to the writing desk. The pictures on the wall were different, but I noticed these, too, were in frames that were screwed to the wall—apparently a posh hotel doesn't guarantee posh clientele. Her computer was connected to a receiver that I assumed was tuned to the bug in my room, and Amber went directly to the table and turned everything on.

"Maybe we can find out what they're up to," she said, putting the earpiece on and gesturing for me to be quiet.

I paced the room for several minutes before Amber put down the earpiece and shut off the receiver. I wasn't used to being kept in the dark like that, and it wore on my patience.

"Okay, they're gone. This is a real problem," she said. "They're going to keep watching your room. It won't be safe to go back there now."

"What? Amber, I need to know the whole story, and I need it now." I was holding back a wave of frustration while I struggled to understand the situation. Amber was clearly upset, but if I didn't know what was happening I couldn't help her. Or me.

"Yes. Yes, I know," she said, and now that we were in a relatively safe spot she sat back to tell what would be a longer story. "Okay, here's how it started. A few months ago Lisa and I met for lunch at a restaurant down in Alexandria. It was a bit far for both of us, but we wanted to get away for a while. We were just talking, you know, sharing office gossip, that sort of thing. I told her about this eccentric guy at our office—Borgman—and how he seemed to be working very hard at something in total stealth mode, but I knew he was doing it because he would check his code into my archive using fake project names.

"You were already suspicious about his project?"

"Oh, no. I mean, I was just telling her about how strange some people can be in that office. Anyway, Lisa was a data analyst in an FBI office not far from here, and she started telling me about a guy in her office, a bad comb-over named Scanlon. Special Agent Larry Scanlon. Lisa thought Scanlon and a couple of his guys were working on a stealth project, too, which I guess is what brought him to mind. Then, in the middle of her story, Lisa looked up and said, 'oh wow, there he is now. That's him!' I looked across the room to where she was pointing, then I said, 'I don't believe it! Lisa, that guy he is with is Borgman!'"

"Doesn't sound like random chance, does it?"

"No, not at all. Well, Borgman and Scanlon left, but seeing them like that made us curious, so we sat there for a while piecing things together. It was just speculation, but as we talked it got more and more interesting. You see, Scanlon is a lead agent in the FBI's WCU—white-collar crime unit. About a year ago, Borgman and his team were assigned to help the WCU on a corporate fraud case, simulating what would happen if various rules were broken to see if they could figure out how the scam was operating. The case had fizzled, lack of evidence, but as we talked we realized that each of them had started working on their secret projects just after that case was dropped."

"You think they were working together?"

"It seemed that way. Anyway, we talked about it from time to time after that. Last week I told Lisa about Borgman's telephone meltdown, and I mentioned your name. This morning she had to go into the office on some overtime project, and she overheard Scanlon's people talking about an office being searched. She heard your name again, and she knew it couldn't be a coincidence. She called to tell me about it, and said she was going to Internal Affairs. But someone must have heard her—a hour later she was killed in a hit-and-run outside her office!"

The whole story would have sounded fantastic if it hadn't been deadly serious. Borgie was a lot of things, but I never would have thought he would do anything criminal. “So you think Borgie was working with Scanlon on something illegal?”

“I don’t know, Roger, but everything I do know makes me think they were working on something together, and that Borgman was killed because of it. Do you think you would be able to tell what it is by looking at the code he put in the archive?”

“Humph,” I scoffed out loud. “You’re the second person this week to ask me to work on someone else’s code. It would be hard enough with the final body of code to study, but just looking at the pieces? I don’t know until I see it.”

“Wait. Someone else has been asking you to look at code?”

“Yeah, a few days ago. A guy asked me to look at a simulation. Sounded like it was hacked together somehow and now he needs someone to make it work. I told him I might be able to take a look after my vacation.”

“Did you get his name?”

“Of course,” I said, and reached for my wallet. “John Carstairs. Here’s his card.”

“John Carstairs,” Amber repeated. “No, I don’t know the name.”

Amber seemed fully engaged for now, but Lisa’s death was still just sinking in. The loss of a close friend would take a lot more time to process. Meanwhile, I was feeling like the reality rug had been yanked out from under my feet. Not one to panic easily, I was more intent on solving the puzzle than on rash action, and it was in that vein that I began thinking about next steps. The most obvious was to get what we had come for: my computer and software. After that, we needed a plan.

"How did you know the people downstairs were FBI?"

"It was Scanlon and two other guys. They're probably the ones from the WCU that are working with him on whatever he's doing."

"I'm going to need my computer," I said. "Can you tell if they've all left?"

"It isn't safe, Roger. They said they were going to watch from the room across the hall. Can you use mine?"

"No, I have special software on mine. Proprietary modeling tools. If I'm going to analyze his code I'll need them." I started pacing the small room again, searching my imagination for alternatives.

"Is there any other place you can get those tools?"

"They're custom tools we built at the Institute," I explained, but then I had an idea. "Wait, maybe I can use yours after all. Let me try something."

I booted up Amber's computer and did a quick check of the system. It was identical to mine right down to the hardware options. Then I checked the wireless connection.

"I set my system up this morning before going out. Unless they messed with it, it should still be running. At home I connect to it wirelessly from my desktop machine, so I should be able to do it here, too." I opened Amber's network control program and a few moments later I could see my computer's name come up on the list of available networks. The Wi-Fi signal between our rooms was weak, but it still showed about half-speed. Then I entered my password to create a peer-to-peer connection. The good news was that my computer had all the installation files I needed on its disk; the bad news was that they were large files. It was going to take a while to copy them to Amber's machine.

While we waited I tried to digest the information had so far. There were a lot of moving parts to the story. I knew I didn't have them all yet, but the overall picture was starting to form in my mind. What I didn't know was what, if anything, I could do about it all. I needed Amber to fill in some of the gaps.

"Okay, so Scanlon—and, I guess, others on Scanlon's team—are doing something illegal, and they were using Borgie to build a tool they need to make it all happen."

"I think so, yes."

"Borgie had a falling-out with them on the phone, and then he was killed. Now this Carstairs seems to want whatever Borgie was working on, but he needs help making it work. Maybe, that is—we really don't know if he's involved at all."

"Sounds right, though."

"What was Borgie so upset about on the phone that day?"

"Not sure. I only heard the last part of the call, the loud part, and then only Borgman's side of it. He was yelling about wanting off a project, but I don't know why."

"Okay. So with Borgie gone they need the program he was building. They think I might have the code, but I don't. You actually do have the code, mostly, but they might not know that yet. Anything else?"

Our conversation went on like that for a while as my custom software suite flowed silently across the ether. The major points having been made by this time, we were now looking for any remaining bits and pieces of available information, but were finding none. The problem was defined, at least as far as possible, but the solution was another matter. Logically, now as at lunch, it seemed more and more important to get access to Borgie's code and his recipe for its assembly—what we call a "build file." Then we had to figure out what it was designed to do, and then we had to find someone we could tell, tell them, and stop whatever Scanlon and his crew were up to. Just as simple as that.

So far, I thought with a wry chuckle, my vacation was a bust.

At the same time, as her adrenaline subsided and her natural poise returned, Amber had become, well, interesting. We seemed to have forged an instant bond, one that would take months in more common circumstances, if it happened at all. I supposed it was natural, an artifact of a predicament that caused two strangers to become mutually reliant. We seemed familiar, sharing inner thoughts and feelings, and while I wasn't the slave to testosterone that my friend Jerry seemed to be, I became aware that I could vividly recall her touch on my shoulder at the bar and again on my arm in the rotunda.

Amber's voice brought me back to reality. "Did you get what you need off the computer?"

"Just a while longer," I said, and then looked at my watch. "I guess I won't be touring the museum after all."

"I get pretty conflicted about that place anyway."

"'Conflicted'?"

"I'm from the Bible belt, Roger. Everything in that particular museum is either based on evolution or is about things that happened long before creation. I mean, I'm not stupid, but it's hard when I was raised to believe otherwise."

I couldn't help but smile. That conflict was completely unnecessary, yet many people suffered from it.

"It's not funny, Roger. It's easy for you; you're a man of science."

"No, not funny at all. I am a man of science," I agreed, "but I have pretty deep religious roots."

"Really?" That revelation had her curious. "How do you manage the conflict?"

"It's really a matter of logic. If you assume the universe was created, it's logical to assume it was created as a scientifically consistent system—everything emerging from a simple set of physical, chemical and biological laws. Among other things, that means it would have to have been created with all kinds of evidence of things prior to the creation. Otherwise we'd have proof of creation, so we would no longer have freedom of choice in what we believe. Religion would be superfluous. The way it is, we can choose to believe the religion or not. In religion, that choice is everything."

"But don't you believe in science?"

"It's a great model for understanding and managing the world; the best we've come up with so far. But that doesn't mean things had to have happened that way. I mean, if we had been created yesterday, complete with memories and everything else in place, how would we know? So I like science, I find it very useful, but I recognize the difference between fact and truth."

"You're a philosopher, Roger. Interesting."

I smiled again. "Well, I really did want to see that museum," I replied. I wasn't sure if she meant my philosophy was interesting or me, but before I could explore that question the last few bytes were finally transferred to her computer with an audible "beep."

"It's done. We need to get out of here."

"Yes, but how? Scanlon's people are watching for us."

"So far they think I've been walking around the mall playing tourist without a clue as to what's going on. My guess is they're just waiting for me to get back to my room, maybe watching in the lobby, too, just in case. We should be okay if we sneak out through the garage or through a service entrance."

The bigger question, of course, was where we should go. I pondered that one for a couple of minutes while we packed up Amber's computer and a shoulder bag of personal items. The only answer I came up with was very short-term, but it was enough to get us moving.

"Let's go shopping," I suggested. "All my clothes are in my room; if I can't get in there I'm going to need a few things. Besides, once this Scanlon sees I'm not coming back to my room he'll start trying to track me down. I may not want to use my credit card much longer." In fact, it would be risky to use my cell phone as well, probably beginning sometime that evening. Time was not on our side.

"Perfect," Amber responded. The prospect of shopping seemed almost therapeutic for her. "I know just the place."

As we walked quietly through the lower level of the hotel, I had another idea. Assuming this situation would be cleared up soon, I decided I might as well keep my things safe. Using a hotel courtesy phone, I told the front desk I had been called away, and asked that they have someone pack up my things and hold them with the concierge for a few days. They were happy to oblige.

We left the hotel undetected, as far as I could tell, at least, then walked the a few blocks to the subway. DC's subway system is a marvel, clean and efficient, and we soon arrived at Amber's chosen shopping area. My first order of business was to find an ATM and withdraw as much as possible to avoid leaving a credit card trail for Scanlon to follow. That money, I hoped, added to the cash I already had on me, would be enough for the rest of the week's needs.

The clothes shopping took a little longer. I picked up socks and underwear quickly enough, but shopping with Amber meant adopting a more pensive approach to my outer wardrobe than I commonly took when alone. I didn't mind; a temporary respite from intrigue was welcome by that time. It gave me time to consider our next move, as well as a chance to observe my newfound partner in what appeared to be her natural habitat. Shopping, I learned, could actually be enjoyable with the right companion.

By the time Amber had selected the last of my immediate needs it was time to eat, and time to face reality once more. We walked—strolled, really, in subconscious procrastination—until we found an inviting restaurant and made ourselves comfortable in a corner booth. It was a small place, the kind of coziness that attracted both locals and those seeking local color, offering an unpretentious menu of meats and potatoes and soups, with fish and crab cakes for variety. I chose a plate of roast beef, having left an unfinished lunch at the museum, and Amber opted for similar comfort food. My scotch arrived along with Amber's wine, and after first sips we readdressed the situation at hand.

"By now I suppose Agent Scanlon is starting to wonder what's taking me so long to get back. He probably assumes I'm having dinner. He'll get more curious soon, though."

"Do you think he's curious about me, too?"

"It's hard to say," I replied. I wished I could be more reassuring, but it was best to deal with reality instead of false hopes. "If Scanlon is a rogue agent he would have limited resources. Of course, he was somehow aware of the search at my office, but the agents who responded to that call were local guys just doing their job. He may not even know about you yet. The trouble is, if they are responsible for Lisa's death they'll be anxious to know how much she knew and whom she may have told, and you will be in her phone records."

"Then we can't go to my place, Roger. The hotel is out, too. Any ideas?"

"Well, Scanlon will be watching for me tonight, at least until he realizes I'm not coming back, so your apartment is safe for a little while yet, I think." I noted her welcome assumption that we would be staying together. "Just to pick up some things, though; we wouldn't want to stay there. I don't know where to go from there yet, but I do know I need to see Borgie's code. Can you get in to your archive from outside the office?"

"I'm not sure," was her reply. "I really haven't had a need to do that in the past. I don't actually do much with the code itself; I'm really just the librarian, you know? I only see the code when I'm doing a build for someone."

"You do the builds, too?" My hopes rose for a moment, as the person who could put all the individual code elements into a final program would be very helpful in piecing together Borgie's work.

"Yes, but not for this program. Borgman was doing that all by himself. But, now that you mention it, I did use remote access once, almost a year ago, so it can be done. We were working in a different building during an office remodel."

Our food arrived and was attacked with gustatory vigor. Stress and fasting had given us strong appetites, and the conversation slowed to the few words per minute that we managed between mouthfuls. It gave me a moment to have an idea, one I wasn't sure would be palatable under the current circumstances, but having no other prospects I decided to test the waters.

"You said Lisa lived in your building. Is her place real close to yours?"

"Not next door or anything. Her place is at the far end of a separate wing and down a floor. Why?"

"I don't suppose you two shared keys?"

“Yes, we did, but...oh. You mean stay in Lisa’s apartment? Oh, Roger, I don’t know...”

For a moment I was sorry I had brought it up, but then Amber surprised me.

“I suppose it would be a safe place, though, wouldn’t it? I mean, Lisa and I were always looking after each other. She’d like it, I think.”

That decided, we finished our meal and headed back toward the subway. On the way we stopped at a phone shop and purchased a pair of pre-paid cell phones, the shopkeeper clearly believing we were married—but not to each other. Fidelity, after all, is one of technology’s more frequent victims.

By the time we arrived at Amber’s building I had given her careful instructions on how to leave her apartment if she saw anything unusual. Amber let me in the door at Lisa’s end of the building and gave me the apartment key, then walked around front to the main entrance. I climbed the stairs and entered the apartment, waiting in the entryway for several minutes while Amber collected her things. I had only seen Lisa for that one fleeting moment in the hotel lounge, but her apartment gave a very good impression of her. It was clean and straight, without looking obsessively so, well-furnished, considering she lived on a budget, and sprinkled with pictures and memorabilia that included a few shots of her with Amber.

There were three soft taps on the door, and I opened it for Amber, who carried a large black plastic bag full of clothes and other items.

“You saw someone?”

"Yes. Impossible to tell if they were looking my way or not. I didn't want to take any chances, so I did what you had suggested: I left to 'take out the trash.'"

As Amber looked past me into Lisa's home she fell silent. I watched as she walked through a once-familiar apartment that now felt strangely foreign to her. The loss welled up in her eyes again, and, in spite of my anxiety to see Borgie's code, I gave her a few minutes to miss her friend. Considering the circumstances, I thought Amber handled things very well.

After that period of reverence, we set up Amber's computer on the kitchen table and logged into the wireless network. Unfortunately, we were unable to access the IAR archive. The remote access system was in place, we could see, but the password Amber had used months ago was no longer valid. It was frustrating for me, and it was the end of a long, difficult day for Amber.

"I'm going to turn in, Roger. I'll be in the guest room; I couldn't sleep in Lisa's bed tonight."

"Sure," I agreed. "I'll be up for a while, then I'll be on the couch."

With Amber settled in I set up her computer and started a log. It had struck me that at some point there would be an investigation into Lisa's death, and here we were leaving all kinds of evidence in her apartment. I wanted to create an account of what we knew so far and why we were there so our presence would be easier to explain if needed. Besides, it would give me a chance to sort things out and put thoughts in order while everything was still fresh in my mind.

I finished the log in less than an hour, encrypted it and sent it to myself by email so I'd have a copy on my mail server. Feeling spent, I made myself as comfortable as possible on the couch and drifted off to sleep, my mind awash with thoughts of uncertainty and intrigue. It was a light sleep, as is common for me in strange surroundings, and it was easily penetrated by a noise from the other room.

Investigating, I walked to the guest room door to hear Amber's soft crying. She was feeling the loss of her friend, and I decided to simply return to the couch. Before I could turn to leave, though, she spoke.

"I'm sorry to wake you, Roger. I just feel so terribly alone now. Lisa and I were so close." The tears subsided. "I'm just so glad you're here."

I wasn't sure if she meant here in the apartment or here in her room, but I sat on the edge of the bed to apply what comfort I could. When that comfort produced a gentle kiss on the forehead she looked up at me and returned the kiss, fully on the mouth. As good as it felt, warm and sensual, I had to gently pull away.

"You're upset, Amber. I can't take advantage of that."

"Yes, I'm upset," she whispered. "But I was praying you would come to me tonight. It's okay; I'm old enough to handle myself."

Hers were not the pleading eyes of a woman desperate for escape. Hers were eyes of passion, of abiding hunger. I initiated another kiss, laying myself next to her as pulses rose with anticipation. Our frames conformed one to the other, hands seeking and finding and caressing. Eventually she reached further, giving clear indication of her intent and finding me fully prepared to fulfill her. I let her set the pace, her body sensitive and responsive as if each touch, each taste produced an impulse. With patient restraint I used those means to take her through increasing heights until she was finally sated in an explosion of carnal appetite. Only when she at last returned to earth did I indulge a more selfish motive, replacing patience with predation. As I did, she repaid my earlier attentions with unrestrained enthusiasm, deftly shifting position and stance to afford every opportunity for satisfaction. She was strong, she was resilient, and she was entirely successful.

4

WATCHDOGS

Morning light was summarily ignored until after eight. When I did awake, it was to a diverse array of thoughts and mental images, each vying for attention in my groggy mind. One thought won easily, as I brushed against a hip and felt it press dreamily back against me. That particular thought consumed another hour of our morning.

While waiting for my turn in the shower, I turned on a Sunday morning news program, hoping the diversion would force the morass of unanswered questions to wait just a little longer. As I would have expected, had I thought about it, my state's senatorial race was an important topic at the national level. Any change in candidates could precipitate a shift in the delicate balance between parties. It appeared that the soon-to-be-former Senator Wyecroft was as liked in DC as he was at home, and, while Hanover had become the heir-apparent, he was obviously seen as a lesser offering by those in the national know. Hannover's candidacy wasn't openly questioned by the press so much as it was met with a cautious "well, we'll see" attitude, and I feared my home state's representation was destined to slip a notch or two as the baton was passed. The one area where he seemed active was the economy, which the show's moderator used to segue into the next topic.

The wealth gap. It had been a topic, on and off, ever since post-tax season statistics showed a dramatically smaller percentage of the population holding a dramatically larger percentage of the nation's wealth. Although both were staunch conservatives, Wyecroft and Hanover seemed to diverge on the issue. Wyecroft's concern was that corporate boards of directors had too often become good old boys' clubs, contrary to their fiduciary responsibility to shareholders, and he had pushed for greater boardroom transparency. So far, at least, Hanover had expressed no interest in pursuing that, or any of Wyecroft's initiatives. I could only sigh, my opinion of Hanover unchanged by the panel's discussion.

Amber emerged from a cloud of steam in a robe and turbaned hair to join me on the couch.

"I gave it some thought in the shower, Roger," she announced. "I think I should go in to the office today and make a copy of Borgman's code."

I had the same thought, but had been holding out for a better, less risky, idea. "I think you're right. We'll need a plan, though. Does your office have safeguards against people copying code?"

"Only for classified programs. Other than that, if you have a valid password for the project it's filed under, you can pretty much get what you want. Anything more would really get in the way."

"Good. How long will it take to make copies?"

"Not long, but I'll have to boot my computer, find all the files...we better plan on a half hour to forty-five minutes."

"Hmmmm. Can you get me inside as your guest?"

"Sure, that's no problem. You'll have to show your ID, though."

"Yeah," I said as I pondered the implications. "Okay, let's do it."

After I got cleaned up, Amber grabbed a key ring from a peg in the kitchen and we went down to the lot to find Lisa's car. "In for a penny, in for a pound," I told myself; it was callousness born of necessity, but Lisa didn't need the car any more than she needed her apartment at that point.

Amber's office was several miles from the apartment, but the Sunday morning traffic was light and we drove into the mostly empty parking lot well before noon. The employee entrance was open, and Amber introduced me to the guard as an old friend.

"Hey, Mick. Quiet here today?"

"Sure is. That's fine by me, though. Your badge? Thank you. Now, who do we have here?"

"My friend Roger from back home. Just doing a quick tour, if that's okay, plus I have to get something ready to give Elle in the morning."

"No problem at all. Sir, please show me some ID, and step around the corner so I can get your picture."

I did as asked and a few moments later we were walking down a long, partially lit hallway toward the main work area. The IAR was a cavernous space, and looked even more so with only one in every five ceiling lights turned on for the weekend. There was enough light to see, of course, but the impression it gave was of a dark, foreboding sea of cubicles interrupted only by a grid of columns and an occasional conference area. I couldn't imagine it being productive; on a normal workday any attempt at serious concentration would be in direct competition with the noise and bustle of hundreds of co-workers.

"I'm right over there," Amber said as we got near her workstation, then pointed to her left. "Borgman's office was back in that corner. That's where the system analysis group was."

" 'Was?' "

"Yes. The group is being disbanded. Even if they could find someone with Borgman's talents, it would be too expensive. I also think his...well, his eccentricities made them less interested in continuing the function. Even the people he hired were pretty high-strung, so it would be starting from scratch if they did try to replace him."

I looked at the corner she indicated and saw a manager's cubicle, meaning a cubicle with taller walls and somewhat larger floor space. A small brass plate near the doorless entrance said, simply, "Dr. Borgman." Such government-issued accommodations were Spartan compared to those enjoyed at the Institute, but I supposed it was all relative.

Reaching her desk, Amber when right to work, turning on her computer and immediately plugging in her smart phone, presumably to recharge it while she copied the files. She explained that she had to dig a little to identify all the files, and then it would take several minutes to copy them all onto her flash drive. I looked around her workstation for a few minutes, noting a picture of her and Lisa in a collage over her desk next to several IAR training and achievement certificates. Beyond that there was little to hold my attention while she worked, and I decided to have a look at Borgie's office.

His office was much like the man, I thought, at least the man I remembered: small islands of order in a sea of chaos. He had a high-backed chair, a larger monitor than any at the desks around his and a personal printer, luxuries that I imagined were afforded the upper echelon at the IAR. These, along with the computer and a few other items, had been labeled and made ready for reassignment. Glancing at his bookcase, I was surprised and flattered to see binders containing all my published papers and articles. Apparently I had made a more lasting impression on Borgie than I knew.

As I reached out my hand to grab one of the binders I reminded myself of the risks we assumed by coming here. Scanlon and his guys believed I might be working with Borgie, and here I was, leaving fingerprints and who knows what else in Borgie's office, visiting surreptitiously on a weekend with pictures at the guard's desk as proof, and escorted in by the one person who actually did have Borgie's simulation code. We knew of these risks before we left the apartment, of course, but they felt more tangible standing there in Borgie's office.

I spent a few more minutes exploring. Nothing was locked; nothing seemed hidden or suspicious in any way. If Borgie had any secrets they were most likely to be found on his computer, but I knew that would be password protected. Eventually I gave up, returning to Amber's desk just as she was finishing.

"I got all the files he had in the archive, Roger," she told me. "If any are missing it's because he hadn't checked them in yet."

"Great. Let's find a place to look them over," I responded, and we walked with quickened steps toward the guard station to sign out.

"Thanks, Mick," Amber said to the guard as we signed the log. "See you tomorrow, I suppose."

"Good meeting you, sir. Enjoy the rest of your weekend."

Just as that exchange was being spoken I noticed a dark sedan roll up and park next to Lisa's car, curiously avoiding several more convenient spots. It may have been nothing or it may have been something; I had no way of knowing but I didn't like the odds. I nudged Amber and tilted my head toward the new arrival, and tried to offer a pretext for us to avoid the newcomer.

"Oh oh," I said, my voice filled with dismay. "Amber, could that be...?" The sole occupant of the car had begun walking the 50 yards or so to where we stood, but he couldn't see us through the reflective glass.

"Oh. Um...yes, I think it is. Mick? I think my ex just pulled up in the parking lot. He's jealous and kind of a bully, you know? I don't want him to see us here."

"No problem, Amber. I'll distract him for a minute or two. Just stand over there—through the first set of doors and around that little corner. I'll let you know when you can sneak out."

Amber gave him a conspiratorial smile and we positioned ourselves as directed, watching the newcomer pass within ten feet of where we stood and then through the inner door to the guard desk. I couldn't hear what was said, but in a moment Mick pointed to the alcove where he had taken my picture, the man stepped out of sight, and Mick waved us on.

As we jumped into the car I asked if she knew who the man was.

"I'm not sure, but he may have been one of the guys I thought might be watching when I went to my apartment last night."

"Is he one of Scanlon's people?"

"I don't think so. Lisa said there were only two of them, and he had two guys with him at the hotel yesterday. This guy wasn't one of them."

Great. Another unknown to throw on our growing heap. At least there was only one man. If someone intended to do harm, I thought, there would be more of them.

We drove out of the lot, looking back and not seeing anyone running out to the black sedan. It appeared we had evaded him, but we opted for a less direct route back to the apartment anyway. On the way we passed a coffee shop, and we decided to get a sandwich and take our first look at Borgie's code.

The shop was a small, brick-walled room with linoleum flooring and older furnishings that gave it a fifties diner kind of look. The coffee aroma was thick and inviting, and a deli case held a variety of sandwiches, cookies and other snacks. Amber took my order and some cash and left me to boot up her computer while she got the food. Plugging in her flash drive I felt a moment of hope, as if the answer to the puzzle was about to pop up on the screen, but I knew that wasn't realistic. What I saw instead was a directory of files, all written in a common programming language, but all with names only Borgie would understand. "Sharedist." "Compyield." "Valthreshold." I opened file after file, and was just beginning to get an idea of how they were organized when a shadow crossed my table.

Looking up I saw two men, one of whom took a seat opposite me and the other next to me, effectively blocking any exit. Amber had seen it, too, and I saw her fade back into the hallway that led to the restrooms. Outside the front window was another dark sedan, similar to the one at her office but not the same. Somehow we had been followed.

The man across the table from me was taller, with calculating eyes and an air of intensity. He had a threatening look, one that told me he was the type who didn't care how far he would have to go to get what he wanted. "Please stay calm, Dr. Morgan," he advised. "We need to talk with you. Where's the woman you were with?"

"I dropped her off at a subway station," I lied, calm on the outside only. "What do you want with her?"

"Nothing, now." He reached across the table and pulled the flash drive from the computer. "I suspect this is what we needed from her. Now it's you we're interested in."

I looked from him to the man next to me. He was shorter, but had the build of a weightlifter. His face was contorted, with a broken nose and a low brow, and his neck seemed to spread from just below his ears out to his wide shoulders. He hadn't spoken yet, and I could tell he wasn't cast in this role to deliver lines. His broken-toothed smile told me two things: he was physical, and he enjoyed it.

"Who are you?" I asked the first man.

He ignored my question. "You have been working with Dr. Borgman at the IAR. He was doing an important project for us, a project that he failed to complete. We're going to need your help to finish it."

"I haven't been working with Borgman," I said. "And I wouldn't have a clue how to finish his project."

"I see. You haven't been working with him, and yet you came here to DC, you searched his office, and you have all the software he was developing right here," he sneered, waving the flash drive. "Stick to software, Dr. Morgan; as a liar you stink."

"Who the hell are you guys?"

"We represent Dr. Borgman's…um…benefactor. Replete. The simulation system you've been working on is for us. Borgman was very well paid, and now we want the system."

"Replete? I swear I don't understand. Replete with what? Borgman worked for the IAR."

The guy sitting next to me finally spoke. "Maybe he really doesn't know what's been going on. Borgman must have kept him in the dark."

"Yeah, well, Scanlon was supposed to keep Borgman in the dark, too." Then, turning to me again, "None of that matters now. Borgman is gone, but he told us you were the guy who could finish it up. So 'tag, you're it,' Doc. Now let's go."

The guy next to me closed the computer and slid it into Amber's bag. Then he grabbed my elbow in what felt like a steel clamp and pulled me to my feet. Once they had me out the door it was just a few steps to their car, but there was a problem. A group of teens had double-parked next to the sedan and were now leaning against the passenger door, joking and shoving one another and generally acting like punks. My strong-arm companions pushed into the small group with me in tow, resulting in the kind of loud confrontation these kids seemed to enjoy. The grip on my arm loosened, slightly, and the owner of that grip set down Amber's computer case to push a kid aside and open the car door. About that moment I heard the quick beep of a car horn and saw Amber waving me toward Lisa's car. Swinging my arm around I broke free, and, before my would-be captor could respond, I grabbed the computer bag and leapt behind the sedan and into Lisa's car. We sped off, noting that it would take at least a minute before they would be in pursuit.

A series of sharp turns and accelerations had us several blocks away by the time I imagined they would again be looking for us. "That was lucky," I said. "Those kids really saved me."

"Not luck. I found them messing around in the parking lot next door and paid them to make a diversion. I told them my boyfriend was being hassled by a couple of jerks and needed help."

I looked at her with renewed admiration, then saw we were about to pass by a large gas station. Almost shouting from the excitement, I asked Amber to turn in and pull up to the pump furthest from the street.

"Is your cell phone turned on?"

"No, it's off. Why?"

"They found us way too easily," I explained, and jumped out of the car. Frantically, I ran my hands under the bumpers and inside the wheel wells, concentrating on the side next to the sedan at the IAR parking lot. While I did, Amber was approached by another driver, a tourist who was lost and seeking directions to Annapolis. She held back her anxiety long enough to explain how to find highway 50, waiting to see what I was doing and watching the street for any sign of the sedan at the same time. A moment later I found what I expected: a small box with a short antenna that was magnetically attached to the frame. We had been tracked, and surely we were still being tracked at that moment.

I jumped back in and told Amber to take off, indicating a route away from the coffee shop while I hastily explained what I had found.

"What do we do now? Abandon the car?"

"Nope. In fact, I imagine those guys will be on their way out of town in a couple minutes."

"What? Where are they going?"

"Annapolis," I said, and gave her a big grin. It only took her a moment to realize what I had done and return the smile. Our relief was short lived, however. "But now we're back where we started. They have the software."

"I manage a software archive, Roger. I always keep backups."

"Yeah, well, I wish we had a backup now."

"You didn't hear what I said," she responded with a mischievous look. "I said I *always* keep backups!"

"What? Where?"

"On my smart phone. I zipped up the whole directory and put it on my phone."

I could only laugh with relief, then she said, "Now, grab our sandwiches, would you? They're on the back seat."

We drove for a little while, but with nowhere really to go we decided to return to Lisa's apartment. As a precaution, we parked in front of another building in the complex and walked the short distance between. It was early afternoon, bright and sunny, and I felt totally exposed even on the wooded walkway. Still more shaken by my near abduction than I cared to admit, we couldn't get inside soon enough. When we did, I went right to work on the computer, taking the memory card from Amber's cell phone and copying it onto the computer. Following her back-up example, I also archived the file by encrypting and emailing it to myself, as I had done with my log file the night before. Finally I began opening the files, and spent about a half hour skimming through them before Amber got impatient.

"What are you seeing, Roger?"

"I'm seeing a lot of things, both good and bad."

"Good first."

"Okay. Borgie's code is compatible with the Institute's simulation tools. That's huge, because, if it wasn't, we'd have no chance of running anything. Also, and this is fascinating for me, Borgie designed this with the same general style and structure as we used back in school. I mean, it has evolved some, but he still architected the code pretty much like we did back then. That would make it a lot easier for me to work with the code, if I had any clue what I was doing. He also did something very cool here."

"What's that?"

"He built a recursion engine into the code. You see, these simulations spawn hundreds, sometimes thousands of tiny programs, each representing one player in the emergent system. We call each one an 'agent.' It's like having one small program simulating each bird in a flock. The problem is that, when the number of agents gets large, the simulation gets very slow. It looks like Borgie found a shortcut using a technique called 'recursion.' It works very fast, but even for the writer it feels like walking through a house of mirrors. Trying to figure out how he did it would take a lot of study, but I don't really need to know that just now; we need the 'what,' not the 'how.'"

"Okay. Bad news?"

"Yeah, there is plenty of that, too. First, there are a couple of hundred files here. It would take days, at least, to sort through them all. Second, he didn't name them in a way that helps me figure out which ones are important and which ones, for example, just hold data. Third, the build file—the one you use to put all these pieces together into a program—is still missing. This is going to take some… wait… this is interesting."

I had opened a file and found a list of variable names that actually sounded meaningful. Within these names were several terms that seemed to be used often, terms like supply, bbl, blend, ppg, mpg, kwh, and many more. These terms were used to define variables that drove the individual behaviors of the many agents, and they seemed to have a general theme.

"This is about energy, I think. See these? Every one of them has something to do with electricity, gas…hold on… yeah, it all seems to be oil-related energy."

"Oil. That's a good start, Roger. What else?"

"It's interesting. This file is about energy, but others seem to focus on other things. Maybe it's still related to energy somehow; I can't tell." I continued looking, but other than getting a feel for how the system was structured I didn't see any more clues as to its use.

I finally had to take a break from it, and paced the floor to stretch my legs. Without source code staring me in the face I was able again to mentally step back from everything and consider the whole situation. We had learned a little; not much, but there were clues. We knew that whoever was looking for us was working hard at it. It had taken only minutes for them to learn we were at Amber's office. Also, there were more people involved than we thought; the three we saw that day were all new to us. That reminded me of something said at the coffee shop that I didn't understand.

"Amber, does 'replete' mean anything special to you?"

"I know what it means, if that's what you're asking."

"No, no. Is it the name of a company or something like that?"

"I don't know, let me do a search," she said, and turned the computer to face her. "I'm not finding much, Roger. Here's a health food supplement...a self-help book...here's a blog article about mega-rich CEOs. Hmm. Well, there's no company by that name that I can see. What is it supposed to be?"

"Not sure. Go back to that last one a moment," I requested. I explained my inquiry as I skimmed the article. "Those guys at the coffee shop said something I didn't quite get about Borgie getting paid by 'Replete.' They referred to it as Borgie's benefactor."

At first glance the article was just a typical internet rant, in this case condemning rich people for the sin of success. As I got deeper into it, though, certain elements caught my attention. There were references to the "Replete Group," and the article included a short list of executives that were suspected of being members, along with their compensation packages. Conspiracy theory or no, this guy had done a lot of homework. "Do you see anything special about this list?"

Amber read for a moment, then pointed out a name that caught her eye. "Here's Hamilton Grant at Reicher Oil, but I suppose you'd expect the CEO of the second-largest oil company to be on a list like this."

"What's special about him?"

"Probably just coincidence, but he was the target of the white-collar crime investigation that Scanlon and Borgman were working on just before all this started."

"Really. Was he playing with gas prices?" There was a lot of speculation in the news that soaring energy prices were being manipulated illegally.

"No, stock prices. The SEC thought Grant was doing something to pad his bonus. The SEC brought in the FBI, specifically Scanlon's WCU, and Scanlon brought in Borgman's team. Borgman's job was to simulate what happens when various rules are broken so they could maybe see how he was doing it."

"Interesting. That could definitely work."

"Well, if Grant was doing something, he had plenty of motivation—look at this guy's comp plan."

I looked and gulped. The guy's bonus alone could fund a modest space program.

Amber continued. "Anyway, everyone thought there was a strong case, and then one day Scanlon just dropped it, claiming there was no evidence of any crime. Lisa told me not everyone on his team agreed, but the investigation was stopped. Just after that Borgman began working on his private simulations, and that's about the same time Lisa started noticing Scanlon's behavior."

Another piece of the puzzle was falling into place, and this time it was more than a piece of blue sky.

"Amber, I think Scanlon and Borgie may have been working for Reicher Oil."

My reasoning was paper-thin, but there had to be some link between Borgie, Scanlon, and Reicher Oil. I stood and again paced across the room, averting my eyes from anything that could distract me, and began mentally arranging what we knew so far. Scanlon investigates Reicher's CEO. Borgie does a simulation for Scanlon. The case is dropped, then Scanlon and Borgie begin working together on something, but what? Then there's Hamilton Grant himself. Rich, powerful, highly motivated to break a few rules for personal gain. How was he doing it? The answer must be in Borgie's simulation. Borgie sends me a card—not his official card, but one he created himself. Why? He was working on something, he told Scanlon about me, and then he sent me this card. He was telling me something.

I went back to the blog and re-read the short article, paying more attention to its mention of the Replete Group. The term was used only a few times, and the article seemed to be written for an audience who already understood the reference, leaving little information for a newcomer like myself. Eventually I widened my search to other articles on the site, and as I did I began to get a feel for the organization behind it.

This was the web site of the Wealth Gap Monitor, a self-proclaimed watchdog group headquartered just across the river in Virginia, whose purpose seemed to be railing against inequities between the very-upper class and the masses. Their site featured an extensive listing and analysis of our nation's highest earners, and besides the blog they hosted a bulletin board with a number of discussion threads. There were too many to read in detail, but the ones I skimmed were full of posts condemning the rich for their success. That was not surprising, of course; many felt jealousy and resentment when comparing their lot to the mega-rich. What I found more interesting was the ominous message that had been repeated at the end of some of posts: "Beware the Replete." With each instance my curiosity intensified, but as far as I could tell there was no definition of what the group might actually be, giving it the aura of a "he who must not be named" metaphor of evil. I finally quit in frustration and began considering instead what our logical next step might be.

Looking up from the computer screen, I saw Amber's face, watching me patiently as I reviewed the site.

"So where do we go from here?" she asked, echoing my thoughts.

"We need to know more about this Replete Group," I responded, a skeletal plan forming in my mind. "Replete is one key. Hamilton Grant is another. These guys at the Wealth Gap Monitor are the best lead we have left."

"Okay, so let's talk to them." Amber was right, we needed to get to them somehow, but it seemed a lot easier said than done.

"Well, the site says they're in Falls Church, Virginia. That's just across the river, but there's no address. Here's an email address, but we may never get a response. Especially on a Sunday."

"Nothing to lose, Roger."

"Yes. Nothing to lose."

I composed an email to the Monitor, making my best effort to entice a fast response from them. The message said simply:

"Have recent info on Hamilton Grant. Need to share ASAP. Must meet."

I followed the message with my new cell number and sent it, only half expecting any response. Chances are whoever owned the mailbox wouldn't see it for days, and even then might not be inclined to meet a stranger on what he considers so sensitive a subject. Next I tried searching internet phone listings for the Wealth Gap Monitor, and found nothing remotely close. I did find a few references to it on other websites, but they merely pointed me back to the Monitor's home page without supplying further information. I was in the middle of the search when my phone buzzed on the table.

I had a text message. The timing was a pleasant surprise, but the content was what I should have expected. It said: *"Who r u? Why asap?"* The message came from a number in a distant area code, most likely using a service that keeps the sender anonymous.

"Tell him there have been two murders!" Amber said.

"I don't want to scare him off. I mean, he's already a conspiracy theorist—chances are he has been stocking up on canned goods for years already. No, what guys like this want most is validation. Grant is the way to get to him. I'm going to try again."

I tapped on the frustrating little numeric keypad of my disposable phone, eventually producing a coherent text message:

"am 1 of grants victims. know what he is doing. must act now."

Okay, it was sent. I had no way of knowing if the message would be received, if the guy I sent it to would believe me, or if he would be at all willing to risk meeting us. It felt like letter to Santa Claus, with only a dream of a response. For the next several minutes we waited, nursing false hope before releasing a sigh and looking for some alternate plan of action. I even debated whether to send another text message, but as I reached for it my phone buzzed again. He would meet us, in public, at the Einstein statue in one hour.

We found the Albert Einstein memorial in front of the National Academy of Science, just across Constitution Avenue on the north side of the mall. The memorial was nestled in a small grove of trees and shrubs, letting most passing tourists walk by unaware. I had to appreciate the choice; whoever we were meeting knew this spot would be public enough to feel secure yet quiet enough for us to talk. It presented a logistical problem for us, though. The memorial stood on one of the most traveled routes in the city and adjacent to the center of the National Mall. Even in mid- to late-afternoon, Sunday tourism put parking at a premium. The congestion forced us to circle the block more than once, and I was about to have Amber drop me at the memorial when a wearied family slumped into a minivan and left an open spot just a block from our destination.

We nearly trotted the short distance, arriving only two minutes late and finding a half-dozen or so people gawking and talking about Einstein and his achievements. They all appeared to be vacationers, and my attempts at making eye contact with the adults among them only drew quizzical looks in return. Anxiously, we looked around the small site and craned our necks up and down the street, not knowing if we had missed our contact, if he was just later than we were or if we had simply been tricked.

We eventually settled down, accepting our apparent fate, and found a place to sit and ponder our next move. While we spoke, I began to notice the memorial itself and the strange behavior of the other visitors. The memorial was a large, bronze statue of Albert Einstein sitting on a semi-circle of granite steps. In front of it was a circular pavement that held a map of the stars. One by one, people stood at the center of the circle and spoke to the statue, each time resulting in a wide smile and laughter. Amber and I looked at each other and shrugged in bewilderment, until, as the last of the visitors finally drifted off, I couldn't resist. I stood in the center of the circle and addressed the good doctor.

"Maybe you could explain what is happening, Dr. Einstein," I said, and immediately realized what the others were laughing about. Standing at the center of the circle put me at the focal point of sound reflecting off the steps, sending every whisper back to my ears with an unearthly buzz, as if I were speaking into a long tube. I laughed like the others had, quickly inviting Amber to experience my discovery, when I noticed a man had emerged from the trees behind me. He was not a tourist, rather he looked me in the eye and waited for my surprise to pass before he spoke.

"I understand you have some information about Grant," he said. "I'm Chuck. What do you have?"

He was a young man, I guessed in his late twenties, and his style of dress—buttoned shirt, cargo pants, and high-topped tennis shoes—made him appear nerdy and out of place, a babe in the woods.

That changed, though, when I looked at his face. He was intense, and, theory or not, he certainly appeared to take his conspiracy ideas very seriously.

"I'm Roger; this is Amber," I replied, and indicated a spot near the end of the monument steps where we could chat in relative comfort and privacy. "It looks like we've run into some trouble."

The mention of trouble made Chuck's eyes open wide behind his bow-rimmed glasses, alarming him to the point that I thought he might get up and leave. Chuck was genuinely worried—about what I had no idea, but I began to appreciate the fact that he was meeting with us at all. I quickly reassured him, hoping to settle him back down while he made quick, sharp movements to search shadows and recesses for hidden danger.

"It's okay, Chuck. Honest. We're here alone. Nobody but you knows we're here. It's just that a situation has come up that we're at a loss to explain, and it has something to do with this Hamilton Grant." That seemed to earn his provisional attention, so I continued. "A man I know, an old friend, was doing some contract work for the FBI. He was doing some analysis for their investigation of Hamilton Grant at Reicher Oil."

"When?" He was insistent. "When was this?"

"About nine months ago," Amber told him.

"I *knew* it! They're finally catching the bastard. Do they have proof? Is he being charged?"

"No, no not yet," I told him. I tried to speak calmly, hoping to find words that wouldn't spook him, but with enough urgency to elicit a response. "Do you have much information on Grant?"

He looked at us with renewed suspicion. "Yeah, we have some. Who are you guys? You said you had information for me."

Amber and I exchanged looks, deciding non-verbally how and how far to proceed. There was a thin line to tread, on one side losing our new friend for telling too little and on the other side losing him for telling too much. The only rational solution was to turn over our cards one at a time, being careful to avoid scaring him further. I decided to start by showing him vulnerability.

"Okay, look. I'm new at this sort of thing, but Amber and I have gotten messed up in something we don't understand. I'll tell you what we know so far, but I'm going to need a little information in return. Deal?"

"We'll see. What do you have?"

"A story about Grant. We don't have proof—yet—but we know it's true," I told him what we had learned, withholding names and any mention of the two deaths. Chuck's guard slowly dropped as he devoted more and more attention to allegations against Grant. It took less convincing than I had expected. He was more than eager to believe the story, and when I got to the part about a corrupt FBI agent teaming with Grant he nearly achieved an adrenal orgasm. Even without documented proof, Chuck's world of conspiring evil-doers was being validated by our tale.

At the end of my story I explained that we, Amber and I, were currently being sought, and the only knowledge we had of our pursuers was the guy at the FBI (whose name we did not share) and an odd reference to Replete. Then I described how our search for Replete led us to him, and his face instantly darkened.

"I've told them a thousand times not to mention Replete in their damn posts," Chuck said. "We're supposed to be hunting, not hiding. If Replete comes after us we'll have to shut the whole damned thing down!"

"I understand," I said. I didn't understand at all. "Who is this Replete Group? Is Grant part of it?"

Chuck looked at each of us in turn, paused, then seemed to decide just how far he was willing to guide us.

"Okay, I'll tell you this much. Look at our site and you'll find a spreadsheet. It's a list of the über-rich. The ones we know—or at least believe—are in the Replete Group have a little mark by their name. Grant is one of them; in fact he's like a charter member. Replete is like club, you know? It's a support group these guys join, and each member helps all the other members make more money. Just look at Reicher Oil's board of directors. Half of them are CEOs of other big corporations, and most of them are in the group, too. It's a total economic bloc, man, and the members are sucking billions out of the economy." At that point Chuck seemed to catch himself, his zeal having taken him further than intended.

I challenged him, hoping to draw out as much information as I could. "You mean it's an interlocking directorate? That's it?" That arrangement is an ethical quagmire, at best, although not uncommon. Even so, it didn't seem like that would be enough to cause what we were seeing.

"No, okay?" Chuck sneered at my naïveté. "That's not 'it.' These guys aren't just board-room buddies. They pay big time to be in the group, like five, maybe ten percent of their income. In return the group will do anything, and I mean *any*thing, to make each member successful. And the members are in it deep. They do what they're told, or else."

"Or else what?"

"Remember J. Foster Shipley, the CEO whose yacht exploded north of Australia not too long ago?"

I remembered it. Shipley ran one of the largest consumer appliance manufacturers in the country. News reports gave fuel vapors in the engine room as a probable cause, and the story dropped from the limelight without any final evidence one way or the other. It was just the type of unknown that could cause a feeding frenzy among the Chucks of the world.

"You think Replete was behind that?"

"We know it. That guy was trying to get out, and they nailed him. We saw the whole thing, man. He must have developed a conscience, and they had to take him out."

"Who's behind it, then? Who runs Replete?"

"No, that's it, man. It's all I'm going to say. Thanks for the story on Grant, but I can't help you against Replete. If they are after you, and you'd better hope they're not, you're way too hot for us. Don't contact me again."

With that, Chuck stood and left through the same grove of trees that had hid his entrance, moving swiftly before I could marshal any attempt to stop him. I felt a void when he was gone, as if the hollow echo off Einstein's steps were the mocking of elusive knowledge. We had not learned all I'd hoped. Still, it was more than we had known an hour earlier. And, in spite of the summer heat, what we had learned was chilling.

Small groups approached as we sat there, mostly couples and young families, each going through the ritual of addressing the statue and each displaying the requisite reaction. I felt as if I were watching through a window, peering from some precarious perch into a simpler world, a place of innocence and abandon. These people were pursuing simple pleasures, enjoying what would have been a beautiful summer weekend, had I been free to notice, while Amber and I struggled against a danger that seemed to grow and evolve at every turn. We watched those tourists for a while, exchanging few words as we devoted mindshare to digesting Chuck's information and deciding yet again on a next move.

Eventually the stone steps became uncomfortable, signaling our time to leave. I looked up from my thoughts and found Amber sitting there, quietly watching, patiently allowing me a moment of decompression. The day's events had distracted me from any prurient thoughts, but as I looked at her, composed and trusting, I was reminded of the single positive aspect of my trip so far. I put my arm around her and kissed her forehead, earning a warm nuzzle in return, and offered the only rational course of action I could think of.

"Let's go for a walk," I said.

Amber smiled and stood, intuitively understanding that I needed more time for my thoughts to percolate to a more actionable plane.

"Where to?"

"Let's just be tourists for a little while, okay?" I asked, and, stretching my legs, we set off across the street and toward the west end of the mall.

A cool breeze met us as we left that grove of trees, refreshing us and offering welcome relief to the throng of foot-weary souls who slowly dragged themselves in the opposite direction after a full weekend of sightseeing. Shadows were lengthening, and the demographic make-up of the people around us was noticeably changing from families to more intimate pairings. The ubiquitous street vendors were shutting down their trailers full of pretzels or t-shirts or soft drinks and heading home. The resultant mall was more sedate, somehow more of a presentation of national identity than the near-carnival atmosphere it had had just a few hours earlier.

Amber took my arm for a while as we walked, holding it without clinging, at once drawing and giving support as we wound along shaded paths toward the Vietnam War Memorial.

"How can people be so greedy?" she asked. It was more a statement of exasperation than a question. "Those CEOs already make thousands of times what others make, and still they want more and more."

"Hmmm. Maybe we should have asked Chuck about membership in Wealth Gap Monitor," I said in a mock-serious tone.

"No, really," she replied. "They're unbelievable."

"Yeah, it's an ethical travesty. Still, we should be careful where we put the blame. It may not be as obvious as someone like Chuck wants to believe."

She gave me a questioning look, so I offered some explanation.

"Well, if a CEO gets overpaid, whose fault is it? The CEO's? He or she is accepting a paycheck; the board of directors sets the pay. I mean, if the Institute decided to double my pay, I'd accept it. The CEO is trying to earn all he can, like anyone else. As long as they aren't cheating, well, I'm envious, but I'm not outraged. But the boards of directors? I have a hard time finding sympathy for them. They have a fiduciary responsibility to look out for the shareholders, right? When they pay out unreasonably large salaries and bonuses, those shareholders are getting screwed. If shareholders had honest representation, or maybe even some direct voice in executive pay, I doubt those salaries would exist."

"Why does a board of directors do that? You'd think they could save a lot of money…"

"Very true, but officers and boards are pretty incestuous. The board sets the pay, but a director of one company is often an officer in another, so they have a lot of motivation to keep officer salaries high. It's a culture of excess, and the good ol' boys take care of their own, I suppose. Compensation is one area where boards don't really represent the shareholders' interests, and that is why shareholders need a stronger voice in it."

"And the CEOs are innocent?"

"Ha! I'd be surprised. At best they're trained to respond to their bonus plan. They're going to do those things that get them the highest income, right? They're working for themselves when maybe they should be working for the investors and employees. The ethical line is a complete blur, so we probably shouldn't be surprised when it gets crossed."

"And just where is that ethical line?"

"You know, I've always been surprised at how hard it is to find a good definition of ethics. I'm no expert, but I've thought about it a lot. I suppose anytime a person is given time, money and resources to serve one purpose but instead uses it to serve his own purposes, that is unethical. The same thing applies to the typical employee."

"I know what you mean, Roger. I've seen people hide basic information just so a coworker won't be able to do as good a job as they do."

"Exactly. Or a manager who hires people based on their race or gender, or for some other personal reason. Ethics isn't always about money. In fact, I think it's more about honoring one's obligations—acting in the employer's best interests, that sort of thing."

I had often pondered ethics, amazed, as I had said, that such an important concept had such poor definition in most circles. At that moment, though, I was more impressed at how Amber and I seemed to agree in yet another dimension. This woman was very, very interesting.

There was a conversational hiatus as we neared the Vietnam War Memorial. The memorial was formed by two long triangular sections of granite wall, jet black, forming a large chevron set below the surrounding grade. A walkway took visitors down from one end to a low point at the center and back up to the other end. The wall was engraved with the names of men and women who fell either in that conflict or because of it, a tribute to them and a reminder of the terrible cost our nation had incurred. Among the visitors we saw were relatives and former comrades in arms, several wearing caps with braided bills or embroidered unit numbers. A few stood quietly near the wall, some gently touching a name etched in the black stone, while others struggled to comprehend the enormity of the complete list of the fallen. The mood was deeply somber, and we passed through quickly and quietly.

When we had gotten a respectful distance from the memorial Amber opened a different topic. "So, what is the pet project you planned to work on during your vacation?" she asked.

"A simulation study I started a while ago; never finished. Never had the time for it, I guess. It's one of those things that I can find interesting while others, well, maybe not so much."

"What is it about?"

"It's about the effects of bad ethics on the economy, how it all adds up to be a bigger cost than we think."

"I'm sorry, but isn't that already done? I see articles every so often about the overall cost of crime."

"Well, that's true, there are those who estimate the overall cost of crime, but it's not the same. What they are doing is adding up all the estimated losses based on current crime rates and comparing it to the gross domestic product or something similar. And it's always a big, scary number, but it's not the same. The cost of bad ethics is more subtle than that."

"How is it different?"

"Here's an example. Say that for some guy ten percent of his decisions are self-serving. That doesn't sound too bad; just one out of ten aren't right. Now imagine two guys like that, working together, and their output is based on the decisions of both. Suddenly only eighty-one percent of their joint decisions are sound. With five guys, it's down to less than sixty percent. With ten, only about a third of their decisions can be trusted—and we don't know which third!"

"Like error propagation, right?"

"A lot like that, yes. But now the cost to our economy is the difference between the GDP we really have and the one we *could* have if people behaved ethically. It's the opportunity cost, and it's pretty big. It happens every time a salesman shorts you one part out of a dozen and you have to run out to buy another. It happens every time a buyer gives out a purchase order to a friend instead of the best business partner. It happens when workers knock off early, collecting pay for time not worked. You can't add these things up like you can crime reports."

"And your simulation will be able to add them up?"

"Ha! Well, no. I'll make a lot of educated guesses, and I suppose that means the simulation will suffer from error propagation, too. I have a lot of interesting data the Institute collected on a job once, though, and I'm curious to know what it all implies. It's just for my own edification."

"So is there any hope for our economy?" Amber teased.

"Well, the simulation isn't done yet, but, yeah, I think we have a few years left. What about you? What keeps you busy outside work?"

"Oh," she smiled, "I play some tennis, I like to meet people, things like that." She downplayed it, but then she went on to tell me about her volunteer work, her continuing education, and more. Amber wasn't one to sit still for long.

We chatted like that as we walked, Amber's goal of providing distraction being effectively met for those few minutes. There was more to it, though. Amber and I had been foisted on each other by circumstance. Now, as we each learned more about how the other felt and thought, we had a brief opportunity to consider the relationship outside the frenzy and intrigue that had forged it. For my part, I saw potential. The physical and cosmetic attractions had already given way to a more cerebral appreciation and caring. As for Amber, well, I could only hope—but the right signs were there.

We soon reached the western end of the reflecting pool and the steps of the Lincoln Memorial. The reflecting pool, which over the years had degenerated into an eyesore and a subject of complaint, was receiving a facelift. Dirt walking paths on either side of the pool were being replaced with concrete walks, and the pool itself was being cleaned and refurbished. Even in its current state the scene was impressive, the still surface of the water mirroring the WWII memorial, the Washington Monument and even the US Capitol building. I wanted to return to see the same scene after the project was completed.

At the end of the pool, watching silently over the length of the mall all the way to the seat of our government, sat the famous statue of Abraham Lincoln, a larger-than-life tribute to a larger-than-life man. We climbed the steps for a closer look, reading the inscriptions of his Gettysburg Address, his inaugural speech and other works, and feeling genuine awe at the commitment and sacrifice that held our nation together so long ago. His words showed steadfast commitment to weathering the worst storm in the nation's history, to surviving and rebuilding in spite of unknown dangers, a message that felt relevant as I considered our current plight. I supposed that was a characteristic of most words of inspiration: universal truths with universal application.

Leaving Lincoln, we approached the Korean War Memorial, a grouping of lifelike statues depicting soldiers slogging through a Korean field. There was a stone wall beyond the statues, etched with shadows of more soldiers. There was also an inscription I like to remember from time to time. It said, simply, "Freedom is not free." Back home, patriotism was a quaint concept rarely thought about during days typically spent in a self-involved haze. Not that people weren't patriotic, but sometimes it seemed we kept our patriotism in a drawer. Here it was a palpable element, a lesson to some and a reminder to others. More than ever, I hoped I would be able to come back and experience the vacation I was now missing.

As we passed through that memorial the sun dipped noticeably lower, signaling time to head back to the car, re-enter the present and address the challenges we knew awaited. Amber held my arm again, and we allowed our conversation to return to our immediate needs and the actions required to fulfill them. We spoke calmly and with detachment, as if our lives didn't depend on our next steps. In fact, in the near-twilight and in this postcard-like setting, it would have been easy to let ourselves forget our problems. The closer we got to the car, though, the less viable procrastination became. In fact, the thoughts I had been mulling subconsciously had pushed their way back to the surface, and as we left the mall I walked with lowered head and furrowed brow.

"You look like you've made up your mind about something, Roger," Amber gently prodded.

"Yes, I think so. At least, I've reached a couple of conclusions. I'd been thinking about simply finding someone, some authority, so we can hand over this whole matter and be done with it. But we can't. Not yet, anyway."

"Because…?"

"Well, first because we lack any kind of proof. Borgie's death was suspicious, but Lisa's was apparently staged to look like an accidental hit and run. The guys at the coffee shop this morning are gone; besides, they didn't actually do anything before we got away. What would we tell police? Then there's Chuck. Not to be, well, uncharitable, but I don't think he'd be a strong reference in our police report, you know?"

Amber nodded her agreement.

"Then there's the 'who' part of the problem. Would we tell the police? SEC? FBI? Honestly, I'm not sure where to start. And, by the way, if Lisa's last call was to their Internal Affairs people we should be leery of them, too. Chuck may be trapped in his theories, but, if he's at all correct about Replete, they have the kind of resources that could tempt just about anyone."

More nods; a noted decrease in enthusiasm as each problem was stated aloud.

"Okay, so those are the things we can't do. What is it we *can* do?"

"Well, first off, we need to stay the course with our original strategy. If we can find out what Borgie was up to, all the other questions will be easier to answer." I hoped. "But Chuck gave us a second path to explore. Remember when he said 'just look at Reicher's board of directors?' I know he wasn't being literal, but that's exactly what I think we should do. I think I know how we can find out who is behind this Replete Group; who the members are, anyway."

"So what do we do?"

"We need to research Reicher Oil. I don't suppose you know of a place nearby where we can work for a while?"

"Well, most of the better hotels have a small business center for their guests, but we'd probably need to be registered. How about a college library? The main library at Georgetown never closes."

I gave her a squeeze with a kiss to the top of her head. "You're a genius. But first we need to pick something up."

Minutes later I was sitting in the car across the street from my hotel, praying that I had guessed right. We needed my computer as well as Amber's if both of us were going to work on this problem, and, while I didn't think anyone would be watching the hotel for me now, it seemed much safer to have Amber retrieve my things from the hotel concierge. That assumed the hotel had gathered them up as I had requested, of course, and that they'd be willing to give all my things to a woman who just happened to have my business card. For her part, Amber did what she could to change her appearance on short notice, pulling her hair back and donning a pair of reading glasses—not the most sophisticated disguise, but if anyone was watching primarily for me, she would likely go unnoticed. At best, though, this was a calculated risk, and I reasoned that the sooner she emerged from the building the safer we were.

Time passed. Then more. I began looking over my shoulder and peering into cars parked around me, but there was nothing to see. Of course, that didn't mean we were safe, and I felt a paranoid tingle creep up my neck as I waited.

At the end of an agonizing wait, Amber stepped out of the hotel carrying my computer bag and towing my suitcase. I started the engine and prepared to turn into the hotel's front entrance driveway, but before I could move Amber did something unexpected. She raised her hand in the air and hailed a cab from the line lurking near the hotel entrance.

The unease I had felt minutes earlier quickly grew into alarm. Something was wrong, but following her closely certainly wasn't the answer. I reached for my cell phone to call her, then paused with uncertainty. Suddenly every course of action seemed unsafe. All I could do was sit there, powerless, and hope Amber would contact me.

I didn't have to wait long. My cell buzzed, and Amber spoke in hurried sentences.

"Roger, I think there might be a problem. I saw someone slip something into your suitcase before they brought it out to me."

"Could be another tracking device," I reasoned. "Where are you headed?"

"North. Did anyone follow me out?"

"Not that I saw. They probably think they don't have to follow; the device will lead them to me. Have the driver drop you off and I'll pick you up."

"Okay. Head north to M street and go west; I'll have him drop me at M and Wisconsin. It's on the way to Georgetown University."

I turned north, realizing as I did that this was the first time since meeting at the Museum of Natural History that Amber and I had been apart. The separation was uncomfortable, a feeling rooted in much more than our mutual circumstance. Amber had become important. My foot strained to bear down on the accelerator pedal, and I had to consciously fight the urge for fear of being stopped in Lisa's car without explanation. Sunday evening traffic was light, but the traffic lights didn't know that. At every intersection the semaphore seemed to sense my anxiety and purposely turn red to fuel my frustration. Every actual minute became a virtual hour until I finally saw her and pulled over.

"Amber, what happened?" I demanded as soon as she was in the car. We had put my suitcase in the trunk on the hope that any kind of transmitter would be defeated when enclosed by metal; still, I steered north on Wisconsin, not wanting to approach our destination at Georgetown University if we were in fact being tracked.

"I just walked in, told them you would unable to return as you had hoped and asked them to check you out and give me your things so I could get them to you. Then the desk clerk heard your name and whispered something to the concierge. Roger, it was Valerie, the woman that checked you in the night you arrived. She's the one Lisa and I had paid to tell us your room number and stall a few minutes so I could place the bug. I was scared to death that she recognized me, but, if she did, she didn't say anything. Anyway, I watched her in the reflection of a big brass sign, and she put something in the top pocket of your suitcase."

It didn't take long to decide that we needed to open the trunk and find whatever waited. If it was a tracking device, we should be able to find and dispose of it far faster than anyone could locate us and dispatch their agents. Even so, I felt as though I had a poisonous snake in the trunk, unconsciously avoiding bumps and potholes while looking for a place to stop.

A few blocks later I pulled into the long drive leading to the National Cathedral and found a spot to pull over. Ah, the cathedral. This was another thing I had planned to see while on vacation, yet another site that would now have to be deferred to some later opportunity. Built in the classical style but just completed in 1990, the building was a thoroughly modern rendition of the large Gothic churches found throughout Europe and England. The main entrance was a large archway framed by two enormous spiked and spired towers, behind which was a cross-shaped floor plan large enough to accommodate the Washington Monument laid down the center aisle. The outer walls were supported by ornate flying buttresses, and the entire edifice was of white stone with massive columns and intricate carvings in every nook. It had taken eighty-three years to complete, and I could only give it a cursory glance while exiting the car to inspect my viper-infested luggage.

Even with our logical minds appreciating the time it would take anyone to lock on to a signal, marshal resources and arrive at our location, our nerves were on high alert. We popped the trunk lid and quickly zipped open the upper pocket, ready to disable any unknown device and speed away as if silent stealth helicopters were just moments behind us. What we found, though, was not at all what we expected. Valerie, desk clerk extraordinaire, had printed out my final bill along with a number of phone messages I had received and sent them along in my luggage. At the bottom of the bill she included a personal note: "I hope you enjoyed your stay; please call next time you need accommodations." She signed it with a tiny heart over the "i" in Valerie, turning her message into the kind of double entendre that would catch the eye of the average male guest. I smiled at that; Amber didn't, instead giving me a raised eyebrow followed by a terse "Let's go."

Before starting the engine I took another moment to skim over the messages, reading the subject lines and sender names and the details of the more important few. As I had turned off my cell phone, callers had tried to reach me at the hotel, leaving messages that had been automatically transcribed for my convenience by the hotel's speech recognition system. Nicki had called to follow up on my office break-in; no news, but I should remember to speak with Ariel when I had time. The next two were from Cynthia, chastising me for not having my phone powered on and asking where I had been. Ariel called, also informing of the break-in and asking if I might participate in a conference call later in the week. Apologies for the interruption, of course, but business was business. The last call was from Cynthia again. She was flying to DC to see her new client, and wanted to meet for breakfast and advice. The rest of the message implored me to turn on my phone so we could coordinate time and place. I didn't think about it at the time, but, aside from Nicki's message, it was strange to receive so many business calls over a weekend. As vacations went, this one seemed doomed on multiple levels.

We found Lauinger Library not far from the main university gate. Although it stood in the staid brick-and-ivy setting of Georgetown University, Lauinger had a contemporary and open design both inside and out, and we found ourselves climbing to an upper floor before finding a suitably remote spot where we could work without disturbing any Sunday-night students or drawing unwanted attention. I was surprised to see so many others on a summer's Sunday evening, although I supposed some of that was because, as a student, I had spent so little time in the library myself. My technology courses had been far less dependent on library resources than law or the political sciences.

Once settled, we quickly booted up both computers, connected to the library's wireless network and downloaded the table of CEOs from the Wealth Gap Monitor site.

"How are you at building a database?" I asked Amber.

"Not bad. I can do a simple one pretty quickly. What do you need?"

"How long to make one that can import Chuck's table and then let us type in more records?"

Amber counted the number of fields and asked for twenty minutes. While she worked I pulled up the annual report for Reicher Oil, searching for the list of board members and corporate officers. Next I did a search on each board member's name, looking for other positions they might hold. Several of them were on boards of similarly sized companies, as we had been told, although it was interesting to see how they crossed over to different industries. Reicher's board included directors that also served companies in food, manufacturing, electronics, transportation and finance. "Okay, Chuck," I asked to myself, "where's the problem? It's not like their board members are creating a monopoly by consorting with the competition."

When Amber's quick database was up and running, we imported Chuck's spreadsheet, filtering out any names that didn't have the footnote symbol that marked them as members of the Replete Group. There were thirty-three entries. Then, one by one, we went down the list and did the same thing I had done with Reicher—looking up the corporate directors and officers and mapping them to positions in other companies.

The work began as a tedious and daunting task, searching for and copying the names and positions of those thirty-three people times the eight to fifteen other board members at each company. That could easily mean over four hundred names to research if there was no overlap, and, even with two adept keyboarders, I feared the project would take days. Luckily, we found a "who's who" type of site that gave a bio for many of the people we were researching, complete with board memberships. That sped up the work considerably, and within another half hour a pattern emerged, a pattern that both simplified the process and gave us a foretaste of the results we sought.

"Look at this," I said, interrupting the rapid clicking on Amber's keyboard. "So far we've only done fourteen of the CEOs, but I've got eight…eleven…no, twelve board members with dual roles within only eight companies. What's more, five of them are on Chuck's list as CEOs of other companies. I don't think we're going to be researching several hundred people here. In fact, it's looking more like a hundred, tops."

"Not even that," Amber told me, and pointed to her screen. She had performed a simple query into her database, and the pattern I had detected was suddenly quantified. Eliminating people with only one board membership and focusing only on companies that held two or more of the remaining people, we were only dealing with forty-five names or so.

Now that we'd hit our stride, the work went faster, and an hour later we had gotten through the list. It was crude research, and we could have missed people or overlooked board memberships or other roles, but there was enough data to see a pattern. We had identified twenty-five companies, each drawing four officers or board members from a pool of fifty names. All but three of the names on Chuck's list were in our results, but those superfluous entries consisted of J. Foster Shipley, the CEO who died in a yacht explosion, and two others who had retired or otherwise left their posts. I didn't know how Chuck had created his list, but so far we were confirming his data and adding names he had yet to identify. Some of those fifty people were on other boards, outside the twenty-five companies we had identified, but that appeared unimportant; in fact, it was probably to be expected. The important point was that there was too much symmetry in what we had found for it to be the result of chance: exactly fifty people, exactly twenty-five companies, and each company having exactly four officers or directors from the list. This configuration had to be by design.

We had unmasked the Replete Group.

Amber and I sat back in our chairs, giving our backs a rest while we stared at the data and tried to divine its implications. Chuck's conspiracy theories seemed much less farfetched now, making me wonder what other things we might have misjudged about him. More importantly, we had identified Borgie's "benefactor," as my strong-armed friend at the coffee shop had described Replete. The Group had been paying Borgie and Scanlon, and probably others, to do something they felt was important enough to kill for. We still had no idea what it was they were paid to do, but we were getting closer. I could feel it. I just couldn't prove any of it.

At that point I wanted to do a careful study our database, possibly adding other information like market data on the companies involved, and see if there was any evidence of manipulation or other mischief. A part of me wanted to grind away through the night, anxious to arrive at some theory that could explain what this was all about, but that was fast becoming impractical. The work was intricate, and as fatigue set in our efforts had become noticeably more error-prone, requiring more and more taps on the backspace key and making the job more frustrating than productive. The work would have to wait, and we decided to back up the data, pack up the computers and head back to our home base *pro tem*.

We had focused on our work so intently I had failed to notice the population of students dwindling, leaving all but the most dedicated—or maybe the most desperate—to burn midnight oil. We slipped out quietly to avoid disturbing their muse, crossing the library threshold and stepping out into the warm embrace of fragrant night air. The campus grounds were alive with wide lawns and trees and shrubs, adding life to the air that the controlled library environment lacked. We had a quarter moon above us, and a bright field of stars in spite of the light and air pollution of the city around us. Warm and cozy, it was the kind of summer night that I would have enjoyed staying up to enjoy in other circumstances, sitting on my balcony with a nice scotch in hand and with a friend or two who would chat and pontificate and help solve all the world's problems. But that was another reality. In ours, Amber and I passed through the campus gates into darkened streets, with shadows forming a visual metaphor for the unknowns that lay ahead. We walked on aged cobblestones past exclusive row houses and found the car, hardly getting so much as a glance at the history-rich neighborhood we traversed.

Amber was quiet as we left the Georgetown area. For several minutes I thought she might have fallen asleep, the long and complicated day finally overtaking her. I took the opportunity to simply look at her, appreciating the understated beauty she possessed even crumpled against the car door, and as we glided through the nearly empty streets of DC toward Amber's apartment building I thought about just how connected we had become. We had known each other for two days, yet a timeless bond was forming.

She stirred shortly before we neared the apartment complex, and I felt her hand come to rest on my right thigh. She stroked gently, and I found myself hoping that we would end the day as it had begun, a much needed intermission from our emotionally draining quest. Amber was sensing the same opportunity, her dreamy eyes suggesting we find a moment of diversion when safely inside. I smiled inwardly, and outwardly, I'm sure, and my foot unconsciously pressed nearer to the floor as we made our final approach.

We were less than a city block from the entrance into the parking lot when the hand on my leg tensed, her fingers gripping me and snapping me out of my carnal reverie.

"Something's wrong," she said. "Pull over a minute."

"What is it?"

"Lisa's apartment. I turned off the lights before we left. Did you turn them on again?"

I pulled over to the side and forward to a spot that gave us a view of the entire length of Amber's building through the trees.

"No. I mean, at least not on purpose." Looking at the building I counted up to Lisa's floor and, sure enough, there was a light on. "You're right. It's on."

"And look at that," she pointed toward the other end of the building. "When I got my things from my apartment I was pretending to take out the trash, remember? I had to leave the light on so it would look like I would be right back. Now it's off."

"Which one is it?"

"The far wing, one floor higher than Lisa's, third and fourth windows from the left. The one on the left should be on."

I looked to confirm, and our eyes alternated between her apartment and Lisa's as we absorbed this new development, unsure if it was real or the result of tired and over-cautious minds. We were both looking at Lisa's window when something more happened.

"Did you see that?" Amber asked?

"Yeah. Lisa's light just went out." Okay, we had a new situation on our hands. "Hang on a minute."

I pulled away from the curb and drove past the entrance, then turned onto the next street and found a spot where we could see the parking lot in front of the building. The sight was chilling, for one who knew the implications: it was a dark sedan, discreetly parked off to one side and away from the building.

5

ALLIES AND ANSWERS

We sat for a few minutes, Amber and I, taking stock of our options. Whoever was looking for us had somehow learned we had been using Lisa's apartment, and had apparently searched both there and Amber's home. Moreover, they were still in the building, and we couldn't be sure if the car we saw in the parking lot was the only one we had to worry about. We could find a hotel, but even when paying in cash a hotel required a credit card—unless it was one of those nasty hotels that rented by the hour. Credit card transactions were easily traced, making it simple for Agent Scanlon to find us. The unhappy prospect of sleeping in the car was looking more and more likely when Amber offered up an alternative.

"Ronnie," she said. "Ronnie will take us. He would have done anything for Lisa, that's certain."

"Who is Ronnie?"

"Oh—he's a Canadian who works at the embassy near downtown. He was chasing after Lisa pretty hard, but he's okay; just smitten. Lisa had that effect on guys." Amber gave a shy smile and dropped her eyes, and I wondered if Lisa was the only magnetic one of the pair.

"You think he would take us in? Our story is pretty hard to explain."

"I think so. I mean, we don't have to explain everything. Lisa and I stayed there once after a party. It's not the main embassy building, so it's all pretty casual. Anyway, all he can do is say 'no,' and, besides, there's nowhere else to go. What do we have to lose?"

"Then Ronnie's it is."

We drove off quietly, thankful that Lisa had chosen a fairly nondescript car in dark green, and even though we were pretty certain we had not been seen we didn't relax until we were well away. The Canadian embassy properties were back in the heart of the district, so we retraced our path as Amber dug her cell phone from her purse.

"Hello, Ronnie, it's Amber. Are you still up? … Good. I'm so sorry to bother you, but I need to see you. Have you heard about Lisa?... I know. I can't believe it either. But, Ronnie, there's more to the story. I need to talk to you. Can we stop by?... Oh, a friend of mine is here with me. Roger. I'll explain when we get there. Would it be okay if we stayed the night?... Thanks, Ronnie. You're the best! We'll be there in twenty minutes."

"All set," Amber told me, and then outlined quick directions.

"So Lisa and Ronnie were close?"

"Not as close as he wanted to be. Lisa was cooler than he was, always saying he was too intense at times. Besides, she had already gotten burned by the 'terrible twos.'"

"What's that?"

"The 'terrible twos?' Two-year transients. DC is full of single men and women who are only here for about two years. A lot of them are government types, like staffing a congressman for two years, or maybe working a couple of years as a lobbyist. Or they might be military. A lot of times military people have an even shorter stay. Then there are foreign diplomats, like Ronnie. So many people who are only here for a short time and they have to move away with little or no notice. The whole thing makes dating in DC a minefield. Very non-committal, you know? I mean, you can't expect healthy adults to live like monks for a couple of years, but these circumstances make a lot of people get a little crazy. Women as much as men, I think. Anyway, Lisa kept it pretty casual with Ronnie, at least most of the time."

Interesting. I wondered where that put me, having been in DC only since Friday evening. But, then, our circumstances were different.

While the Canadian embassy proper was on Pennsylvania Avenue, Ronnie and other embassy staff lived in a stately manor home the Canadian government owned on the northwest side of the district. The mansion was used as a residence as well as a venue for informal parties and other non-state affairs. The home was an older three-story of brick and stone in a neighborhood of equally large and impressive homes, each with mature trees and carefully manicured grounds. I didn't know if this was the "foreign soil" type of embassy property, but I did notice they had security cameras at the pillared entrance and on the circular drive where we parked. We grabbed my bag and the computers and walked to a front door that opened as we approached. A man, dark-haired with chiseled features and square shoulders, greeted us and invited us in. Behind him were two other men, who appeared to have a security role. The foyer was large, intended to accommodate a number of guests, I thought, and it gave the impression of old money more than of political institution.

"Amber. Good to see you. I'm so sorry about Lisa. Heard it on the news last evening. I tried to call..."

"Thank you, Ronnie. This is my friend, Roger. Roger, Ron Ward."

"Ronnie, please," he said while shaking my hand. He was smiling when he said that, but at the same time he had something in his eyes—a wary look that told me he didn't like to be crossed. I supposed it was an occupational necessity, the alpha wolf's need to establish ahierarchy. "Come inside where we can chat."

Ronnie led us into a large room with comfortable furniture where we could sit and talk. The ceilings were high, twelve feet or so, framed by a wide crown molding and supporting a crystal chandelier that hung over the center of the room. One wall held portraits—the Queen, the Prime Minister and the Governor General, above a panel of dark wainscoting. A large window dominated another wall, and a fireplace on another. The whole room evoked the formality and elegance of a bygone era, reasonably maintained but generally outdated. When he invited us to sit, Amber and I took the sofa and Ronnie faced us in an overstuffed chair.

"Would you like a drink? We have an excellent port for our special visitors. Jason? Some port if you don't mind."

One of the men I had seen in the foyer, a barrel-chested man with short cropped hair and a square jaw, stepped over to a table and picked up a crystal decanter. Ronnie was being overly gracious, perhaps keeping us off guard until he could determine who and what we really were. It didn't take long before he asked direct questions.

"Now, Amber, what brought you here at this time of night? Is it to do with Lisa? On the phone you said there was 'more to the story.'" Ronnie adopted a concerned look, and leaned forward to better focus on what he was about to hear.

"Oh, Ronnie. You know Lisa thought the world of you, don't you? You were very important to her."

"Yes, well, thank you for that. She was a very special lady," he replied. "I had just tried to see her on Friday, you know, but she was busy, as usual. It's hard to believe she is gone." Amber's eyes welled up as he said this, and I watched quietly as they took a minute or more to discuss Lisa and honor her memory.

"Do you have the funeral arrangements?" Ronnie asked.

"No, I don't, I'm sorry. In fact, I don't know what has happened to her at all. I had to go. I wasn't safe…" Her words had the desired effect; Ronnie's demeanor had quickly been transformed from grief to concern. "Ronnie, it wasn't just a hit-and-run. Lisa was murdered!"

A moment of shock set in, and Ronnie automatically called for an explanation when we were interrupted by Jason, who approached Ronnie and whispered in his ear. Then Ronnie gave us a hard, cold look.

"Amber, you need to be very straight with me now. Am I harboring criminals here?"

"What? No, of course not. What's happened?"

"Jason ran the plates on your car—Lisa's car, actually. Standard procedure here. The police have a BOLO out on it, a 'be on lookout' notice. I'm sorry, but you need to tell me what you're doing here, right now, or you'll have to leave."

Special Agent Scanlon had apparently enlisted the unwitting aid of the DC police in finding us. Ronnie didn't say there was a BOLO on myself or Amber, though, which was curious. In any case I had been silent long enough. "Ronnie, Lisa and Amber stumbled on to something that involves a rogue FBI agent. Moments after he found out she knew something, Lisa was killed. He knows about Amber, and he also thinks I have some information he needs. We have been hiding out in Lisa's apartment—figured it was the last place they'd look—but tonight someone was there searching the place. We're just now starting to understand what this is all about, but we're not nearly done yet and we need a place to spend the night."

I had compressed a lot into five sentences, and Ronnie stared at me as he digested it. For a moment it wasn't at all clear if he believed me or not, and, even if he did, I couldn't be sure of his reaction. He could simply send us away, or he could call the police and wash his hands of us. At the end of that moment, though, he decided to engage himself in our intrigue. Maybe his ability to judge character, honed by his service in the Canadian diplomatic corps, had allowed him to test us somehow and find us true.

"Jason," he called, "we're going to need some help. Take Roger's keys and empty out their car, then wipe it down and find a place to park it away from here. We're going to play a little hide-and-seek." Then to me, "I'm sorry, Roger, but that car can't be found on our property."

I handed the keys to Jason, then Ronnie turned to us again, his eyes filled with excitement at the prospect of an adventure that held little personal risk, as if he were being invited to play poker with someone else's chips. "Now, tell me exactly what it is I've just stepped in."

I started talking, finding that it was far easier to share details than to create an abridged version on the fly. I spoke with almost academic detachment, interrupted at various points as Ronnie asked questions or as Amber added subtleties or clarifications. I didn't take time to relate everything that had happened, such as my office break-in or the things I had gleaned from Borgie's software files, but there was enough for Ronnie to understand our plight. He also sympathized with our dilemma: there was simply not enough hard evidence to bring in any law enforcement. Yet. By the time we had stated and confirmed that point it was very late, and Ronnie, now a steadfast ally, called an end to the discussion.

"Well, you will stay here tonight, of course. Tomorrow, well, we'll have to see what tomorrow brings. Only one guest room is available, so you'll have to make do." He watched me as he said that, giving just a hint of a smile, but I was too tired to react. Instead we just gathered our things, climbed the long, wide staircase and located the door to our room.

While the main level of the mansion had been maintained in its original, classic style, the second floor had been divided into modern suites, each outfitted with a private bath. Ours had separate rooms for sitting and for sleeping. We had a large, king-sized bed, a masculine four-poster which we occupied in short order. We held each other for a moment, kissing gently, but earlier thoughts of intimacy had been supplanted by fatigue, and we quickly fell asleep.

Even though we had turned in only a few hours earlier, I woke early. My mind was racing, and I laid there for a time recounting step-by-step each event from the time Amber and I met at the museum until the present. I was groggy, managing hazy recall at best, and I retraced those memories multiple times without revelation. We had learned many things in that short time, but there was something more, something I had seen or heard but had either missed or dismissed. It was a whisper, persistent and frustrating, as if someone were taunting me with inaudible answers to desperate questions.

My mind continued to work more or less aimlessly as I stretched myself into full consciousness. I began to appreciate how completely the present circumstance had transported me out of my normal life. I hadn't even thought about the office or my projects or anything back home since meeting Amber, with the small exception of the phone messages. Just days earlier I had been shuffling between meetings, each day feeling much like the last. Now I was waking up in a Canadian mansion, lying next to a woman I hadn't known existed three days earlier, and searching desperately for some way to save myself and her from an unknown evil. Yeah, it wasn't the vacation I had planned, but I had still managed to get away from it all.

With that wry thought I slipped out of bed and padded my way to the window to greet the day. It was bright outside, and I carefully pulled back a corner of the curtain to avoid shocking Amber from her sleep. Squinting into the morning sun I got my first daytime look at the upscale neighborhood. It was still quiet, with dew-covered cars parked in driveways and newspapers lying on driveways. No wonder; the screen on my cell phone told me it was only a few minutes past six AM. I wished I had slept longer, but at the same time this was an opportunity, a chance to get a head start on what was sure to be a challenging day.

I cleaned up and dressed as quietly as I could and was out of the suite before Amber stirred. The hallway was filled with the inviting aroma of coffee and toast and sausages, and I became acutely aware that we had missed dinner the night before. When I reached the bottom of the stairs, I followed my nose to a dining room where the housekeeping staff had set up a buffet for residents and guests, and I gratefully accepted an invitation to break my fast. I was not the first to eat that morning, but as I didn't know the other gentleman I sat alone with a newspaper to keep me company.

My still-groggy eyes passed over a story about Senator Wyecroft twice before it caught my eye. When it did catch my eye I had to shake my head; the man's troubles had continued through the weekend. It seems he had planned a Sunday news conference to discuss his support for his replacement candidate, Ron Hanover. While that support would normally have been guaranteed, some political insiders had reported an apparent rift and speculated that Wyecroft was about to shift positions. There were rumors of "political and philosophical differences," but rumors were not unusual in modern politics. The press wanted, even needed, a little drama injected here and there to drive viewer interest, drama the press could conveniently attribute to faulty intelligence gathering by some unnamed reporter if events turned out otherwise. Still, it seemed to me—a most casual political observer—that Wyecroft's and Hanover's divergent platforms made such a rift possible. Maybe it was true, maybe not, but in the end we wouldn't know for sure. The conference was cancelled on the news that Wyecroft's aged father had passed away early that morning, the victim of a heart attack. Wyecroft's office instead released a statement expressing his continued support of Hanover and gratitude for the many condolences his family had received.

By the end of the article I was alert. Food and coffee and the brightly lit room had drawn me out of the haze. I was able to focus on my situation with a degree of intellectual detachment, and I used that focus to once again define the problem and seek potential solutions. Some facts and a few plausible theories were slowly accumulating, each, it seemed, spawning another question for my list. Someone in the Replete Group was trying very hard to do something very wrong. What was it? They had co-opted FBI Agent Scanlon, along with at least two others. Why? Their scheme involved a custom simulation Borgie was working on. What did it do? I still didn't know, but I was beginning to get a sense for it. I sat like that for a while, juxtaposing bits of knowledge with further questions, but now, awake and refreshed, the questions were less frustrating. Instead, as often happens, the questions themselves were suggesting the next course of action.

Just as I finished my second cup of coffee, Amber walked in and chose a small plate of fruit and a muffin. Amber, I decided, must be a morning person—bright, alert, and well-groomed, considering the only makeup she had was what she carried in her purse. She placed her hand on my shoulder and said "good morning," then sat across from me so we could chat. We were just a few words into our conversation when Ronnie entered and pulled a chair up to the side of the table, the staff delivering his morning brew as I gathered was customary.

"Good morning," he began. "I see you found the amenities. Did you rest well?"

"Very well," Amber replied. "Thank you so much, Ronnie—you're a life saver. I don't know where else we would have gone last night."

Ronnie looked at us one at a time, as if watching a tennis match. "Excellent. Have you decided what your plan is now?"

He didn't say it, but I suspected part of his concern was whether we expected to return that night, and at that point I had no idea how I would answer if asked.

"I have been thinking about that. I'm pretty sure we're on to something with the data we gathered last night. There's a pattern or trend in there that should tell us what's happening, but it will take some more study. I think I want to get back to the library and work on it this morning."

Amber agreed. "Ronnie, can someone call us a cab?"

"Oh, that's not necessary. We can spare Jason for a little while. I'll catch a ride to the embassy with Mrs. Martin."

"Thank you! We should have him back to you by mid-morning."

"No, no. I'll ask him to stay with you for the day. I'm just going to be in meetings anyway. Besides, Jason can be very useful at times." Ronnie didn't say it, but he was obviously concerned. He was offering us security more than mere transportation, and I fully appreciated the gesture.

"That's very generous, Ronnie. Thank you!"

"My pleasure. Jason will meet you at the door in fifteen minutes," he replied, then leaned in before continuing. "Now look, I know I haven't heard the whole story yet—no, it's okay, that's what it's like in the diplomatic corps—but even I can see that you're into it about as deeply as you can go. Your friend is dead, and now Lisa is gone. I've already done about all I can, save one piece of advice: don't be a hero. Find out what these people are up to and take it to someone in a position to help."

"You've read my mind, Ronnie. That's exactly the plan."

"Ronnie," Amber said, "Do you think you can find out the arrangements for Lisa?"

"Of course. I'll email them to you later today."

We grabbed our computer bags and got to the front door as Jason came up the drive in Ronnie's embassy limo. In moments we glided out the drive and down the street for the short trip to the library. Obviously there were benefits to life as a diplomat, and I found myself wondering how Lisa had been able to resist the creature comforts that came with Ronnie's attention.

When we got a block from the manor, Jason surprised us with a talkative side I never would have expected, given what we'd seen the night before. He was humorous and jovial, sharing anecdotes about the people he had seen at the manor and the interesting situations they had gotten caught up in, all told in the classic Canadian accent. No names, of course—his position required discretion—but he shared a string of tales in a way that told us he truly enjoyed his work. There was a French Canadian VIP who screamed at Jason for delivering a shaker of black pepper when what he needed was toilette "pepper." There were regular parties in the great room on the main floor that often ended in the room Amber and I had shared. There was even a small group of young Canadians who had tried to stage a demonstration by camping on the front lawn naked, and Jason and his team had to physically carry them off. "Now I ask you," Jason said with an impish grin, "where were we *supposed* to grab them, eh?" Through it all, Jason's love of country was readily apparent, and we learned that one didnot make even remotely disparaging remarks about socialized medicine, Canadian beer or especially hockey while in his car.

As entertaining as Jason was, my mind was increasingly anxious to re-engage in our problem. I smiled or chuckled on cue, at least I think I did, but my real focus was on the puzzle we were trying to solve, on Borgie's code and on the Replete Group database we had built the night before.

During a rare pause in Jason's monologue, it occurred to me that it would be safe to turn on my smart phone to retrieve messages as long as we were in transit, and in a few moments I had downloaded a series of calls and emails. Before turning the phone off I happened to glanced at one of the icons, and when I did I suddenly remembered that elusive something that I had sensed when waking up that morning. It was something that was said by the guys who had tried to grab me in the coffee shop, just after they mentioned Replete. They were talking about me having to complete Borgie's work now that he was gone, when one of them said "…so tag, you're it."

Could it be that simple? Could I have been that obtuse all this time? I stared at the application icon that had caused this epiphany. It was a "tag" reader, an application that used my phone's camera to read a tag—similar to a 2D bar code, but in the form of a picture that was linked directly to a web site. A picture such as the unlikely logo printed on the business card Borgie had sent me before he died!

"I don't believe it!" I exclaimed.

"What?" Amber's first thought was that we'd run into a new danger.

"Borgie's message. I've been carrying it around this whole time!"

I quickly retrieved Borgie's card from my wallet and Amber shared my excitement as I pointed the camera and activated the application. Just as I thought, my phone was immediately taken to a website Borgie built shortly before he died, a private site for my eyes only. It and the business card were an act of desperation, and Borgie had nearly outsmarted himself with his arcane approach to security. He had scribbled "you're it" on the back, and he would never know how close I came to missing his clue entirely.

We were only blocks from the Georgetown University gate nearest the library, and I put my phone into "airplane mode" so I could leave it turned on and read my messages and that web address without the phone broadcasting my position.

"I think we've got it," I told Amber. "I think Borgie is giving me the build file, the key to his simulation code!"

"Does that mean we can run his simulation?"

"I don't know yet, but this has to be the key we've been looking for!" then to Jason, "It looks like we're going to be in the library a while. Thank you so much for the ride, and please let Ronnie know we'll pick up the rest of our things when we can."

"Mr. Ward asked me to take care of you," Jason responded. "If it's okay with you, I'll drop you off here, run an errand or two, and pick you up around noon, eh? You can call my cell if you need anything sooner."

"Perfect," I told him, and we exchanged numbers so we could coordinate any change in plans.

We practically ran from the main gate at Georgetown University to the library, fueled by the belief that Borgie's clue would lead us to a quick resolution. Lauinger, a florescent-lit cave the night before, had been transformed into a vibrant space with daylight streaming in through large windows. The few desperate souls we left there had been replaced by students who looked refreshed, adding life and activity to the tables that stood next to long rows of shelves. It was still early, though, at least on student time, and we found our isolated table waiting for us unoccupied.

As quickly as possible we booted up our computers and typed in the URL to Borgie's website. Borgie had been in a hurry, and the page we saw was nothing more than a paragraph:

Hello old friend. Glad you found this. As I said when I called, just hit the link at the end and enter your name. The password is your old nemesis. See you inside.

I hadn't received his call, of course. Apparently Borgie had planned to tell me about this site by phone rather than rely on the business card alone. He may have had no idea the trouble he had gotten himself into could be fatal.

I hit the link and entered my name—Borgie always called me "Morgan"—and stared at the password request for a moment.

"Okay, so who was your nemesis?" Amber asked.

"He was. We had referred to each other that way from time to time; the competition between us was no secret, but the term 'nemesis' was an exaggeration. Mostly."

I entered "Borgman." Nothing. Then "borgman," not knowing whether it was case-sensitive. Again nothing. Then I smiled and entered "Borgie." It worked immediately. Borgie had used a password that anyone he had met after grad school would not easily know or guess.

Again we were presented with a simple page of text, and Amber sat close beside me as we read in silence.

Morgan,

First, don't call me. Read this whole thing before you do anything and you'll understand why. I'm into something pretty deep here, and you're the only one I can trust to tell about it. I suppose damn few people would understand it anyway.

Here's the deal. I got tasked to help the FBI figure out how the CEO of a large oil company was scamming the system to make his bonus outrageously big. I built a sim of trading rules, oil market dynamics, and his compensation plan, and I figured out how the greedy SOB was doing it. The lead FBI agent dropped the case for some reason, but from my end it seemed like we had the guy nailed.

A few weeks later, the same FBI agent asked me to do some moonlighting for a pile of money, sponsored by something called the Replete Group. He said it was part of some top-secret case that couldn't go through normal channels. I did it; I mean, I get government wages here, you know? Anyway, it was almost the same sim I had already done for him, but bigger. They wanted me to assume the same comp plan but with the market dynamics for a bunch of other companies.

Here's the good part. They wanted to run this sim without needing a big computer. That's what everyone wants, right? Anyway, I found a way to do it. I built a super-tight recursive engine and optimized the simulation code to run on it. Morgan, it works! It can run a sim with up to fifty parameters and five hundred agents on a high-end multi-core PC. Not huge, but definitely big enough to for a lot of jobs. This could really be something important.

Here's the deal. I'm going to publish it all as soon as I can. What I need is for you to help verify the system before I publish. I'll own the idea, but I'll put your name on the paper if you help me out. Think about it, man. The whole field of emergent behavior simulation will explode when people can run their sims on any decent PC, you know? This is huge! We can change the whole science.

There's one other thing. It turns out you were right, man. Back in the day you warned against using simulations to manipulate people. A couple of weeks ago I found out what this sim is all about. I think this FBI agent is helping Replete force bigger bonuses for a bunch of execs. I'm not sure who or how, but when I told him I wasn't going to help anyone break the law it turned ugly. Real ugly. The bottom line is we have to keep this quiet until I figure out how to handle Replete and this FBI guy. Until then, only contact me on this site. That's important, Morgan. There's a link below where you can leave messages.

The other link is for the code library. I'm trusting you, Morgan. It's not finished yet, but the main parts work; just compile and run. You're going to love it, man!

—B

Several large pieces of the puzzle just fell into place. Borgie had finally been seduced and, wittingly or not, had stepped to the dark side of our field. All the debates, all the warnings, all the out-and-out arguments from our post-grad days came flooding back as I shook my head at his ego-driven, and apparently greed-driven, mistake. I wondered how much he had been offered to sell his soul like that. Replete had incredible resources; after all, they were able to buy Special Agent Scanlon and at least two of his team. A big paycheck would have made Borgie feel important, but I doubted that was enough. The chance to do something technically impressive, though, that was something Borgie's ego would have found hard to resist. I had the odd feeling that, behind it all, Borgie had been hoping to impress me.

Borgie's note did several things for us. It confirmed that Replete and Scanlon were behind our problems. More importantly, we now knew what this system was designed to do. Even Borgie hadn't had the whole picture—you needed to have the full Replete membership roster to get that—and I guessed that Scanlon didn't have it all, either. Nor did Chuck and his fellow conspiracy theorists. As I thought about it, chances were that even the individual members in Replete only knew their small part of the whole. The complete scheme was probably known only to a very few, the masterminds behind Replete who maintained a veil of secrecy so they could hide tens, maybe hundreds of millions of dollars in fraudulent income. Now it was also known to us. We had knowledge Replete would kill to contain.

We had been quiet for several moments, our heads nearly touching as we read and absorbed Borgie's note. When we got to the end we turned to each other, moving in unison and then talking over each other in our excitement. Now we just needed to run Borgie's code and verify that it did as he claimed. Then we needed to study the Replete roster and, if possible, learn who might be behind it all. Then we needed to figure out what we were going to do with that information. That last part was the murkiest of all, but we weren't ready to face it just yet anyway. Just knowing these steps felt like progress, as though the end of our ordeal were drawing nearer.

A glance through the code library Borgie had included confirmed what he said. Everything we needed to compile the application was there, including the all-important build file. That was the missing link, the piece that told the compiler how and where all the other files were used when building the final, executable simulation.

Using my computer and the tools I had brought from the Institute, we began building the final executable program. The process was semi-automated, but still took several minutes, time I used the time to peruse the messages I had downloaded to my smart phone. Most of the texts were a series of increasingly anxious messages from Cynthia needing to ask something before a big meeting near DC that afternoon. I had five to ten minutes before the compiler would be finished, so I decided to see if I could help.

I walked down to the main entrance on the excuse that I didn't want to disturb other students by talking on my cell, but the truth was I didn't feel comfortable talking to Cynthia while sitting next to Amber. I had no further connection to Cynthia outside of work, but she represented a part of my past that didn't need to be intermingled with my present.

"Roger? Damn you! Where have you been?" My call had found Cynthia fairly wound up, it would seem.

"I've been preoccupied. What's going on?"

"I've got a new client here and I absolutely have to talk to you before the meeting this afternoon. Where are you?"

"Can't we talk on the phone?"

"Not really, no. Roger, this is a huge contract and I need you to see what I'm pitching to them before I stand in front of them and make a fool of myself! Where are you?"

This was exactly the wrong moment for me to make any time commitments, so I tried again to help her without physically meeting. "Just email your presentation and I'll have a look."

"Damn it, Roger, I need to see you! Where in hell are you?"

"I'm at a library over in Georgetown—long story. Look, I can't leave now. Send me your presentation and I'll call you back, okay?"

A heavy sigh. "Okay, Roger. I'll send it in a few minutes."

I returned to our table just as the compilation process ended, and launched my email program so I would be alerted when Cynthia's presentation arrived.

“I’m going to be interrupted for a few minutes when I get an email,” I explained, and Amber simply nodded her acknowledgement.

We were both eager to run Borgie’s simulation. I knew it would probably be more efficient for one of us to test the simulator and the other study the Replete Group database we had created, but it would have been impossible to tear either of us away at that moment. Besides, I rationalized, it was useful to have two sets of eyes on each task. As we huddled together in front of my notebook screen, I launched the simulation with a ceremonious keystroke.

The first thing we saw was a user interface with several drop-down lists allowing the user to select the options for simulation. One list held ticker symbols, the three- or four-letter mnemonics designating a company’s name on the stock exchange.

“Hold on,” I said. “Fire up your database. This list looks familiar.”

Amber launched the database and immediately confirmed my observation. The ticker symbols referred to the same twenty-five companies as were in the Replete Group.

We toyed with Borgie’s user interface for a while, getting a feel for what the simulation used as inputs and what we could expect as outputs. The system was context-sensitive, meaning that each time we selected a particular company the other options became items specific to that business. Another page allowed a user to enter information for a given company, specifying current data—very inside information, I was sure—that the simulator would use in producing its results. Still another page let the user define relationships between member companies, things like major contracts or debts; another let you define members and their roles in various companies. That last part hadn't been populated yet, as Borgie probably didn't have that kind of information.

As Borgie had hoped, I was incredibly impressed with his innovative simulation engine, the piece he wanted me to help verify for his paper. Even on my relatively modest notebook computer the system ran quickly and flawlessly. I supposed it would slow somewhat as various data fields were populated, but even so, a reasonably high-end PC would have no problem. Borgie had been a true genius to the end.

What that engine was simulating, though, was incredibly complex. Manipulating the bonus for one CEO involved actions by other members in other businesses, actions that might impact their own incomes for which still others needed to compensate. Each action caused ripples across the network of executives, and each ripple required action. In a much smaller scheme all these interdependencies might have been manageable, but Replete was doing it on a grand scale. When complete, this simulator was intended to model actions and reactions involving all fifty executives and twenty-five subject companies. Replete had built a interlocked microcosm of a business world that played by Replete's rules, and Borgie's simulator was going to be the control panel for the entire system.

I wanted to spend much more time testing and analyzing Borgie's simulator, but we had already learned what we needed for our immediate concern.

Having an initial understanding of Replete's scheme, we turned back to the database and began searching for more clues that might indicate who was involved and what—if indeed there was anything—we might do about it. This was a two-computer job, as it had been the night before, with one used for managing the database and the other for research into names and affiliations and anything else that seemed relevant. Amber had complete mastery of the database, and I found myself at moments simply watching her as she efficiently added fields for new data or queried the existing data to produce various views of the data. Soon we could name the industries where Replete had a presence, we could see how many Replete companies were in each industry, we could list the shortest path through their network from one executive to another, and more. The key we sought, though, still eluded us. We had no clue as to who was running Replete.

Hopes ran high and fell again a dozen times over as we worked. Each time we found a new clue keyboards clattered rapidly; each time our path turned into a logical cul-de-sac there was a silent pause. Activity came in a series of waves that started rapidly and eventually slowed as we began running low on ideas. Finally, Amber slumped over her keyboard and I sat back in my chair to search the corners of my head for another idea to pursue.

Lost in thought, I was barely aware when someone approached our table. I first ignored him, assuming it was just a passing student, but took more notice when he came to a stop at the end of the table nearest me. In my peripheral vision I saw Amber look up at the new arrival, and, following her gaze, found myself looking into a most unexpected face.

"Good morning, Dr. Morgan," he said. "I'm afraid I must interrupt you again. We have very little time."

I was stunned. "John Carstairs," I said almost in reflex. Then, as the implications of his presence hit me, I said, "You're behind all this? What the hell do you want from me? How did you find us?" I fully expected thugs to emerge from the stacks and grab me at any moment.

"I'm behind none of it, but the men you fear are already waiting for you outside. You need to trust me, and we need to leave. Right now. Can you do that?"

"What do you mean? Why should I trust you?"

"Listen, please. I'll answer all your questions when we get out of here. For now here's all you need to know. My name is not really Carstairs, it's Shipley, John Foster Shipley, and there are people outside waiting for you to come out. I don't think they'd try anything inside the library, but in a few moments they will most likely have someone in here doing reconnaissance. You need to leave right now. They're not at the rear entrance yet, but if they think you know about them they will cover every exit and we'll have no way out."

Shipley. This was the dead CEO from the exploded yacht, the incident Chuck had mentioned. "Can you prove you're Shipley?"

"There's no time for that, Morgan. Look out that window and you'll see what I mean."

Amber was closest. She went to the window and looked out, then turned and gave me a grave nod before quick-stepping back to our table. "It's the two guys from the coffee shop yesterday, and they have a couple of friends with them. He's telling the truth, Roger!"

In time it took Amber to look outside I had found Shipley's picture on the "who's who" site we had been using. He had changed his appearance—added glasses, colored his hair and removed some facial hair—but it was Shipley. "Yeah, it's him. Here's his pic. Let's get out of here," I said, and we packed up the computers and walked to a south side staircase as quickly as we could without creating a commotion that others might notice. Once outside we ducked into an adjacent building and quickly walked to the far end before stopping to talk.

"Where to?" I asked Shipley. "You have a car?"

"We'd have to walk past them to get there."

"Give me Jason's number," Amber said. "There's a safe way out of here."

In moments she had dialed her phone. "Jason, it's me, Amber. Are you far from the campus?... South of the Key Bridge? Excellent. If you don't mind, could you pick us up on Canal Street at the Exorcist Steps? They're near the end of the bridge... Perfect. We'll be there in a couple minutes."

"Follow me," she said, and turned toward the landmark she had given Jason. Within minutes we had walked down Prospect Street and reached the top of a long flight of stone stairs that descended from the bluff-top campus down to Canal Street, forming a narrow slot between a stone wall and another of red brick. "They call these the Exorcist Steps because they were in the movie," she explained. Then to herself, "I hope that's not an omen."

We scurried down the stairs in tandem, paced by Shipley's slower feet. Jason's car pulled up just as we reached the bottom of the steps, and Shipley looked to me for verification before we emerged from the staircase. Even then, he carefully peeked out, looking up and down the street before walking into the open. Shipley was being careful; he felt as much at risk as Amber and I did.

There was the normal traffic on Canal Street, but no ominous dark sedans that we could see and we quickly crossed the walk and climbed in Jason's waiting car.

"Jason, this is Foster Shipley. He'll be riding with us if that's okay with you."

"No problem; my pay's the same either way, right? Where are we headed, folks?"

Of course, none of us had thought that far ahead. "Up the Parkway," suggested Shipley, "if you can find a convenient place to turn around."

Jason looked at Shipley over his shoulder and smiled. "Oh, this looks convenient enough I suppose. Hang on folks!"

With that he found a gap in the oncoming traffic and snapped the wheel sharply, executing a U-turn right in the middle of Canal Street. It was clear he was an expert driver. It was also clear he had no fear of being stopped for his illegal maneuver.

"The most feared thing on DC streets," he told us, "is a car with diplomatic plates. Other drivers avoid us like a tax audit! Sorry, couldn't help but show off a bit."

Shipley gave me a questioning look. "Canadian embassy driver," was all I had for him. "Oh, and this is Amber Meadows. She works with the Interagency Resources."

Shipley looked from Jason to Amber, then back o me. "You've been in DC since Friday night?"

"Yes, that's right."

He gave an appreciative nod. "Okay, I have a small place just off the parkway where we can talk. It's only a couple of miles from here, will that do?"

"Sounds good. Jason…"

"You may want to wait on that," Jason said with new urgency. "That car behind us looks like what Mr. Ward was warning me about. They've been with us since Canal Street." He indicated them with his eyes via the rearview mirror, and all heads turned aft.

"Do you think you can lose them?"

"I can sure try. But I have to warn you, these diplomatic plates have a down side. Cops usually won't bother to stop us, but we can be spotted a mile away. Hang on."

Jason drove normally for another block or two, just long enough for me to loosen my grip on the door handle. Then in a flash we went from leisurely urban cruise to derailed rocket sled as we pulled around a left-turning vehicle and headed up Connecticut for a block. I was thrown against the car door, then pressed into the seat back as we accelerated. Stealing a look over my shoulder, I could see our pursuers; it looked like we had bought only a few car lengths with that first maneuver. A short distance later another sudden left took us on Calvert, then a right, left, right at increasing speeds as the dark sedan struggled to keep up. These were urban neighborhoods, residential mixed with small retail, complete with pedestrians and street lights at major intersections. Jason moved like an ambulance driver, maximizing our speed wherever possible yet slowing as necessary to preserve bystander safety. Streetlights were minor impediments to Jason as he expertly threaded his way through holes in any cross traffic. Congestion was more of a problem, but he moved around other vehicles like a cheetah chasing a prized buck. If I had thought about it I would have been more than impressed with his skills, but at the time I was holding my seat belt with one hand and the door handle with the other, knuckles white and teeth clenched. Amber and Shipley were in the same state, eyes wide open and muscles taut as we slid from side to side in our seats and tried in vain to anticipate the jerks and twists that threw us around the car's interior. Looking back I could see the people we had passed, shaking fists and cursing us after we cut them off or blew by at high speed. Most had a momentary look of surprise that quickly dissolved into anger, often accompanied by a one-fingered expression of dismay.

Over my other shoulder I could see the dark sedan had fallen another half-block behind us. At the moment I again faced forward, Jason pulled hard to the left and then right again to avoid a double-parked delivery van. I was taken by surprise, sharply knocking my head against the window. Amber saw it, or maybe just heard it, and turned to check if I was hurt. She couldn't do anything more, as it would have required her to release one of her hands and risk the same fate herself. I shouted that I was okay, the high volume more a result of the wild commotion than of any ambient noise.

Shipley, I noted, had pressed himself back in the corner of the rear seat, pressing hard against the door and holding on with ashen face and sardonic smile. Our eyes had met once or twice, but both of us were too preoccupied for more.

Looking back one more time I found relief. Oncoming traffic had neatly plugged the lane next to the delivery van we had just passed, and the dark sedan was unable to pass. Jason saw it too, but made two more quick turns before slowing to a sane pace. As we passed Wisconsin Avenue he turned to me with a surprisingly calm expression and asked for instructions. "It looks like we've lost them for the moment," he said. "Where would you like to go from here?"

The ordeal had lasted only a few minutes, but the adrenaline would be with us much longer. Hands slowly let go of straps and handles, and blood started flowing back into faces and fingers. It was a few moments before rational thought returned, and a few more before we had an answer for Jason.

"Take us to my car," Shipley said. "It's parked a few blocks from the main gate in front of Georgetown." It wasn't clear if he was inviting us to go with him or abandoning us to our own resources.

"You're leaving, then? That's it?"

"No, I am not. We have a lot to discuss, Morgan, but I think our friends back there will be looking for this car. Better to use mine and get safely inside my place, if that's all right with you."

I had no plan at that point, and few options other than simply bailing out. Amber's eyes met mine in agreement, and Amber asked Jason to take us back to the neighborhood outside Georgetown U. It was a short drive, as it turns out, as the wild ride we had just taken had brought us nearly full circle. Once there we couldn't thank Jason enough for his skilled help.

"No problem," he replied. "Good to stay in practice, I guess. As long as I didn't put a dent in Mr. Ward's car, we're good!"

"Please tell Ronnie we'll be by for our things later," she added as we pulled ourselves out of the vehicle. "I'll try to call this evening."

We said our goodbyes, Jason expressing his protective instincts as he advised us on a quiet back-street route and things we could do if spotted again. Before he finished, he looked at Shipley with a touch of suspicion, and I had to admit I was feeling it as well. Had Shipley saved us, or had we saved him? I wanted to trust him—in fact, we needed to be able to trust him—but trust was an earned commodity. Those thoughts took only a moment, but Shipley saw something in my face that prompted comment.

"Don't worry, Morgan. I'll explain it all when we get to my place."

With that he unlocked his car and we climbed in, but as we pulled away from the curb my curiosity broke its bonds.

"How did you find us in the library? Nobody knew we were there."

"I'm afraid I learned it from your colleague, Ms. Holt."

"Cynthia? She's working with you?"

"Not exactly. After you spoke with her this morning, she called her new client, the Replete Group, to tell them where you were. I have a man keeping an eye on her. I'm sorry, Morgan, but I don't think you can trust her."

"Who is it, Roger?" Amber interrupted, and I took a moment to explain.

"Cynthia is a program manager at the Institute. She had called to say she was in town to meet with a big new client, and really needed to have me review her presentation. That's the email I was expecting earlier."

"My guess is the email never arrived," interjected Shipley.

"You're right. I waited for it, but… Come to think of it, she was anxious to know where I was when I spoke with her. Even her emails and text messages asked that same question, over and over. Damn! Cynthia was handing me over to Replete?"

"Yes, but she probably didn't know why they wanted to find you. She was probably told you were simply ducking their calls while on vacation. And I'm sure they paid her nicely for the information."

I thought about Cynthia for a moment. Where Borgie's weakness had been ego, Cynthia's was greed. She wanted money and she wanted power, and I wasn't sure she was able to distinguish between the two. They had equal value to Cynthia, each being a source of the other in her mind. Then I thought back a little further, to the night before I left when she surprised me at my home. She had been after my itinerary then, also, and had asked several questions about Borgie. That whole evening had been staged to get information from me! There was more, though. I had also seen her talking with Shipley in the hall just before I left.

"Yes, that's true," Shipley explained when I asked about it. "I had visited the Institute that morning hoping to intercept you before you left for the airport. Your boss, Ms. Ming, referred me to her in the hope Cynthia could fulfill my needs in your absence. I've gotten ahead of myself, though. This is my place here; let's go inside and I'll start at the beginning."

We pulled up in front of a three-story row house in a meticulously maintained neighborhood facing an equally manicured green space called Kalorama Park. The home was narrow like its neighbors, and had a lower-level walkway from the street through to a back yard. The façade was dominated by a large bay window that rose the full height of the building, and there were two short flights of steps that took us to a small front patio and then into the home.

Once inside we found a different home than one would suspect from the curb. It was actually two row houses wide, the intervening wall having been opened to form a spacious and comfortable floor plan. On the left side of the foyer rose a long staircase, and on the right was a formal sitting room. We were greeted in that foyer by Donato, Shipley's Man Friday, I assumed, who ushered us to a table in Shipley's study where we could talk and set up a computer if needed. I got the impression that Donato had worked for Shipley for some time, but I also noted that Donato referred to him as "Mr. Carstairs."

Shipley took a moment to ask Donato to serve a small lunch. While he did that, Amber turned to me and asked the question I was already pondering.

"How much can we trust this guy?" she whispered.

"Haven't decided yet," was all I could respond before he turned back to us. Shipley seemed sincere, but his interests didn't seem exactly aligned with ours. He knew something of what was happening, though, and he seemed to know about the inner workings of Replete. We had to at least hear what he had to say.

When Shipley turned back to us he read the question on my mind and addressed it. "I've asked Donato to address me as Carstairs for now. In fact, I ask you to do the same. Officially, Shipley is missing and presumed dead, giving me a degree of freedom and security that would otherwise be impossible."

We each nodded our assent, and then it was Amber who steered us back to the real topic. "Okay, I'm lost here. Both of us are, I think. How are you involved in all this?"

"Of course. Let me explain. But, to be honest, I suspect you may have more information than I do."

With that, Shipley launched his monologue.

"Do you remember the Enron scandal? Of course you do. Billions in market value were lost when that story broke. What we're looking at here could make that seem like a liquor store robbery, if we're not careful. No matter how big you think this is, it's probably bigger. Big enough to kill for, many times over. Always remember that!

"Now, you already know I was the CEO of Rumsley Industries up until a few months ago. For several years the company was doing well under my leadership, well enough that I was making good money. It wasn't outstanding money, though, at least not compared to what CEOs of similar companies were making during that time. I had some good advisors and we were making a lot of progress, but I wasn't doing as well as I wanted on a personal level. I know what you're thinking, but it's all relative. Even a billionaire feels unsuccessful next to a multi-billionaire, you know? There is never enough.

"Anyway, about two years ago I had a dinner party on my boat. There were a number of business associates on board, including one of our directors. At one point in the evening this director told me about a great opportunity, a unique 'investment club' called the Replete Group, all very exclusive and designed for the special needs of people in my position. He described it as a 'proactive wealth-building network' geared for the elite. 'Proactive.' That was the key selling point, the thing that made it interesting. High level execs, well, they like to feel they have control.

"A few days later I had my first meeting with Ian Wallace. Ian founded Replete. The man is a genius, the kind of guy with incredible vision and a knack for making things happen. He also had a value proposition that was pretty hard to beat. He promised that, if I invested in the group and followed their lead, he would double my compensation within a year. Double. That, my friend, was a lot of money.

"The deal worked like this. Replete would provide a new employment contract for me and the legal support to negotiate it with my board. Once it was in place, all I had to do was continue doing a good job, follow some 'group directives,' and pay my dues. The dues were high—ten percent of total compensation—but it was a small price to pay for a *guaranteed* doubling of my total income. Think about it. No matter how much you make, an eighty-percent net increase feels like a lot of money. Ian was just the kind of person that could make it happen, too. And the guarantee? I'd get all my investment back if my income didn't at least double.

I had an idea where this story might be headed, but I still had to ask. "What did he mean by 'group directives?'"

"Well, that is the whole point, the part that makes Replete work. From time to time I would get a phone call. Nothing in writing, only voice. The caller would ask me questions about various transactions and things, then he would tell me to do something that I assumed would help some other member of the group. Never myself; always someone else. Nothing blatantly criminal; not by itself, anyway. In fact, it all seemed completely innocuous. I would be asked to accelerate a major purchase, or maybe delay it. I would be asked to stall an acquisition, or invest funds in a certain corporate bond, or change the timing of a product announcement. Sure, it was manipulating finances a bit, but nothing illegal and nothing out of the ordinary for the leader of a large company. Ian had thought it out very well. Of course, I was on the boards of a few other companies, and I would get directives for those as well. Different things, things a director could influence.

"Pretty soon I noticed things happening at Rumsley. The board approved my new comp plan with surprising ease. Some of our key suppliers were being incredibly generous just when we needed it, and major customer programs seemed to hit at just the right moment. I was asked to take a couple of risky actions, but each time things magically worked out perfectly, and my bonus plan soared."

Donato carried in a tray of food, creating enough of a pause for us to consider what Shipley was telling us and to ask a clarifying question or two.

"So, you were manipulating the business to increase your compensation," Amber said. She sounded a bit judgmental, and I have to admit I had a hard time withholding judgment myself.

"Well, first of all, Ms. Meadows, that is how a bonus plan works. It motivates an executive to do things that improve his personal income, right? There's no crime in that—well, not usually. But, in any case, that wasn't how it worked. The actions I was asked to take would benefit officers of other companies, but not myself. Ian and his staff coordinated the whole thing for the mutual benefit of the members. Other members of the Replete Group did things to bolster my comp plan, but there was nothing that could be traced back to me. Like I said, Ian is a genius."

I was no lawyer, but it seemed that Replete's plan went far beyond the innocent workings of a bonus plan. They were manipulating giant businesses, perhaps influencing the entire market, for personal gain. Shipley needed to rationalize it in order to sleep peacefully, I supposed, but I did not.

"But you decided to get out, didn't you?" I was remembering what our friend Chuck had said about the boat explosion.

"Not exactly. I'll get to that in a moment. Within the first year, Ian made good on his promise. My comp more than doubled. It paid for a number of homes like this one, I upgraded to a bigger boat, a faster plane...life was good. Very good. Too good to last, I suppose. I have a sixth sense about these things. Just to be cautious, I began moving assets into accounts owned by an alter ego I had set up just before my divorce: Carstairs.

"Anyway, the only other person I knew for certain was in Replete was one of Rumsley's directors, Hamilton Grant, who also happens to be CEO over at Reicher Oil. Nice enough fellow, but not the kind of sharp mind you'd put at the helm of a big corporation. Comes from a powerful family—it works that way sometimes. Anyway, Ham does things in a clumsy way, and I'm sure that's how he executed the instructions he got from Ian. He probably shot his mouth off to the wrong people once or twice, too; I know he told me things he was supposed to keep quiet about. Eventually, somebody blew the whistle on him, and next thing you know he was being investigated by the FBI's white-collar crime unit. He told me all about it, giving me updates over a couple of months, when suddenly the investigation was dropped. When I asked him how he got out of it, all he'd say was 'Ian fixed it.' I knew he was telling the truth; Ian is capable of most anything.

"Then one day I was asked to divert some R&D funds from a major project and, at the same time, sign a letter of intent that committed us to a huge software purchase once contract details were ironed out. Those directives didn't feel right. For the first time I was being asked to do things that could come back to haunt me, so I consulted my attorney. I told him pretty much what I've told you about Replete, about all I know, actually, and he strongly advised me to get out. I didn't want to, of course; the money was much too good to simply walk away, but I did talk to Ian. I told him those particular group directives were a problem, and that I wanted to explore some alternatives with him.

"Within a week I took a big hit. A key supplier really screwed me, right out of the blue. That night I got a call from Ian. I had twenty-four hours to execute my directives. Ian gave, and now Ian was taking away. I did it, but I also called Ian and gave him hell for it. Next thing I know I was on my boat just off the Great Barrier Reef at about five AM when boom!—no more boat."

"How did you escape?"

"Luck. I had been awake, jetlag, and was out near the bow when it happened. Donato was also on deck, just down the port side if I recall, talking with the crew. He was thrown into the water right next to the dinghy. It was Donato who saved me, pulling me out of the water just moments later. Good thing, too; the reputation those waters have for sharks is well-deserved. We trolled around the wreckage until help came, but Donato and I were the only survivors. That was when I decided to be Carstairs for a while.

"Since that day I've been looking for a way to bring down Replete. I want that damn Wallace's balls in a jar. And it can't happen soon enough. Until Ian goes down I have to remain Carstairs, and, dammit, I want my life back. Now!" Carstairs hit the table in emphasis. Point made.

"Okay," he continued after a breath, "so I've been working on this for the past couple of months. I've made some good progress, but I sense that after today things might finally move more quickly."

"What progress have you made?"

"You, first of all. Both of you, in fact."

"I was hoping we'd get to that part," I told him. "Just how did you find out about me?"

"I started by researching Replete, of course, and found there was very little to go on. Ian was careful to cover his tracks. When I started I didn't even have his phone number; I'd lost my cell in the explosion, and I couldn't go back to my office. However, Ian had used his lawyer to help me negotiate a new employment contract at Rumsley. I hired a private investigator to watch the lawyer, and that led me to an opportunistic weasel named Scanlon. Special Agent Larry Scanlon of the FBI, the man who had been investigating Ham Grant."

Amber and I gave each other an "aha!" look.

"You recognize the name?"

"Yes. He had been working with a friend of mine on a project for Replete."

"Borgman, right? I'm aware of him. When Ham Grant was under investigation, Ian recognized the risk to Replete, so he bought himself some protection: he put Scanlon on his payroll. I'm sure he didn't come cheap, either. FBI people are pretty dedicated, even those like Scanlon, but I suppose everyone has a price. Anyway, I think that's where Ian first learned how useful a simulation can be.

"You see, Ian had a problem. The basic idea behind the Replete Group was ingenious, but when he scaled it up the whole thing got very hard to manage. He and a small staff have to constantly analyze and plan and issue those so-called group directives all manually. When Ian found out about Borgman's behavioral simulations he realized he could improve the whole process, test the directives to make sure they did what he wanted before taking any action. So he paid Scanlon to contract Borgman to build a much more comprehensive program, one that could be used to simulate the entire group."

"It's hard to believe Borgie would work for Replete," I said. "I mean, his job was strictly doing government work."

"My guess is that Ian was using Scanlon to make the whole thing look like a top-secret FBI project. Borgman didn't know what it was until he was almost finished."

That part agreed with what Borgie had said in the letter on his website. "So Borgie's program was supposed to make Replete work more efficiently?"

"I think it was even more than that. Remember, it's always going to be bigger than you think. With Borgman's software to help, Ian planned to get more than a cut from each member. He also wanted to manipulate the stock prices of the companies he's working with. A little 'proactive portfolio management.' He would not only *have* inside information, he would *create* inside information. This guy's net worth would go from huge to staggering!"

I looked at Shipley with narrowed eyes for a moment. He wasn't telling us everything. "To know all this you must have a contact within Replete. Not just a member, but someone who works directly with Ian."

"Yes." Shipley gave me a smug look. "And no, I won't divulge that detail."

I locked eyes with him, but I saw it would go nowhere and decided to let him finish his story. "So, how did all that lead you to me?"

"Your friend Borgman was nearly finished with his software when he figured out how it could be used. He called Scanlon and had a meltdown, during which he said you were the only person besides himself that could make the system work. My contact was able to copy some of the code, and that is what I wanted you to look at when we first met at the auditorium."

The auditorium. The DOT presentation. The meeting Carstairs—Shipley—and I had had in the wings when he asked me to delay my vacation and have a look at some code. That entire event seemed a lifetime ago.

"Do you know exactly how big Replete is?" I wanted to double-check the data Amber and I had gathered.

"I know there are quite a few members. Twenty, thirty, maybe more. Why?"

"Actually, there are fifty," Amber interjected. "Fifty members, each holding two officer or director positions in a pool of twenty-five companies."

Now it was Shipley's turn to be surprised. "You're sure of this?"

"Reasonably certain," Amber assured him.

"Then you two have made phenomenal progress in the past few days. And we are facing a phenomenal risk."

"What's that?" I asked.

Shipley waved his hand palm upward. "The risk of Pyrrhic victory." He gave a small sigh of frustration before explaining himself. "How can Replete be stopped without shaking the very foundations of those companies? And how can twenty-five of the top companies in the country be shaken up without causing economic collapse? Think about that. If just a few of those companies failed it the entire market would take a big hit. Something on this scale? This could ruin Wall Street, and create a pall of investor distrust that would hang over our heads for decades."

I had considered that problem, but tabled it for later consideration. I was more interested in figuring out what Borgie had been up to. Now that we had a pretty good idea of Replete's plans, this question had to be addressed. In fact, I was starting to understand that, like Shipley, I would not have my life back until that question was answered.

"Now," he continued, "I think I have been more than fair. I've shared nearly everything I've learned about Replete over the past few months. In the past few days you have apparently learned some things I have yet to uncover, and I need to you share them with me." Shipley's eyes narrowed as he said this. I was more comfortable with Shipley at that point, but my guard was still up, as was Amber's, and I wasn't prepared to show all my cards just yet.

"I understand. Actually, the story begins with Amber and her friend Lisa. Replete killed Lisa last Saturday."

Shipley gave Amber a sympathetic nod, and, with a tilt of my head, I prompted Amber to tell her part of the story. She began with the lunch where she and Lisa had seen Scanlon and Borgie and took him up to the point of Lisa's death. Amber was concise and articulate, neatly encapsulating intricate details clearly and succinctly. It was a highly abbreviated version, compared to what she had told me back in her hotel room, but the salient details were all there.

I already knew her story, of course, and as she told it to Shipley I found my mind drifting, paying more attention to her than to her words. She had been ripped out of a normal world, her best friend was murdered, and she was running for her life with a stranger, me, as her only support. Yet, she was able to sit calmly and describe it all with poise and precision. I was impressed with her all over again, so much so that she nearly had to poke me when it was my turn to speak.

In the interest of time, my story was, well, less of a story and more of a listing of the events that brought us to that point. I told Shipley how I had been nearly kidnapped at a coffee shop, that the kidnappers had mentioned Replete, how our search led us to Chuck the Conspiracy Theorist, how Chuck's website gave us the first clues to Replete's membership and how Amber's database program and a little spade work had allowed us to figure out the complete roster, the companies involved, and the board and officer positions that linked those companies together. As I spoke I realized how much we had accomplished in that short time. I also found myself watching Shipley's face at various points in the tale. His reactions were genuine, and I found myself increasingly comfortable sharing details with him. In the end, I suppose I had shared about all we had.

"Excellent, Morgan. Truly excellent," Shipley said, and I could see he was coming to respect us as well. "That's it, then?"

"There is one other detail," I added with a sly smile. "We have Borgie's program working. Most of it, anyway."

"That is incredible! You mean Borgman had actually completed the system?"

"Well, no," I told him. "We got his code to compile and generate an executable program, but it isn't complete. Several of his source code files are empty placeholders where actual code had yet to be inserted. The user interface seems to work, and it does simulate a few of the companies in Replete, but not many. Each one is incredibly complex on its own; getting a complete system up and running was an ambitious goal, even for Borgie."

6

THE CHAMELEON

Letting Shipley know about Borgie's program was cathartic. We had told all our secrets, so now we could be more at ease, no longer needing to guard our words and reactions as if playing hide and seek with the truth. It felt as though we had reached a milestone. We had joined forces with Shipley, aggregating resources in a common quest.

We had also reached a strategic turning point. Until now, Amber and I had been groping in the dark. We had learned a lot—a combination of research and dumb luck, I supposed—but our actions had been reactive. We had been looking over our shoulders, always fearing the next brush with Replete's nefarious agents. Now, for the first time since this had begun, there was hope. We had the knowledge and information to fight back, the means to be proactive in bringing all this to an end. That alone was enough to bring a temporary sense of relief, a sense I could see was reflected in the others as well. We had moved from desperation to hope and empowerment, and it felt good and refreshing. But empowerment to do what? As before, the foremost problem was to define a plan. It was easier in some ways, having the information we now had, but at the same time more difficult as there was now a third vote, another cook in the kitchen. I could only hope Shipley's goals and ours were aligned well enough to minimize dissent.

We spoke about this for a few minutes, seeking consensus in an approach to solving the problem. Shipley, coming from the rareified atmosphere of the corporate executive suite, was accustomed to hearing facts and making decisions, and I was initially concerned that he might presume a similar role with us. I was uncomfortable with that prospect; Shipley wasn't the guile-less, mutually supportive personality that had allowed Amber and me to cooperate so well. As we spoke, though, he seemed to consciously keep any natural overbearance in check. Shipley had valuable information to share, but seemed to show less interest in listening to ours. For a while, I think, both he and I were being careful not to step on the other's toes; a political nicety, but one that did not make for a productive relationship. It was Amber who finally steered our thoughts in a more useful direction.

"What do we believe Ian's interests are in each of us?" she asked. "I mean, I know he wants Borgman's program, but he must know by now that he can't get it from me. He doesn't even know Shipley's alive, and he knows you, Roger, are on the run. He can't still think he'll get the system running, can he?"

"Excellent questions," I replied. "We need to understand his current motives. I don't think we're going to like them, though."

"Nor do I," agreed Shipley. "I may be the lucky one here. As long as Ian thinks I'm dead, I'm off his radar. If he learns the truth, he'll stop at nothing to kill me as quickly as possible. I'd be the biggest security risk he has."

"As for me, well, there are probably two answers," I said. "First, if he thought there was any chance at all, he would probably want me to finish Borgie's program. I'm not even sure it's possible, by the way, but that makes things even worse: if he thought I was lying about that he'd just keep applying pressure and I'd have nothing to give. Second, from what the guys in the coffee shop said, they already think I know everything Borgie knew. If he knew how much we've learned about Replete, though, he'd consider me a threat. You too, I'm afraid."

Shipley then shared an observation. "We're all a threat to Ian, but I think Ian has another problem as well. It's the 'guaranteed to double' promise that got him in trouble. A smaller increase might have been easier to produce, but actually doubling the income of fifty execs means everything he does, *everything*, has to work out perfectly. He must have zero tolerance for error. That's why it upset him so when I questioned his last directives, and that's why he panicked and killed Borgman and then your friend Lisa. My guess is he's nearly desperate. He needs Borgman's program, or something like it, to keep Replete running, and he stands to lose many millions if he fails."

"He couldn't be running Replete by himself, could he?" asked Amber. "He must have some help."

"You're right," Shipley responded. "Ian's smart, but he can only do so much. I know from before that he has a few others to help with the day-to-day work so he has time to manage the membership and set strategy. The others probably know as little as possible about what they're really doing. Compartmentalized information, that sort of thing."

I sat back and listened to them, absorbing their theories while mulling over one of my own. Shipley had direct knowledge of Ian, and he had invaluable insight, the product of his experience leading a corporation, I supposed. Amber was pragmatic, challenging and testing each idea with keenly logical analysis, the IAR technical administrator collaborating with the corporate officer. Amber held up her end as well as Shipley, refining his thoughts and offering her own. They continued like that for a few minutes while I made up my mind; then, when they paused for a breath, I broke my silence.

"We need to take the offensive," I told them.

They both turned to me, expecting, I suppose, a level of detail beyond what I had to offer. Frankly, I didn't yet have a specific plan of action, but I did know I had no wish to live in fear of every dark sedan that passed by. We had been forced by circumstance to play the fox, but those circumstances had changed when we pooled our knowledge with Shipley's. It was time to play the hound.

Shipley broke the momentary silence my statement produced. "What did you have in mind?"

"So far all I have is logic," I replied. "Up to this point, Replete has held the advantage. Ian may have considered each of us was a threat, but none of us knew enough of the puzzle to actually *be* a threat. Now that has changed. We know what he is doing, we know what he wants, and we know what threatens him."

"We also have no proof of anything," challenged Shipley. "And let's not forget that risk of success we spoke about."

"I haven't forgotten. And I know we lack proof. In fact, I think that's just where we should start."

"What do you mean?"

"I mean Ian is guilty of two things that we know of: corporate manipulation and murder. Replete Group operations are pretty complicated, and it would be hard for us to get any proof against him by ourselves. Murder, though, that's a different thing. If we had evidence that Ian was behind two murders we'd stop Ian, and that would put a stop to the Replete Group."

"Roger, you're exactly right!" Amber declared.

"Maybe he is," Shipley's eyes narrowed, "and maybe not. It's a lot easier to say we'll get proof than it is to actually get it. Do you have a plan?"

"I don't have the complete answer yet, but we do have two things going for us. One is surprise—Ian doesn't know about you yet. The other is irresistible bait."

"Oh, Roger, you don't mean that you…"

"Wait," Shipley interrupted. "We can't launch an offensive with just the three of us. We need more. A lot more."

"What else do we need? We're on the run, Shipley, all of us. Time is not on our side."

"We need Borgman's program," he responded. "All of it, in working order. That's what Ian wants. With it, we hold all the cards; without it we have nothing he wants."

Shipley held me in a cold stare, and I could do nothing but return the look. Apparently with Amber debate was acceptable, but, with me, it was not. I came to realize that it wasn't because he had more respect for Amber; in fact, it was the opposite. Shipley saw me as competition for authority. Amber, in his misogynistic mind, was not. I would never understand how a person's intellectual or leadership value could be gender-dependent, but knowing how Shipley thought helped me better understand him and how to deal with him.

The real problem, though, was Shipley's logic. Completing Borgie's program might not have been possible, but, even if it was, it could take weeks or even months. And then what would we have that we didn't have already? The program Amber and I had gotten working in the library clearly showed what Replete was doing. Adding more companies to it wouldn't prove a thing. Besides, we would have tampered with that evidence. The only value it could have would be to Replete. The more I thought about it, the more I knew that working on Borgie's program was a long detour I didn't intend to take. I also realized I was feeling disappointment. Minutes earlier I had been relieved to have a new member on our team, but now…

I found myself pacing around Shipley's study, trying to explain my issue with working on the program while at the same time trying to get Shipley on a path more complementary to our own. We needed proof of what we knew, we needed to locate Ian, and we needed to turn him in. Then we needed to figure out what could be done about the Replete members, if anything. All told that was a big challenge for us, even with Shipley's apparent resources; without them it looked like K2 standing atop Everest.

Shipley's resources did appear sizable, attesting to his (or his attorney's) ability to hide assets in the Carstairs name. The home I stood in was large for a row house, professionally furnished and decorated. From the window behind Shipley's study desk I could see a carefully tended yard space with comfortable-looking, and probably unused, lawn furniture. There were two late-model SUVs parked further in back, although one had quite a bit of body damage to the front end, the only imperfection I had seen so far in Shipley's home. That aside, everything was impeccably maintained in a manner that required trained staff. If this was but one of several homes 'Carstairs' kept, he was doing okay.

For her part, Amber shared my concerns, both about Borgie's program and about Shipley's logic. Neither she nor I felt comfortable wasting time on the program, yet Shipley was resolute. In his mind, Borgie's program was everything. His tactic in this debate was to dig in his heels until others yielded out of exasperation, using intransigence to wear down opposition. In fact, the more we discussed it, the more emotional Shipley became. For all the progress we had made in the past few days, we were now at an uncomfortable impasse.

In time the conversation simply stopped of its own accord. Shipley had said all there was to say from his side, and Amber and I failed to sway him with our rationale. As much as I disliked the oversimplification of "biz-speak," the only short-term solution was for us to "agree to disagree." Even as we reached that point, Shipley was still bursting with adrenaline, his frustration barely distinguishable from rage. Amber looked bewildered, and I, too, was at a loss. I had spent my life dealing with strong-minded people, but, in my technical world, logic was usually able to resolve disagreement. That wasn't the case here, and I had begun to ask myself why. My only answer was to question the man's motivation.

Again, it was Amber who put us on a more pragmatic path.

"Well," she said, "we need to start thinking about tonight, Roger. We're still homeless, you know."

Shipley immediately jumped in. "You'll want to stay here, of course. There is plenty of room, and all the resources we need to work out of this mess. In fact, would you like to see the guest room?"

Amber looked to me for our joint response, unsure of her level of comfort after our protracted debate with Shipley.

"That's very kind, thank you," I said. "But we'll need to get some things. Mine are at the Canadian residence from last night. Amber has nothing but her purse. Maybe a quick trip to a mall would be in order?"

"I'll have Donato drive her," Shipley replied, his angst having subsided enough for him to play the gracious host again. "And, naturally, I'll pick up any costs. Donato?" Shipley left the room to make arrangements, and I had the first chance to speak with Amber alone since we left the library.

"How are you holding up?" I asked, keeping my voice just above a whisper.

"I'm okay, but I don't understand where he is coming from. Your plan makes much more sense, Roger. What does he hope to gain?"

"I'm not sure. Maybe he just needs to be in control, but it's almost as if he wants Replete for himself. Watch it with Donato, okay? And try to be back soon; I kind of like having you close, you know?" She squeezed my arm, and I had just enough time to place a quick peck on her forehead before Shipley reentered the room.

"It's all set. Donato will take you to the mall and then to retrieve Morgan's bags."

With that we declared a break. Amber left with Donato in the undamaged SUV, and before returning to his study to make a number of phone calls, Shipley showed me to another room where I could set up my computer. In spite of my reservations about both feasibility and practicality, I agreed to take another look at Borgie's program to assess the scope of completing the implementation.

With Donato gone and Shipley in the far end of the house, I had time to sort my thoughts and close any holes that might exist in our theory of how Replete operated. As much as I hated to admit it, I was impressed by the way Ian had designed and built the Replete Group. Even the name was appropriate, each member having so much of everything they could want. Yet, they still wanted more, and were willing to break the rules to get it.

I thought about how the incredible compensation paid these executives was affecting the rest of us. It would have been easy to think of that compensation as a vanishingly small percentage of a major company's total revenue, but I knew that wasn't relevant. Those dollars, if not paid in executive comp, would be profit dollars, adding to that thin margin that was the real reason for any business to exist. As a percentage of profit, the sum total of executive compensation a company paid out could range from high to obscene.

A little mental exercise put it into perspective for me. I imagined a company that made bars of soap, and I assigned reasonable estimates for the company's material costs, sales and marketing costs, transportation and then retail store mark-up. What I came up with was staggering: if the bar of soap cost me one dollar at the supermarket, it could easily take the sale of fifty million bars of soap just to pay for one million dollars of executive salary. Hypothetical, of course, but eye-opening.

The other issue is where that money came from, who the real victim was in this whole scheme. The consumer was one, as prices were raised to support such excess. The investor was another. In the end, they were the ones actually paying the executives. A board of directors, in over-paying for executive services, was simultaneously draining the economy and cheating the very shareholders they were paid to serve. If they could achieve the same corporate results with less cost, i.e., paying less for those top few officer positions, they had a responsibility to do so.

Now the Replete Group had invented a way of making the problem even worse. For fifty top executives, they had found a way of increasing that inflated compensation to a total of over a *billion* dollars. Ian was already getting a percentage of that; now, if Shipley was right, he wanted to manipulate stock prices to make even more.

We had to stop him.

I thrust my hands deep into my pockets and walked down the hallway toward Shipley's study, intent on taking one more run at convincing him to stop pursuing Borgie's program. I planned on approaching him calmly and rationally in the hope that reason would prevail. As I neared the study, though, I overheard Shipley speaking on the phone. I could only hear his end of the conversation, of course, but it was enough to turn on a mental light that, maybe, should have started flickering much earlier.

I had overheard him say, "…won't have to worry about that damned bill. His kid was more important to him after all. He's out for sure this time, so you're it, Senator."

It was too late for me to simply walk away unnoticed. Shipley saw me and quickly but calmly ended his conversation. He was giving me a curious look, and I came to realize I was simply standing in the doorway, processing thoughts while staring blindly back at him. It only took a moment before he spoke.

"You should knock, Morgan."

"You were very convincing," I responded, any hope of concealing my newfound knowledge having been lost. "I especially liked the chase scene. Very realistic."

"I'm not sure I understand." He was fishing, wanting to be sure of how much I knew before deciding on a course of action.

"You like the name 'John,' don't you."

"It is my first name, yes."

"John Foster Shipley, John Carstairs... The Gaelic equivalent is 'Ian,' isn't it?"

"What was it that tipped you off?" Shipley asked me, his eyes showing only confidence in his ability to contain this new situation. That alone would have sent me running, but I knew it would be futile. His man Donato had Amber.

"Sometimes it's a pebble that triggers the landslide," I told him. "Borgie had left me a note that said 'you're it.' One of your men also said that at the coffee shop where they tried to kidnap me. You just used those same words on the phone. It's funny how something like that will become a catch phrase in an organization. Amber and I didn't understand your arguments earlier; now it all makes sense. You want the program to help you run Replete."

I was completely vulnerable at that point, playing flute to a swaying cobra as we each tried to predict the other's next move. I was trapped, and my only chance, in the near term, was to let him believe I could help him with Borgie's program after all. I needed to be more valuable alive than dead, and I needed Amber's safety to be a prerequisite for my cooperation.

"You're right, of course, Morgan. There is no Ian Wallace. I created the Replete Group. I designed it, recruited others into it, and made it work for the past couple of years now. It's a perfect system."

"I have to admit it is impressive. How did it get started?"

"Simple. I was being screwed. Rumsley was highly profitable, more so than most of its competitors, but I wasn't getting rewarded for it. My compensation plan sucked bath water. It looked good when I was first offered the job, I suppose, but when I got the growth started and the profits up I got damned near nothing for it. Ham knew. Ham Grant was on the board. As CEO I was on every board committee except one: the compensation committee—conflict of interest, of course—but Ham was on it. He's a dolt, but even he could see I was being screwed, and with his typical lack of subtlety he told me about it right in front of some friends while we were golfing. Big laugh. But it made me think. I found the best lawyer I could and we wrote up a new contract. Then I got Ham to help push it through the committee in return for me keeping quiet about a few of his indiscretions. It was all too easy.

"Anyway, the contract helped a lot, but it wasn't enough. In order to make any serious money, I needed some cooperation. That's when the lightning struck. I imagined a network of executives all cooperating to achieve the same goals, and then I made it happen. First I recruited Ham, of course. Then I got another, and then another. After the first few I put together a more strategic plan, selecting members and companies that would complement the group as a whole.

"The beauty of it comes from symmetry. Exactly twenty-five companies, complementary businesses that, with a little coordination, can make each other very successful. Exactly fifty execs, each holding two positions in those companies, giving me just enough control to exert that coordination. Finally, a common contract—executive compensation agreement—used by all the executives. That was the key; that made it all feasible.

"I'm sure you understand it, Morgan. It's a lot like your 'flock of birds' example. The Replete Group provides a framework, a set of common rules that binds the execs together and creates a new group behavior."

I understood what he was trying to say, but he forgot an important part: autonomy. For the flock to work spontaneously, each member of the flock had to be autonomous. He was constantly intervening, manipulating. That was one of the problems with creating a hegemonic system: manipulation is a lot of work.

"In just over a year I was making far more from Replete than I was at Rumsley, and there weren't enough hours in the day to do both. At the same time, my dear ex-wife was trying to bleed me dry. That's when I decided to disappear. Very effective, too. It cost me a nice boat, but I got that bitch off my back and was able to put all my time on Replete, all in one shot.

"The problem, though, was just what we talked about before. Replete alone is still more than a full-time job. And there's little room for error; everything has to work perfectly. So, when Ham got his stupid ass investigated, and I found out how the FBI was using your friend Borgman to figure out what we were up to, I saw the light. The program Borgman used in that investigation was just the kind of tool I was looking for."

Shipley's pride had him almost eager to expound on his accomplishments, so I decided to go after more information. "How did you get the FBI to help you?" I asked.

"Not the FBI *per se*, of course. Just a burned-out, disillusioned agent who was tired of seeing so many white-collar criminals piling up money and getting away with it. He came surprisingly cheap, and he was able to convince Borgman and a couple of his guys that he was working on a secret FBI project. Ha! It was all too easy!"

I was having another revelation as he spoke. I tried not to show it, but I needed a little more information to test my theory. "And what happens if the rules change? I know, for example, that there's a bill in the works that would make things like executive pay a lot more open. Wouldn't that shut you down?"

"Yes, yes it would," he smiled. "But you must always remember that Replete is bigger than you think. That bill isn't going to make it into law; it's losing its sponsorship."

So my suspicions were right. Shipley was right, too—Replete was playing on a much larger scale than I had considered.

At that point Shipley seemed to realize he had been telling me a lot, and with a steely look he returned to the present. "Now, Morgan, you have a once-in-a-lifetime opportunity. If you're smart, you'll take it and help me out. I can assure you, the rewards for your work will be sizable."

He had said "*will*" be sizable, not "would," the presumptuous bastard. He believed he was going to get my help, one way or another, and wanted me to think there might be something in it for me. He wasn't planning my demise just yet, but I knew my long-term prospects were poor. I needed to buy time so I could think.

"Well, as I told you earlier, Borgie's approach isn't going to work. I think you knew that. In fact, I think that was why Borgie had a meltdown on the phone the day he mentioned my name. He had painted himself into a corner and needed to lower your expectations, but without admitting he simply couldn't do it. His ego wouldn't let him do that."

"But yet you think you can do it?"

"That depends on what 'it' is. I think…I know…a good simulation program could help manage a system like Replete. It would simulate the effect of whatever potential actions you had in mind so you could see what works before you make a move. A simulation would never be able to define those actions for you. I mean, you could never just run a program and have it pop out a set of your 'group directives,' but it would let you develop high confidence in every move before you commit to it, and let you know the impact on others in the group."

"You could create such a program?"

"Developing the program itself isn't that difficult; in fact, Borgie did most of the groundwork for you already. The trick is knowing exactly what the program needs to do. For example, it would have to iterate, run over and over until the ripples from any given set of actions settled out." I was walking on a razor's edge. It was probably quite apparent that others could code up the program, but I needed to appear indispensible until I found a way out of this.

"But you could do that, correct? You could define the program that would do all the things you described? One that actually worked?"

"I could, now that I know what you need it to do. Borgie didn't have the complete picture. You had kept too much of it secret. He really didn't have a chance to succeed." It was true; I could specify a program that would make his job much, much easier—although it would probably be the last thing I did.

"Tell me, Morgan, how much do you make in a year these days?"

I told him, and he gave an appreciative nod.

"That's a good salary. I'm sure it reflects your value to the Institute. Now, what if I offered you five times that much for this little project? Would that get your full cooperation?"

"Five year's salary for one software spec? That is a lot of money."

"Do you know how much money is involved in Replete?"

"I have some idea."

"Then you know how much it is worth for us to keep Replete running at top efficiency."

"I do. In fact, it may be worth ten year's salary, if I did it right. Even more than that if I were to finish writing the program, test it out and maintain it for you as things change downstream."

Shipley gave me an evil smile, believing that he had found my dark side.

"But, of course, there are a couple of problems." I couldn't be seen as giving in too easily. Besides, this was an opportunity to find out more about the murders. "Borgie is dead. Lisa, too. For all I know, there are others. Why did they have to die, John?"

"You know why. When Borgman realized what we were doing he became self-righteous and wanted out. He called Replete a con game and even threatened to expose us. A con game! That outrageous twit! Replete may be the perfect money-making scheme! We're just gathering up a few cents per share and putting it to better use. Each member of the group wins, and each time they win, well, I win, too."

Interesting how Shipley could conveniently forget that just a "few cents per share" was the total return on investment many shareholders hoped to get. "You killed Borgie because he wanted out?"

Any pretense of civility went out the window at that point. "Damn it, he threatened to expose it all! Do you know what that would mean? Do you realize what that would cost me? I couldn't let that happen. At first I just wanted to have him…well…sequestered so he could finish the work without distraction, but when he decided to resist I knew he had to go. We planned to do it cleanly, far away from here, but

Trevor tapped his head too hard with that little bronze bust over there."

"So the money was worth a man's life?"

"Look, Morgan, this is serious business. We're managing over a billion dollars, all together. It's unfortunate, but people like that can't be allowed to get in the way. Period!" My question had turned Shipley to solid ice, and I was suddenly worried I had pushed too far.

I had. Shipley knew I would never be able to rationalize his actions the way he had been doing.

"There has been enough talk. You will do as I've asked, Morgan, and you'll do it now."

I gulped at the implication. "Why would I want to do that?"

"Ah, well. You might do it for yourself, I suppose, but I'm guessing you're going to do it for the sake of Ms. Meadows. Perhaps my associates can help explain your motivation." His eyes indicated behind me, and I turned to look at two men who had approached unnoticed. They were the men I had met at the coffee shop.

"Take him down to the cellar," he told them. "Remember, Trevor, just a demonstration—for now. Oh, and Morgan, I'll take your cell phone."

I stared defiantly into Shipley's eyes as I handed him my smart phone, which he threw into a drawer. Then he came close, so close I could smell him, and said, "Remember, Morgan, this is what Ms. Meadows will experience if you fail to cooperate. This, and much more."

I was taken to the 'cellar,' as Shipley called it, and found it was actually a completely finished lower level with a fully equipped home theater. Next to it was a workshop that had an exterior staircase up to the back yard. The theater was windowless and sound-isolated, making it the ideal place for what they had in mind. As they pushed me past the shop and into the theater I turned and raised my hands, palms forward, and started to explain that this was completely unnecessary, that I would cooperate fully. I didn't get to the end of that sentence before I was doubled over in pain. One of them, the anvil-fisted one, scoffed and said, "you made us look bad yesterday," sputtering in my face as he spoke. Then he hit me in the solar plexus, completely taking my wind. He hit a third time, and I fell to my knees unable to see or think or hear for several moments.

When I finally opened my eyes, still gasping for air, his friend took over. This man had a more subtle approach. He grabbed my hand, bent it forward at the wrist and then twisted it sharply outward. I went down to the floor completely incapacitated, the torsion on my arm feeling certain to snap a bone at any moment. Then he looked at me, smiled, and kicked me in the floating ribs.

"This is just a demo," he said. "You'll survive. We may get to do this again and again. To your girlfriend!"

They went on like that for a couple of minutes, finding new places to hit, kick, twist or distend. Actually, it could have been longer, but I wouldn't know.

When I was again fully conscious I was sitting on the floor, leaning back against a large chair.

Everything hurt, and it took several moments for me to remember why. My attackers were standing just through the door into the workshop, smoking and arguing about something I neither heard nor cared about at that moment. I needed a plan, and I needed to warn Amber before she walked in unaware and was trapped.

Hanging my head as though still blacked out, I slowly slipped my hand into the pocket furthest from them, shielding it from their sight, I hoped, with my body and legs. I found what I was looking for and pulled it out of the pocket: the disposable cell phone I had purchased on Saturday. Shipley had never patted me down, and there was no reason for him to think I carried a second phone.

I opened the phone and peeked at the time, seeing that I had only been out a few minutes. My hope now was that Amber was still shopping, or, at least, was not already on her way back here. She had already been gone a couple of hours, so I knew I had little time to warn her.

Slowly I pushed the menu key to select text message. I was rewarded with a beep, loud enough to cause near-panic as I quickly lowered the volume. I was deathly afraid they had heard it or had seen my startled reaction. I didn't dare turn my head toward them again, but I didn't see anything in my peripheral vision and I heard no movement toward me. So far, so good.

With painstaking keystrokes, using my left hand and having just a number pad to spell out the words, I formed my message. It read "shipley is replete get away send help."

Next I dialed 9-1-1. I wouldn't be able to speak to them, but I intended to leave the line open and hope they would find me. I punched in the numbers, but before my thumb could press the enter button my hand received a hard kick and the phone when flying, hitting the wall with enough force to dislodge the battery and shatter the case.

"Now, that was clever, Doc," Trevor sneered as he stood over me. "Hadn't you already gotten enough?"

Shipley stepped into the room, having been summoned by club-hands, and Trevor immediately stepped back, deferring to his superior.

"Who did he call?" Shipley demanded.

"He was dialing 9-1-1," Trevor responded. "Didn't get it out, though."

Shipley knelt to my level. "You've been very resourceful, Morgan, and we have had an interesting game of cat-and-mouse. Now it's over. We have a lot of work to do, and I am going to insist on your cooperation. Do you understand?"

"I…I understand," I replied with a cough. What I didn't understand was how long I could give him faux cooperation before he realized what was up. There was no way I wanted to help this man beyond what it took to protect Amber. The problem, of course, was that, as soon as my work was finished, Amber would be finished. As would I. And I had no way of knowing if she even got my message.

"Okay then," Shipley said, and turned to Trevor. "Get a hold of Donato and tell him to keep the girl in the car when he gets back. You're going to take her to the Baltimore location. I don't want them together.

And have Alex get back down here to watch Morgan until we find a place for him to work. Got it?"

Trevor left with a curt nod and his friend, Alex, returned. Shipley left me there, sitting on the floor of his home theater, without so much as another glance. As far as he was concerned, I was contained.

"Some vacation," I said to myself with a humorless chuckle, followed by a sudden pang as my bruised torso signaled its protest.

I wasn't really comfortable on that floor, but sitting there seemed to beat the alternative of trying to get myself up. I decided to defer that attempt another few minutes, as long as Alex would sit in the workshop and read his magazine instead of bothering me in the theater. My mind was foggy from pain and post-adrenaline let-down, but my primary concern was still Amber. From what Shipley had said about keeping us apart, I might not know for some time whether she'd been able to escape, or if she had even gotten my message.

As the fog lifted, I began rehashing the argument we had had with Shipley that afternoon. I had wanted to go on the offensive, a logical strategy, but when I said it I wasn't sure exactly what it would entail. Now I had more information. Shipley had, for all practical purposes, admitted his role in two murders to me. I had also learned of his role in another crime, one that was still playing out. In fact, I believed I had proof of crimes that could put him and the others out of action for a very long time. The only problem was finding a way to do it without getting two of my favorite people dead.

I had no answer to that problem, and eventually my mind drifted to other topics. I found myself judging Shipley in terms of the definition of ethics I had described to Amber back on the mall. Everything he did, including his actions as CEO of Rumsley, had been for himself, even though he was being paid to watch out for the interests of his company. He was devoid of ethics, and that had allowed him not only to commit multiple crimes, but to rationalize them, believing they were simply necessary to produce those self-serving results. I didn't think I could rationalize the way Shipley did. I saw ethics as a discipline, the measure of one's character, the caliber of one's soul.

Out of professional habit, I started putting all that in terms of emergent group behavior. From a group perspective, ethics had very high intrinsic value. It made each member of a group more productive and reliable, giving the group a better chance to flourish and reach its goals. Unethical behavior cost the group—it was a waste, a drain on society. The problem, of course, is that the one being unethical was often rewarded, at least in the short term. Personal benefit at public cost, I supposed, was a universal bane of ethics.

All of that was mere procrastination, I suppose, while I avoided unpleasant thoughts of the dangers Amber now faced on my account. I had only known her for three days, yet as I sat on that floor, the thought of her transported me. She and I were in sync somehow, thinking and acting in concert. She possessed qualities I had missed in other relationships, things ranging from energy and enthusiasm to competence and reliability. Now Amber was being callously used as leverage in Shipley's unending quest for more and more. I had already decided that I could not let her suffer because of me. The trouble was, I had no idea how to prevent it. I also realized that my feelings for Amber could only increase Shipley's control over me.

I noticed it had been a while since I had seen anything of Shipley or his men, save Alex's uninspiring backside as he sat just outside the door reading his magazine (or, at least, looking at the pictures). Some time ago I had heard Shipley pass by the top of the staircase while shouting "I don't care, find him" at somebody, but that was all I had for input in the last hour. Then, at last, something appeared to happen.

I couldn't hear anything, being held in a room that had been deadened for watching movies, but I did see Alex put down his magazine and rise to his feet, his head cocked to one side listening to something happening above him. Whatever it was, Alex only took a few seconds to decide he wanted no part of it. I watched as he shoved his chair aside and dashed toward the door to the outside steps. Then I saw him step back into the room, hands raised, followed by two armed police officers.

One of the policemen put Alex in handcuffs while the other approached me.

"Are you Roger Morgan?" he asked, and I confirmed. "Please come with me, sir." With that they took Alex up the staircase with me escorted behind him, the cop holding my arm as my legs were unsure of themselves on the staircase.

There was a flurry of activity when I entered the front room. Two more officers were walking Trevor and Alex toward the front door, while two more and a detective were beginning a search of the house. The officer that had helped me upstairs stayed with me, along with another detective. The two began asking questions, starting with the most basic.

"I am Detective Morris with the DC Metro Police. My partner is Detective Escobar. You are Roger Morgan, correct?"

"I am."

"And you were being held against your will?"

"I was."

"Were you assaulted?"

"Yes. Yes, I was definitely assaulted."

At that point I saw Amber pushing her way into the room.

"Roger! Are you all right?" While she spoke she ran up to me and gave me a tight hug, and I had to work at not showing my discomfort.

"I will be. Just bruises."

"Oh, Roger, I knew there was something wrong with Shipley, but I thought he was just being a greedy bastard…"

The detective interrupted her. "I'm afraid we have some more questions. Do you know where J. Foster Shipley is at this moment?"

Oh no. "You mean he wasn't here?"

"No, he had apparently left before we arrived. Do you have any idea where he might have gone?"

"No. But he had been talking to Trevor—the tall one. The other guy was downstairs watching me."

"We'll be asking him shortly. Do you know why they were holding you?"

"Yes. I do, and it is a long story, but right now I have some more important information for you. We have two murder weapons."

The detective's eyes opened widely. "Murder weapons? Who was murdered?"

"Please, let me show you," I said, and walked them back to Shipley's study, the second detective joining us en route. "First was the murder of Leonard Borgman. His body was found last Wednesday, I believe, in downtown DC." As soon as I mentioned the name I heard the other detective calling his office for information on the case. "This bronze bust was the murder weapon; Shipley himself told me what happened. I imagine your medical examiner will be able to match it to the wounds. Shipley told me that Trevor, one of the men you arrested, is the man who hit Borgman with it, right here in this room."

The detective carefully picked up the bust with gloved hands, examined it, and placed it in a plastic bag. "Looks like they wiped it off, but we'll see what the lab finds. We're going to have to leave the room, now, so the crime scene team can check for residuals. We'll also need prints from both of you so we can eliminate any we find in here."

As we walked out the detective prompted me for more, "You said there were two weapons…?"

"Actually, the other weapon is just outside. There was a hit-and-run in the district on Saturday morning. The victim was Lisa DeLoit. I think you'll find that the banged-up SUV behind the house was the vehicle that hit her."

The detective gave a quick look to the uniformed officers, who left to check it out.

"Do you know who was driving, sir?"

"I believe it was Donato, but I don't have proof of that. I don't know his last name, but he's the one who was with Amber this afternoon. Is he in custody?"

"Yes. He's been taken to a hospital for observation, then he'll be booked for assault. He was unconscious when they found him."

I looked at Amber, who gave a slight shrug and said, "Jason did it, Roger. Ronnie had him watching over me. I got your message when Donato and I were in the parking lot leaving the mall. When I tried to get away he grabbed me and forced me into the car. Jason saw what was happening and jumped him, and then we called the police."

Detective Morris did a quick recap. "Two murders, two assaults, one kidnapping and an attempted kidnapping. This is going to be some report. Is there anything else?"

"Yes. We have a lot to talk about," I said, remembering Shipley's admonition that however big you think it is, there is more. "You're going to want Shipley's computer, for sure. He's been manipulating corporate execs, bribing officials and a lot more."

"Okay," Morris said as another crew arrived with large plastic boxes of supplies and equipment. "We're going to leave all this to the CSI folks for now. I need to take you to the station to get a statement. Are you up to it, or do you want medical attention?"

"Absolutely I'm up to it," I replied, although my tender gut wasn't quite as enthusiastic. Amber echoed my affirmative, and in minutes we had gathered up our computers and were being escorted through the line of gawking neighbors and into a van headed downtown.

We didn't get any questions on the way to the station. I suppose the detectives wanted a controlled environment where they could take notes, listen more closely, and probably even record our statements. That gave Amber and me a few minutes to catch up. Detective Morris asked that we not discuss the case until we arrived, so we instead spent the time reassuring each other that we were okay. Luckily, Amber had only been grabbed and pushed a bit. We were parking at the station before she was finally convinced that I had no serious damage, that they had intended my experience only as a "demo" to make me more cooperative. There was no need to mention it was a demonstration of trauma intended for her.

Once inside the station we settled into a conference room where Morris was obviously the man of the hour, having found key information—and physical evidence—on two open homicide cases. We were joined by his partner, Detective Escobar, their Captain Levi, and the young woman who ran the recording gear. A steady flow of cops walked by and stared through the conference room windows as news of the event spread through the precinct building.

"Okay," Morris began after the introductions were complete, "please be aware that everything you say in this room will be considered a part of your statement. Remember, you're not suspects here. We need you to be completely open with us. You'll be asked to review the transcription for accuracy when we're done. Understood?"

Understood.

"Good. Then let's start with how these two deaths are related."

"There is a lot leading up to that point," I told him. "Why don't we start at the beginning?"

"Indulge me," he replied. I realized that so far he was only interested in the crimes he already knew about, so I gave him an answer that would cause him to widen the scope. Before we finished, I knew, this case would grow far beyond the local precinct anyway.

"Okay, fine. The deaths of Leonard Borgman and Lisa DeLoit were both ordered by John Foster Shipley as a means of keeping his vast scheme of corporate fraud, bribery and illicit earnings of several hundred million dollars from becoming public."

Morris stared at me with widened eyes, then exchanged glances with his captain and partner. "Maybe you had better start at the beginning," he told me.

Given that opening, I launched into a narrative that told the story of Shipley and the Replete Group, recounting everything Shipley had told us that I was convinced was true. I told them how Shipley was a CEO whose greed convinced him to form the Replete Group so he could extract a percentage of the income of others. I described the intricate and inventive system that drove Replete, and how Shipley became overwhelmed with its operation, how he first bribed Agent Scanlon and subsequently learned of Borgie's abilities. At the mention of Agent Scanlon, Captain Levi beckoned an onlooking officer into the room and whispered instructions that sent him scurrying off on an errand.

Next, I described how Shipley had bribed Scanlon to convince Borgie to write a very special simulation program for a fake top-secret investigation. I wasn't sure exactly when Borgie had learned the real purpose of his code, but I knew that he wasn't truly complicit in Shipley's schemes. Better that he should be remembered as the genius he was rather than as a criminal. It was the least I could do for an old friend who had already paid for any transgressions.

I got to the part where they killed Borgie, and shortly after described how and why they killed Lisa. I also told them I suspected Donato of being the driver who hit Lisa, as the others drove in dark sedans. My guess was he happened to be in the area when they found out about Lisa's phone call and had to arrange her accident on the fly. As I described that logic, a new party entered the room.

"Dr. Morgan, this is Special Agent Jake Lewis, FBI Internal Affairs. I happen to know he was not the person Lisa DeLoit called Internal Affairs, because last Saturday morning he was with me on the Chesapeake in a fishing boat. Jake, you'll get the full transcripts when we're done; for now, Dr. Morgan and Ms. Meadows here are willing to swear some of your agents have been taking bribes."

"Well, one," I corrected him. "Two others have been working with him, but I believe Scanlon convinced them they were on a classified project just like he did Borgie."

"Special Agent Larry Scanlon? From our Rockville office?" Maybe I was reading more than was there, but Jake didn't seem surprised to me.

"That's the one," Amber told him. "I saw him working with Borgman, and we saw him and his men other times, too."

We spent a few minutes recapping Scanlon's role in Replete, during which Lewis made a phone call and summoned more agents.

"Okay, then," Levi took the floor, "This is going to take a while before we can confirm any of the details. I have to ask you to stick around for a while in case we need to ask any more questions."

"Actually, Captain Levi, there's a bit more. Two things, actually. But these are very sensitive. We need to speak confidentially."

The room went quiet for a moment while the captain and his FBI friend looked at each other, telepathically conferring on how much they believed me. I didn't blame them; the entire story so far had been near-fantastic. Now I was telling them I had deep dark secrets that they needed to keep from the detectives and others in the area. In the end they decided to do as we asked, either because they believed us or because they thought we might talk more readily in private. Either way, it was important that what I had to tell them didn't become general knowledge just yet, if ever.

"Morris," Levi said, "you and Escobar take point on the kidnappings and assaults, and talk to me the moment you get lab results on the car and that statue. Carrie, shut off the recorder, take the mike out of the room, and get the transcription typed up forthwith.

Sooner is better, understand? Okay. And have someone bring in more coffee."

With that the captain stood and closed the blinds over the conference room windows. Before he closed the door, though, two more people entered the room.

"These are Special Agents Jefferson and Hanson," Lewis told us. "I want them to hear about Special Agent Scanlon firsthand when you're ready."

"Yes, but this next part is pretty sensitive..." I replied.

"Morgan, these agents have been on the inside on cases you wouldn't believe. Their clearance is as high as mine." Then to the newcomers, "consider this classified for the time being, okay?"

"There are two problems I need to tell you about," I began, "one big and the other bigger. I'm not sure which is which at this point, but I'm going to start with the Replete Group itself. May I boot up my computer?"

In a couple of minutes I had launched Amber's database and turned the screen so the rest could see it.

"I only gave you a brief description of Replete earlier. Here is what's really been happening. See these companies here? These are twenty-five of the biggest corporations in America. Together they represent an enormous piece of our economy. Over here is a list of executives, fifty of them. Each one holds at least two positions within that list of companies. Most are officers at one company, like a CEO or COO, and on the board of directors at another. These people are the members of the Replete Group, okay? For each one of these members, Shipley has been bolstering their income by getting other members in other companies to do things that indirectly benefit that particular member. It's extremely subtle; I doubt anyone would ever have been able to see the scale this is happening on."

"How much money is involved, Morgan?" Lewis asked.

"Well over a billion in total compensation. Shipley guaranteed that each member would make double the income, then took ten percent for his services. He's been pulling in somewhere between one-fifty and two hundred million a year from this scheme. But that's not the big problem."

Lewis spoke for the group. "There's something bigger going on?"

"The problem is the scale of this thing. You see, accusing one CEO of manipulation might cause a blip on the market. Upsetting twenty-five companies of this size could crash the entire stock market. The economy would stagger, and wouldn't recover for years. Shipley thinks it makes him immune because nobody would dare prosecute."

Lewis looked at his friend and said, "Okay, this is a new ball game. This whole case just entered FBI jurisdiction. Any problem with that?"

Levi shook his head. "Gonna need our help?"

"Finish the lab work you've started, if you don't mind, but we're going to want to file those charges together with any others, so don't blow your budget on them. Meanwhile, we're going to have to go meet with the boss."

He was forgetting that I had mentioned two problems. "That was one issue," I said. "There is still one more."

Lewis turned back to me looking like he was on the edge of overload. What I was about to tell him wasn't going to help. Even Amber was looking curious at that point; she and I hadn't had a chance to share this next topic yet.

"Okay," Lewis said with a hint of trepidation, "we're listening."

"The Replete Group relied on two things. First, Shipley got each company to adopt new compensation plans for each of his members. The terms of the new contract paid out bigger bonuses for the kind of things he was able to make happen through the Replete network. Second, those contracts and other boardroom actions had to remain confidential. The execs had to be able to make some hard-to-justify decisions without facing a lot of questions from investors."

"So?"

"There is a bill in the US Senate, the corporate ethics and transparency bill, that would take away Shipley's cloak of secrecy. It is a major threat to him; something that could expose everything he had built. The bill was sponsored by Senator Wyecroft, from my home state, the one who just announced he wasn't seeking reelection. Shipley was behind Wyecroft's withdrawal. The disappearance—kidnapping—of Wyecroft's son a week ago was a warning shot to force Wyecroft's hand. I also think it's possible he caused the death of Wyecroft's father this past weekend."

"Damn, Shipley must be working overtime! You can prove all this?"

"No proof. I only know what I overheard him say this afternoon. I know that Hanover, the candidate replacing Wyecroft, is in Shipley's pocket. He may not be involved in any crime, but he could probably help explain a lot. I'm hoping the proof is on Shipley's computer or somewhere else in his house."

"If it's there we'll find it. Now, is there anything else?"

"That's all I know about for sure, except that Shipley probably holds the record for tax evasion now." I was being less than half facetious. Shipley needed to go down, and I didn't really care which charge did it.

Lewis smiled. "We'll see—it's been done before. But now we have to run. We have an appointment with my boss."

By the time we had left the precinct station and arrived at the FBI office it was late, and they brought in food so we would not have to rush our meeting in Deputy Director Emerson's office. Before we began, Lewis explained the need for discretion, after which Emerson had Amber and me each sign a confidentiality agreement. I hadn't expected that, but I understood. It was the price of being on the inside of the case as events unfolded.

Deputy Director Emerson was a career agent who had risen as high as possible in the FBI without a presidential appointment. As such, he lived on the cusp between the pragmatic and politically nuanced, and he had learned to serve both equally well. He was gracious, playing the role of host to our dinner meeting, but he was also as serious as a heart attack. I quickly learned that if Emerson didn't want others to know his thoughts, they didn't. From the time I began the story until I finished, he said hardly a word. It was like talking to a post.

When I was done, though, Emerson seemed to throw an internal switch. He asked insightful questions that went as far back as the beginning of our tale, referencing intricate details I had given, in spite of not having taken any notes. He cross-referenced my information with details he from Lewis and others, and even asked to see our database. One data field seemed to influence him more than the others: each member's total income had at least doubled at some point in the past couple of years.

Once Deputy Director Emerson decided our story was credible, he asked us to wait outside his office with Special Agent Hanson. He and Special Agents Lewis and Jefferson remained in the office, and for the next forty minutes or so they remained behind a closed door. At one point I asked Hanson if this was part of the normal process.

"This is anything but a normal case," he told me.

At that point the four of us were invited back into the office, and we again sat around the deputy director's conference table where, I noticed, a speaker phone had been deployed.

Emerson spoke directly to Amber and myself. "Okay. The two of you have gotten our attention," he said. "This case has high priority as of now. But there are a couple of things happening where we are going to need your help. Is that a problem?"

Amber and I quickly said "no."

"Good." Then he addressed the others. "Hanson, you're the Special Agent in Charge. You're going to be getting a lot of help on this one; if it's help you don't need, be direct or call me. Got it?"

Jefferson half-smiled at that, then confirmed.

"I want this Shipley found double-quick. Locate all his properties and have them watched by local bureau. We're going to freeze all his accounts—we'll have official paper for that in another hour. This guy lives large, so you'll also want to look for chartered planes and such. And get some agents to pick up the men in custody over at DC Metro PD and get them to interrogation downstairs. The one, Donato, probably has a good idea where Shipley is headed."

"Already in process, sir."

"Jake, you probably better give your buddy Captain Levi a call. We don't have time for another pissing contest over jurisdiction on this one."

"Right away."

"Then, Jake, you're going to get Internal Affairs all over this. I want Scanlon's head on a pike in my outer office *yesterday*, along with any others that took a dime. I want rock-solid proof. Clear? No mercy on this one. The Bureau doesn't need a black eye like this, not on my watch, not ever."

Then Emerson turned to us again. "I know you have had a rough few days. It looks like Shipley was getting Bureau help to track you, and the Bureau apologizes for that. He doesn't have that help now, but a man with his resources will still be very dangerous."

Amber and I exchanged looks as this all sunk in. This still wasn't over for us.

"You mean dangerous to us?" Amber asked.

"Shipley displays a well-known psychological profile. He's a sociopathic megalomaniac, and I'm afraid you two have frustrated his plans for greatness. I'm sorry, but there's a good chance he'll be seeking revenge. That means one of two things. Either we keep you in a safe place until he is found, or you help us find him."

I knew Emerson was dangling bait for me, but he didn't have to. I was more than willing to help.

"What kind of help did you have in mind?"

"Your state party's convention is this week, and Hanover's nomination will be made official tomorrow night. I'll have agents at Senator Wyecroft's home shortly; if they can confirm what you've told us about his kid, if there really is a case of election fraud, we'll tell the party leadership. They may want to delay that nomination until the delegates are given the complete choice. That's about the most we can do without tampering."

"How does that involve us?"

"We have reason to think Shipley may try to meet with Hanover, and he may need to keep his pressure on Wyecroft. Getting Hanover in office is a big part of his plan, and, since he doesn't know that you figured it out, he would feel safe there. We're hoping you might be able to spot him for us. Also, we're going to need this whole mess explained to Wyecroft, and maybe even to Hanover, not to mention the party leadership. Of course, being with our agents means you'll be under our protection the whole time. It's your call."

I looked at Amber. "I'll be able to come back here as soon as this is done. Tomorrow night, most likely."

"No way, Roger. I know what he looks like, too, you know. I'm not going to sit in my apartment flinching every time I hear a car door."

That was exactly the reaction I'd hoped she would have.

Emerson's phone beeped and he answered promptly. After only a few acknowledging grunts he thanked the caller, hung up and looked at us.

"Wyecroft confirmed everything. We're rounding up his family now for safekeeping. I'll be speaking with him in a few minutes; meanwhile, you have a plane to catch." Then to Special Agent Hanson, "wheels up in seventy-five minutes."

In mere moments we were speeding across town, first to pick up my bag at the Canadian residence, then to retrieve Amber's purchases from the DC police station, and then, finally, to Reagan National Airport. There, toward the south end of the airport, was a row of hangars leading away from the passenger terminals, and we pulled up to one near the end of that row. Outside the hangar was a jagged darkness, interrupted at intervals by high yard lights. There were barrels and crates stacked nearby that, combined with airport noise and the heavy smell of jet exhaust, gave a harsh and inhospitable industrial impression. Inside, though, was a different world. The hanger was quiet and pristine, with tools and equipment neatly stowed in cabinets along the wall, an unblemished epoxy floor, and bright lighting from an array of fixtures that virtually eliminated shadows.

In the center stood the object of all that care and attention, a polished white Gulfstream G550 business jet complete with a piece of red carpet laid in front of the steps.

We climbed aboard with Hanson and two others just as the pilot was finishing the pre-flight checklist. Hanson introduced us to Agents James Dorrow and Kelly Wright, and we quickly selected seats and stowed our bags. We were barely strapped in before the aircraft door was shut.

Special Agent Hanson conferred with the others as we taxied to the runway, filling them in on the mission at hand and answering what questions he could regarding Shipley and his dealings with Senator Wyecroft and State Senator Hanover. He didn't get very far before we were in position for takeoff. Moments later we were propelled through an impressive climb, the G550 an agile sports car that easily outperformed the lumbering commercial passenger jets I was used to. I expected to feel more turbulence in that smaller plane, but I felt none as we quickly gained both speed and altitude. I also noticed the relative quiet, likely due to a combination of superior insulation and sound-dampened airflow within the cabin. Even though the FBI's aircraft was not decked out like a corporate counterpart might be (it was definitely missing an onboard bar, for one thing), the VIP treatment was not wasted on us. The plane might have been just a matter of utility for the FBI, but it was a treat for Amber and myself.

When we had achieved an altitude where we felt safe moving about the cabin, Hanson asked me to join his team and give them a firsthand account of the last few days. I stood, and while doing so looked down to see Amber already leaning to one side in blissful slumber. I was envious; my body was giving me constant reminders of Alex and Trevor's ministrations, and I yearned for the basic maintenance afforded by a good night's sleep. Instead, for the next three quarters of an hour I described Shipley's affairs to Agents Dorrow and Wright, stating the facts frankly and also offering my interpretations as I guided them through the complexities of the past days. Agent Hanson was on the phone most of that time, calling and being called about events that were rapidly unfolding both in DC and at our destination. By the time I had briefed the others, he rejoined us to share what he had learned.

Looking at his team members, Hanson asked, "Do you two know Larry Scanlon from the Rockville office? He's in the White-Collar Crime Unit.

Wright knew him, Dorrow knew of him.

"Well, he's in the wind. Jefferson thinks Shipley may have tipped him off. Meanwhile, IA has already had their first interviews with Scanlon's team—Emerson isn't wasting any time on this one. Looks like Scanlon convinced them they were working a special operation of some kind, everything eyes-only, with Scanlon the only one reporting up the chain. Lewis' preliminary conclusion is they're innocent, but those poor bastards will be under IA's microscope for some time."

"Does he have a money trail?" asked Wright.

"Yeah, they already have a list of his domestic accounts. If he tries to access any of them we'll see it.

Won't know about any off-shore money for a day or two."

"Anything about Shipley?" I asked.

"Nothing. His boys aren't talking yet. The lab found some hair and blood that didn't get washed off the SUV, but it will take a day to get DNA results. The damage is consistent with the deceased, though. They also think they'll be able to prove that bronze bust killed Borgman, but they'll need to exhume the body to know for sure. It could be a few days on that one, unless they get lucky—the medical examiner has some imaging that may give an earlier determination."

Dorrow chipped in with, "once the proof is in at least one of them will tell us all he knows for a plea bargain."

"That's a safe bet," Hanson agreed.

"Did they find his Baltimore property yet?" I asked.

"Nothing. They haven't found any others, either, but it's only been a few hours. Tomorrow they'll have a team on it, I'm sure."

"They might want to look under the name Ian Wallace as well." I was stifling a yawn as I said that. "That's another alias he used with us."

"Will do. Best get some rest now, though, Dr. Morgan. The three of us will be working up an op plan, but you have maybe an hour and a half before we land."

I got up and walked back to my seat next to Amber, grabbing a couple of small blankets and pillows from a stowage shelf before settling in. Then I discovered our seats reclined and provided a leg rest, and that was the last thing I remembered before we were on final approach for landing.

I often slept on flights, but rarely well. This time, even though brief, I felt surprisingly refreshed. Changing time zones helped, of course, letting us land and even get to our hotel before midnight. Amber and I decided to save the FBI the expense of our lodging, and instead secured a large suite on the concierge floor atop the hotel where we could splurge on some late-night room service. The extravagance of it paired nicely with our arrival by private jet; besides, I thought we deserved it. At Amber's suggestion, we also sent a glass of wine and a light snack to each of our agents' rooms. I truly liked how her mind worked.

I grabbed a quick shower while Amber sorted through her newly purchased clothes, smoothing out the wrinkles they had got from being carried in a borrowed duffle. Then, while she took over the bathroom, I sat in my plush complimentary robe and watched a late-night recap of the news. There were the usual stories, the economy, of course, and a few local criminals who'd managed to achieve a moment of notoriety. The party's convention was mentioned briefly, then a reporter took time to again describe the Wyecroft-to-Hanover candidate switch, recalling in detail Wyecroft's withdrawal and Hanover's sudden rise to prominence. Nearly a week had passed since all that had transpired, but the reporter described it with a tone of shock and surprise, wringing out any residual drama in hopes of viewer retention. If he found that remarkable, I thought, he should hang on to his socks. Unless I missed my guess, tomorrow's news would leave the man stammering.

The shower stopped and after a moment I heard the whirring of the hotel hair dryer, my eyes drifting from the television screen while I instinctively visualized the scene in my head. The burden of fear had left Amber, having unloaded our tale on the FBI, and, while there was still much to be done, she was treating our current circumstances almost as an exotic getaway. I knew half of it was her attempt to help me shed the stress and forget my bruises, but there was something else. She was happy, which I was coming to recognize as her natural state.

The day's news apparently exhausted, the program degenerated into fluff journalism that no longer held my attention. Besides, I was faced with a distraction. Amber had joined me. Instead of the terrycloth robe and turbaned towel I had expected, she was displaying her new nighttime wardrobe. White, sleeveless and ankle-length, the sheer material allowed for an enticing silhouette as she moved between me and the now completely ignored television screen.

I handed her a glass and she sat down next to me, tucking her legs beneath her and placing her hand on my shoulder. We shared a silent toast, and both of us drew large sips of wine before placing our glasses on the table behind the sofa. It was the first time we had been completely alone—and fully awake—since arriving at the Canadian residence. We had much to talk about, but all discussion was deferred in favor of more primal communication. I reached for her head with my open hand and she pressed her cheek into my palm, then I gently pulled her toward me and tasted her waiting lips. Her body melted against mine, pert with anticipation as she stroked herself against my chest. Then her mesmerizing eyes peered into mine, offering, even demanding, that I take the initiative.

With a gentle pull I turned her around and set her between my legs, reclining her back against my chest and resting her head on my shoulder. My hands caressed her upper arms while I placed warm, full kisses on her cheek and neck. Soon my arms reached around her, and she placed her hands on top of my own, guiding them from one sensitive locale to another and prompting my attention to each. We were like that for several minutes, our breathing heavier and kisses more passionate as we explored increasingly delicious possibilities, until the enthusiasm she felt growing behind her commanded her attention. Then, looking back at me, she said, merely, "bedroom" and stood, leading me in my precarious state to the inner chamber.

7

SURVEILLANCE

There was a short time that night, after our libidinous interlude and before sleep once again overtook us, when we simply talked. Amber, having missed Agent Hanson's information on the plane, asked for and received the latest updates on Shipley and company. She then asked me questions, including some of the same ones I had posed earlier, prompting me to consider them a second time.

Why are we here? Because we can help recognize Shipley, because we can explain events to Wyecroft.

Is that all? We don't know; Emerson is a wily one. He may have had more in mind that he wasn't ready to share.

Will we ever be safe? There was light at the end of the tunnel, but we may not be completely safe until Shipley is put away.

A pause.

Did I know what is worse than dating the "terrible twos"? No, what? Trying to keep a long-distance relationship alive.

With that last statement Amber rolled over on her side, facing away from me. I don't think there were tears, but I was struck by how engaged she—we—already were in this relationship. In that instant I realized how far I felt from my life as a Senior Principal Researcher, how distant the Institute and all its workplace drudgery had become. I could feel the relative solitude I had had, even enjoyed, for the past few years morphing into a sense of isolation. I had left for a week thinking I needed a break; now I was consciously weighing the pros and cons of larger change. I had never spent much energy on life outside the Institute before, but maybe the past few days had given me enough of a wake-up call to get me thinking.

"Then we will have to avoid that," I finally told her.

"How?"

"I don't know yet. Would you like to help me find out?"

"Yes," she nearly whispered, "I would."

Morning arrived via phone call, the unit next to the bed having been left on full volume. Agent Wright, realizing she had awakened me, gave me a moment to collect myself before explaining that SAIC Hanson wanted to talk to us in about an hour to plan the day and telling me where we would find them. I then kissed Amber awake and called for a continental breakfast before heading to the bathroom.

We arrived at the hotel conference room roughly on time. Special Agent Hanson was not impatient with us, but as the team lead he was naturally anxious to begin the operation.

"Have a seat," was his laconic greeting. Then he softened it a little by adding, "by the way, thank you for the snack."

The others echoed the sentiment and we smiled back as we took our places at the long table.

"Okay. I have some fresh information from home." The time zone difference, coupled with

Amber's and my late sleep, had given the home office a head start over us. "First, you were right about Ian Wallace. We've found several properties and accounts under that name. Local bureau agents are checking them out, but so far Shipley hasn't been seen. Also, we got a report on flights in and out of the DC area, and we don't think he left the country. Bottom line is that we're still hoping he's going to show up here."

"I've been wondering about that," I said. "By now he must know you have our story and that you're holding three of his men. Doesn't he know it's over?"

"It really isn't over. That's the problem," Hanson told me. "Shipley has been running Replete anonymously this whole time. As long as he believes he can pull strings from behind a curtain, he has a lot of motivation to keep trying, even if he has to drop current members and recruit new ones. He's had a setback, nothing more. But if he is going to keep trying, he still needs to block Wyecroft's bill, and he doesn't know that we know about that. Right now, that is our trump card."

"What about Supervisory Special Agent Scanlon?" Dorrow asked. "If he's here, wouldn't he recognize us?"

"Lewis thinks he is running for cover, but if he did show up here he'd recognize me, for certain. He has probably seen all of us in our building at one time or another." Then he looked at us. "As for you two, well, he had to know who to look for, so he would at least have had photographs. Let's not take any chances. Dorrow, call the local office and have them send out a team to watch for him."

"Will do, Boss."

"Okay, next. We have a presumptive positive on the bronze bust as Borgman's murder weapon. The suspect, Trevor Maynard, isn't admitting anything, but the other guy, Alex Barnes, slipped in interrogation. He ended up giving an eyewitness account. As for the hit-and-run, they're ready to book Shipley's man Donato. No full confession yet, but he started talking after they brought up the other murders. He has already implicated Shipley for ordering all the murders, including Borgman and Lisa DeLoit."

"Other murders?" Amber and I were not aware of more.

"The crew of the boat Shipley and Donato blew up. US-registered vessel in international waters, so it's ours."

Of course. It's always bigger than I think, I reminded myself.

"Okay, that's it. Now, here's the plan. Dorrow, after you've briefed the local office, meet us at Wyecroft's suite and manage the team there. Remember, it's got to be an invisible fence. Emerson has spoken with the Capitol Police, so they'll cooperate. Wright, meet up with the local guys watching Hanover. Both of you, talk to me every fifteen minutes, news or no news."

Then he turned to us.

"Our part is delicate. Wyecroft is expecting us as soon as we are done here. You'll need to explain to him how Replete works, including Shipley's role, but don't discuss other aspects of the case. After that, if he decides he wants back in like we predict he will, I'll meet with him and the party leadership right after that. You two will go to Hanover's hotel. Wright will meet you in the lobby and take you to the video surveillance room. We're having live surveillance video feeds from Wyecroft's hotel and Hanover's set up in a room in Hanover's hotel. Here's the thing: if Wyecroft gets back in the game, Hanover gets pushed back out, and that's when we'd expect Shipley to show up. Until we know more, we'll need you watching those screens for any sign of Shipley. Understood?"

We understood the instructions, but there were a few other things I didn't fully understand. I waited until my questions would not be an intrusion, and got the opportunity to ask while we were in transit to Wyecroft's hotel.

"How did the Capitol Police get involved?" I asked.

A micro-expression passed over Hanson's face, a suggestion of an eye-roll that let me know this was a subject of some frustration.

"This is one of those jurisdictional nightmares the FBI faces all the time. Senators and congressmen, once they get in office, are protected in DC by US Capitol Police. Any protection at home is between the USCP and the state. Before they're elected, candidates are protected only by the state, if at all. When there's a specific threat, though, or if there is any attempt made on them, the FBI gets called in. Of course, for strictly local stuff in the district they'd probably call the Metro Police. It keeps our lives interesting."

"It must be hard to keep information contained when you have to coordinate with so many people."

Hanson grunted in agreement.

"You also said the Wyecroft part was going to be delicate..."

"The Wyecroft meeting will be interesting, but the delicate part will be with the party leadership. It is not expected to go smoothly. These guys may like Wyecroft, but they hate voter confusion and they sure as hell won't want any whiff of scandal. And, of course, we can't assume Hanover is without support at that level."

I was beginning to see the role of an FBI agent in a whole new light. Hanson probably wished he could simply work crimes the way I often wished I could just design behavioral models.

Wyecroft's suite was a busy place that morning. The outgoing Senator was scheduled to deliver an important speech that evening prior to Hanover's formal selection as candidate, and his room was a blur of aides and writers and party operatives all moving and talking rapidly even though the Senator was not in the room. SAIC Hanson showed his ID to a man at the door who, I assume, was FBI, and then again to an aide who asked us our business. She quickly left the room, and moments later followed the Senator back in. Senator Wyecroft instantly commanded the attention of everyone in the room with the power and presence of a leading man on a set full of minions. I was instantly struck by his bearing and grace as he approached us and offered warm handshakes. This was truly a man possessed of natural leadership.

The Senator invited us into a small anteroom where we could speak privately, and without waiting for prologue asked Hanson to please explain the mission.

"We're on a protection detail at the moment," began Hanson. "I'm assuming Deputy Director Emerson explained what we knew as of last night. As of this morning, as you have probably already learned, we have agents protecting you and your wife here, your children, your home, your mother and siblings. This case has the highest possible priority."

"Yes. The President and Director Monchek called earlier to assure me of that."

"I have also brought Dr. Morgan and Ms. Meadows here to help explain what they know of the situation, if you like. I know time is short, Senator, but if you have decided to return to the race there will be a lot to accomplish today."

The senator knew very well the stakes and the arduous road that lay ahead. Still, this was not a man to be rushed. He looked at Amber and me, then asked a simple yet pointed and astute question.

"How does this 'Replete Group' work?"

The senator clearly wanted the facts, not some rendition of a story, so I went directly to what we knew without describing how we knew it. I described the matrix of companies, executives and directors that formed the group. When Wyecroft asked for a few names I looked to Hanson, who explained that the information was being held confidential pending further action, but that the senator would certainly recognize many of them. Next I described the executive compensation contract, and how that enabled Replete to ensure the success of its members. Finally, then, I described the "group directives" and how Shipley was pulling the strings on one company to effect another.

"That's incredibly complex," Wyecroft observed. "How has he managed it all?"

"We know he has had help, and he has been pursuing a unique software tool to help him manage it."

"How did the two of you get involved?"

I looked at Hanson again, and he gave me a nod that I interpreted as "Okay, but keep it short."

"I am the Senior Principal Researcher for the Institute of Emergent System Analysis. Among other things, we create simulations of complex systems to predict their behavior. Shipley was trying to use such a system to help him run Replete, and for the past couple of days was trying to force us to work on it."

He then looked at Amber.

"He had been trying to get that software system done by a man I worked with. That man is now dead. He also killed my best friend."

The senator took a few moments to express sincere condolences. Then he asked another question.

"Do you believe my bill is the reason he has threatened me and my family?"

"Your bill would shut down Replete and cost Shipley hundreds of millions. Yes, I believe it is the reason."

"Would you excuse me, please."

Hanson, Amber and I returned to the main room of the suite, where silenced staffers watched us with questioning eyes. Minutes later Wyecroft reentered the room and gave them cause for still more questions.

"Agent Hanson, I'd like you to accompany me across the street to speak with the party leadership." Then he pulled his speechwriter over to our side of the room and told him in a low voice, "we're scrapping the speech, Ellis. We're back in the race. You have maybe four hours."

"How do we explain it?" the writer asked, a surprised smile betraying his pleasure.

"You say 'factors contributing to my withdrawal are no longer relevant.' Say that back to me." Wyecroft listened, then said, "good. That won't satisfy them, but it will buy us a little time until we're ready to explain it all. Get going; I'll get back here as soon as I can. And, Ellis, this stays here until I say so, got it?"

We had done it. Wyecroft was re-entering the race.

Before Hanson followed Wyecroft out the door he gave Amber and me a minor change in plans. He asked us to wait in the lobby of Hanover's hotel with one of the local agents and Agent Wright would meet us there.

A short walk later and Amber and I were waiting as asked, although we had no idea why we were there. I assumed it was a political or logistics issue, and grabbed a newspaper to share with Amber while we waited. I was just getting into an article about latest wave of tech gadgets to hit the market when I felt Amber tap my wrist with the back of her hand. I looked up, and she tipped her head toward the group that had just entered the room.

Whereas Wyecroft was given devoted attention when he entered a room, Hanover seemed to demand attention. He strode in forcefully at the point of his v-shaped entourage, asking questions and giving real-time stage direction in a loud, commanding voice. There was nothing to resemble Wyecroft's finesse. Hanover's first impression, on me at least, was of a boorish man who seemed to believe he had tight control over his surroundings.

Their route toward the lobby elevators brought them past us, and while I'm sure he noticed us, Hanover didn't even cast a smile at his possible constituents. Instead he reached for his phone, making a call as soon as he was out of earshot. A man as self-assured and self-important as himself probably didn't feel a need for the social graces the way someone like Wyecroft did.

As soon that call was Hanover was interrupted by another, and after checking the caller ID he quickly pressed the phone to his ear. Then he stopped in his tracks.

"*What?* What kind of news?... I'll be there in five minutes." Hanover was apparently about to receive unwelcome news. We had a pretty good idea of what that news might be, and we exchanged looks as Hanover clapped his phone shut and squeezed it in front of him for a just moment in frustration. His gaze swept the room one more time, then he pulled one of his aides close enough to whisper something that sent the man running off in a different direction. Finally the whole group seemed to pivot as they marched double-time back out the lobby entrance.

With Hanover and company gone the lobby returned to normal. Agent Wright found us there a couple of minutes later and took us to the room where the FBI had set up their surveillance system.

It was obvious when we entered the room that the FBI had had a lot of practice doing this sort of thing. In a brief time they had set up two large screen monitors, easily fifty inches each, and all the equipment required to control and record and communicate with their agents. One of the screens was labeled "Hanover," the other "Wyecroft." On each screen were fifteen or more windows, each representing a camera in a hallway, in a lobby, an elevator or even on an agent's person. The resulting mosaic was dizzying until we acclimated to the show, learning quickly how to mentally select the windows with the most promise of a sighting.

What we didn't see were any views of Hanover's or Wyecroft's suites. Agent Wright explained why that was.

"The last thing we would want is a story claiming the FBI is trying to spy on or, worse, intimidate a candidate for public office. Going by the book is a pain sometimes, but it sure keeps life a lot simpler when we stick to it."

Within a short time we were adept at working with the FBI specialist at the controls. She would scroll back a certain window, zoom in on a face or take some other action when asked, we just needed to learn what those capabilities were and how to request them clearly. She was fast, too, and her ability to create rapid on-screen view changes quickly took its toll on my eyes. Even Amber, who I had started to believe could spot a mosquito at one hundred yards, had to ask that she slow down. When she did, there was an immediate pay-off.

"Well hello there," Amber said to an image on the Hanover monitor. "Roger, does he look familiar?"

The tech froze the window in question and zoomed in for a better look.

"That's my 'ex,' isn't it? The guy who visited my office on Sunday?"

We had stood around a corner just feet from him when he entered Amber's office building that day, but it still took me a moment to be certain.

"Yes, that's him. Agent Wright, you may want to keep track of this man. We think he works for Shipley."

Wright noted the camera's location and began speaking into her wrist, giving a complete description and location to roaming agents until the man left the camera's view. One or more of them would soon be tracking him, leaving Amber and me to focus once again on the screens in front of us. The traffic in various parts of the hotel was increasing as delegates and other convention goers prepared for the official events of the day, causing us to strain at the monitors in our attempt to find our prey. At one point I wished out loud that he would at least wear a striped stocking cap so we would have a sporting chance in our game of "Where's Shipley."

Soon we saw SAIC Hanson escorting Wyecroft and a pair of aides back to his hotel suite. He raised his hand to his mouth, and we heard Agent Wright talking to him momentarily. Then she turned to us and told us what was happening.

"Okay, it's going public now," she said. "All the delegates Wyecroft got from precinct primaries are bound to him for the first vote, and it's a clear majority."

Within minutes there was a noticeable change at both hotels. First a flurry of reporters and crews raced into Wyecroft's hotel lobby and jockeyed for position in hopes of pulling two or three coherent words out of the din when he passed by. There would be no new information, of course, unless Wyecroft decided to preempt his own speech later that day by giving an impromptu press conference, but the media was nonetheless bound to see if shouting his name repeatedly might somehow work to their advantage.

Moments later we saw Hanover and his team pass through the other lobby, looking neither right nor left and wearing scowls that would wilt wallpaper. Seconds behind him came the media, who literally chased him into the elevator before taking over the lobby in much the same way as had been done at the other hotel. The siege was in place.

With a quick reminder for us to keep eyes on the monitors in front of us, Agent Wright turned the room's television set to a news channel so we could hear their version of what was happening.

"...breaking news as we learn that Senator Vincent Wyecroft, who had surprised everyone by announcing his intent to withdraw from the race, will announce later today his decision to remain a candidate. In short written statement received from

Wyecroft's office we are told only that 'factors contributing to Senator Wyecroft's planned withdrawal are no longer relevant.' State Senator Ron Hanover, who had been selected to replace Wyecroft, has apparently just learned of the planned announcement and has yet to release a statement."

There was a moment, for both Amber and myself, I think, when our roles in this event hit home. I was just trying to take some vacation time, and now here I was, responsible in part for a shake-up in state and even federal politics. It was a heady thought, but, of course, we hadn't caused change so much as we had helped prevent it. I didn't expect we would be written up in any historical account of the event.

The activity on the monitors had now grown into a near-furor. Both lobbies were a crowded mix of media, delegates and hotel staff, hallway traffic had multiplied and descending elevators were stuffed with button-wearing conventioneers. It seemed those not vying for prime lobby real estate were headed to the convention center to reserve their spot on the floor for the momentous speech that was still a few hours away. Our eyes danced across the screens, scanning scores of faces each passing minute until forced by eye fatigue to slow down. Luckily, by then much of the traffic had already passed through and the remainder was returning to a more manageable pace.

While the traffic may have slowed somewhat, the intensity had not diminished. If Deputy Director Emerson and his crew were correct—and the appearance of Amber's "ex" told us they were—this was the time when Shipley would be most likely to appear. Amber and I leaned forward into the monitors, and the sounds of wrist-talking agents and droning newscasters faded away until our world consisted of the monitors and the dialogue between us and the agency's surveillance technician. Every few minutes we would have a possible sighting, freezing the frame and zooming in to vet the unsuspecting subject, and then we'd return to skimming mode. At Agent Wright's suggestion we were both placing more focus on the "Hanover" monitor, but even our double-teaming on those windows was not paying off. We couldn't stop, though. At least until Wyecroft's speech was delivered, we were bound to sit and stare under exponentially increasing tension.

Nothing.

By the time Wyecroft's speech was to begin, all timed to satisfy the media coverage, the monitor traffic had dropped to near-zero and Amber and I were exhausted. We had seen hundreds of faces, zooming in on a couple of dozen, at least, but there was no sure sign that Shipley was even in the same time zone. Checking that many cameras for that long in that kind of traffic was taxing, but the feeling of utter futility that overtook us was even worse. And we didn't know how much longer the FBI expected our help.

Finally the lobbies, hallways and elevators at both hotels were near empty. Agent Wright conferred with her radio, then gave us some welcome relief.

"You two are doing great," she said, "but even if Shipley is in the area the chances are he'll be watching Wyecroft's speech. We can take a break until it's over."

There was no argument from us. We got out of our chairs and paced, then sat on the small couch along the far wall, sipping water and snacking on some food one of the agents had brought in. Agent Wright stepped out into the hallway, then turned and told us she was going to stretch her legs for a few minutes.

We also stood and walked the hallway for a moment, but didn't stray far. I wanted to see the speech on the cable news, so we made sure we would get back in the room before the opening applause died down and Wyecroft formalized his announcement. Ellis, the speechwriter, had done an impressive job in the few hours he was given, and the speech wasted no time getting to the point.

"...personal circumstances that once seemed insurmountable have been resolved. And so, I am very pleased to announce that I remain a candidate for reelection and fully intend to serve our great state and the United States of America for the next six years." The arena erupted again, and, while Wyecroft graciously thanked Hanover for rising to the occasion, Amber and I congratulated each other on the role we played in righting a narrowly-averted wrong.

As the speech segued from the big announcement to rhetoric more typical of the venue, we again stood to stretch and decompress our bodies from hours of sitting at the edge of our chairs. Amber had endured as much as I had, of course, but somehow she seemed less affected. Her smile had returned, and her eyes were wide with the wonder and enthusiasm with which she addressed life. Her movements were fluid and unstrained, and she spoke in positive and constructive terms. After all we had been through, after all we had shared, I was fascinated all over again.

The last person in the room with us was Jenn—Agent Reid, actually, the agent who ran the monitors—but she didn't stay long. She excused herself to the small bathroom to splash a little water on her face in anticipation of another round of surveillance when the speech was completed. It made sense that Shipley might be mobile then, if he was there at all, but neither of us looked forward to it. In fact, the thought of it broke my earlier reverie and I pulled Amber close to reassure her that this wouldn't go on forever, that if we didn't see Shipley soon the agents would likely give up on their theory and start looking elsewhere.

I guess it was the distraction of that embrace, but neither of us noticed the door from the adjoining room open until two men had already stepped through.

"I was told I might find you here," said the familiar voice. John Foster Shipley, the man we had been searching for over the past few hours, was now standing conveniently before us. Conveniently, that is, if you were to ignore the guns.

"You're doing your own dirty work now, John? I thought you just liked to pull the strings."

"Yes, I ordered the deaths of your friends. I set up the boat, too—even helped Donato place the charge. But that doesn't mean I won't pull this trigger right here and now. Do you have any idea how much you have cost us? *Hundreds* of millions! All we were doing was helping a few people find success. Replete was the perfect system until you stepped in. Now we're forced to leave it all behind and start over. It's okay, we'll survive. But you sure as hell will not!"

"Amber didn't hurt you, John. Leave her out of this."

"Both of you, into the next room. *Now*!"

"Leave her, John!"

"No! Now move!"

"Sorry, no. You're going to kill us anyway. I'm not going to make it any easier for you."

"Then here it is," said Shipley, and raised his gun toward me, chambering a round as he moved.

Two shots rang out. Then two more.

There was a moment of near silence as I sat slumped to the floor and leaned against the table, my left shoulder feeling as if it had been struck by a semi truck. An acrid smell hung in the air, and I felt more than saw Agent Reid emerge from the bathroom to check the bodies of the two men on the floor in front of me.

Amber was with me, holding my head and begging me to speak to her as a temporary fog lifted from my mind. "I'm okay," I told her, the shock to my body already overriding the pain. I heard Agent Reid calling for the other agents, and then rushing to get a towel to compress against my shoulder. In minutes a flood of agents returned, expertly applying first aid to my shoulder while an ambulance was en route.

That ambulance arrived quickly, having been detached to the nearby arena for the duration of the party's convention, but there was enough of a delay for me to learn what had happened. Shipley had been unaware of Agent Reid's presence around the corner in the bathroom. The first two shots were the two of them exchanging fire, with me caught between. The second two were between Reid and Shipley's accomplice. Shipley had survived with a serious chest wound; the other man had been less fortunate.

While two agents worked to stabilize him, Shipley turned his head and looked at me, his pain as obvious as his struggle to ignore it. "You only...got me," he gasped while forcing a wicked sneer. "Always...bigger than you...think." He attempted a laugh, but no sound came out.

With that Shipley passed out. The agent attending him told us he'd lost a lot of blood and gave the chances of survival at fifty percent or less. By the time the ambulance crew had him on a gurney, they virtually ran from the room and into the waiting truck without pausing for me, a welcome sign that my injury was not considered particularly serious. It was less welcome for Shipley. As we watched the ambulance from the window, we saw it race for a block and a half, then slow and turn off its lights and siren. He hadn't made it.

The influx of agents continued until our room was brimming with dark suits and tight haircuts. Even in those numbers, with many of the agents never having met before that day, they worked the scene as a well-oiled machine, a team that emerged from the rules and policies and training of the bureau. I had moved to the sofa, and from there I could see and almost hear our guardian Agent Reid describing the scene to Agent Dorrow and SAIC Hanson. Reid was from the local office, specializing in surveillance technology, and apparently only carried a gun because it came with the badge. Her face was taut, and her eyes were narrow as she gave a specific account of the shooting, locating her position for them near the bullet hole in the wall. It had only been paper targets for her until now, but she was the consummate professional. Jenn Reid would be fine—once the prodigious pile of paperwork for this was complete.

Agent Wright was with us at the emergency room, and stayed with us through the entire ordeal. I was happy to hear the bullet had missed anything too important, merely passing just under the skin through some muscle tissues before exiting. "Merely." I supposed I could blame Hollywood for my naïveté; the mere "flesh wounds" that characters bounce back from in a scene or two are excruciating in real life. In fact, I reasoned, the nerves are in the skin—a deeper wound might have felt pretty much the same.

Between treatments and trauma we had little time for chat, and I admit to being distracted by such personal matters, but by the time they had my arm bandaged I was again attuned to the situation and gave Agent Wright a curious look.

"Are you on duty?" I asked. "Are we still being protected?"

"We want to keep an eye on you."

"Shipley's dead," Amber told her. "I mean, isn't this over now?"

"We hope so, but there are some things we want to be certain of yet. According to Agent Reid, Shipley referred to a 'we' when he spoke to you. Also, just before he died, he said this was bigger than we thought. We'll want to check that out."

"He had said that several times since we met him," I told the agent. "But it was just his ego talking. 'No matter how big you think my great scheme is, it's always bigger.' Now that he's dead, what does it matter?"

"It could have just been ego. We hope to know soon." Sometimes agents were either gracefully tactful or frustratingly circumspect in their answers.

With that we prepared to leave the hospital, signing forms and accepting prescriptions to ward off infections and "discomfort." The hospital was required to report any gunshot wounds, and Agent Wright gave them a brief statement and her card with the promise of further information should they need it. When it was all done we turned toward the exit, just as a man walked up to us. I recognized him from Wyecroft's suite.

"I'm glad I caught you, Dr. Morgan," he said. "Senator Wyecroft asked me to stop by and check on you. Are you okay?"

I assured him I was fine while he eyed my bloodied shirt.

"Very glad to hear it. The senator has asked me to request a meeting with you back in DC. He is very interested in the organization you described to him and how it might impact his proposed legislation. Will you be returning there soon?"

I looked at Amber and smiled. "Yes," I said to him. "I will be spending time in DC."

"The senator will be at the convention for another day, then back to DC. I'll tentatively schedule time with him on Thursday, if that works for you. May I have your number?" I gave him Amber's pre-paid cell number, remembering that my smart phone was probably still in Shipley's desk drawer. "Thank you. Here is my card, then. Please call me if there are any questions."

8

THE BROTHER OF GREED

We spent that evening in our hotel. Amber picked up some exercise clothes from the lobby shop and hit the hotel's gym with Agent Wright while I stayed in the suite, not wanting to pull stitches. While I waited I scheduled a meal to be delivered on Amber's return and settled in to watch the news.

Senator Wyecroft, having surprised the delegates that afternoon, had just received a decisive mandate from the convention. Delegates, party officials, and even local newscasters were thrilled to see him and his wife standing at the podium, smiling and waving to cheering crowds while the reporter tried to describe circumstances leading up to that moment. When that story died down, there was a surprisingly short item: a shooting at the hotel where State Senator Hanover was staying had taken the lives of two men. Police and FBI were on the scene immediately, but would only say that the shootings were an isolated incident that appeared unrelated to the convention. Thankfully, names had been withheld, at least for the time being.

I had wondered about how the FBI would handle that. Had Shipley lived, I suppose there would have been a long, protracted case and trial that would publicly expose Replete and all its members. The great risk that Shipley had described—the risk of crashing the market and bringing down the economy—had been narrowly averted for now, and hopefully for enough time to find a safe solution.

When the shooting story ended my mind went adrift, trying to predict the near-term future of travel back to DC, my meeting with Senator Wyecroft and my eventual return to work. That last part was particularly murky. I hadn't thought of the office much, if at all, in the past few days. It was almost refreshing to realize that. My vacation, such as it was, had indeed removed office tedium from my mind, providing a greater degree of diversion than I could ever have hoped. Now, however, I was beginning to realize just how far from work I felt. I had helped build the Institute from the ground up. I had a good team there, and a few co-workers I felt were my friends, but still I felt isolated. Just days earlier I couldn't have imagined a better place to work my trade, but now…

My forehead furrowed deeper as these thoughts piled up inside. There was something more, something I sensed somewhere just beneath the conscious plane, that bothered me about the office. Something was wrong, something about the break-in at my office that fateful Friday night. It was something I wasn't ready to admit to myself just yet.

My mind brightened considerably when Amber returned and hit the shower. I began to think about other prospects, about an alternate future and how it might come about. There would be some time to find all that out, I hoped, but perhaps not a lot. My vacation would end soon, and, while tactical decisions might not yet be possible, it would be time to choose a goal.

We ate a light meal, speculating about Wyecroft's meeting and how soon all this could end. At length Amber addressed the real issue on her mind.

"I'll need to get back to work soon, Roger. What do you think about what Agent Wright was saying? Are we going to be safe?"

"A lot safer, at least. Shipley is gone, and his inner circle of thugs arrested or dead. I don't know about Agent Scanlon, but he sounds like the kind that got bought, got exposed, and ran for the hills. My guess is that, if he got enough dirty money to disappear on, he's already long gone. There are still others out there—Shipley wasn't running the day-by-day operations alone—but it sounds like everyone else was kept in the dark as much as possible."

"So when is this over?"

I gave her the best reassuring smile I had. "When we say so, I think. I mean, there will be some aftermath, like depositions and the meeting with Wyecroft, but beyond that I'm not going to live in fear of every dark sedan that passes by. The Replete Group will be shut down, one way or another. They don't have any need for us anymore." I listened to myself say that, and I mostly believed it. There were always risks, but ours were no longer much higher than the average person's.

Our meal complete, I pushed the room service cart back into the hallway and turned to see a glass of wine in Amber's outstretched hand. We sipped and chatted, the discovery phase of our relationship still in process, until the hour combined with the rigors of the day to send us to bed. It was there that I discovered something I had already begun to suspect. Amber, without a hint of guile or hidden agenda, was as insatiable as she was enthusiastic.

The "wheels up" time for the FBI flight back to DC was mid morning after their final meetings with local bureau staff, but the flight time combined with time zone change had us arriving late afternoon. During the flight we had ample opportunity to chat with the agents, and even received a call from Deputy Director Emerson.

"The Bureau is very grateful for your help, and equally pleased that you escaped greater injury," he told me.

"What is your plan for the Replete Group membership?" I asked. It was more than curiosity; I was invested in this. Besides, I knew it would likely involve me at some point.

"I can tell you that we are getting good cooperation from Hamilton Grant at Reicher Oil, as you suggested. Beyond that, this case is classified. We'll be working with the SEC and others on this for some time."

To a degree it was frustrating to be out of that loop, but I understood. The case was between the agents and the perpetrators, and Amber and I were merely witnesses.

"I understand. Both of us will be happy to help out if the Bureau needs. In the meantime, though, I have another topic to discuss with you. Would it be possible to meet in your office while I'm in town? I won't try to discuss this case, but it is a matter of concern for both of us."

"I suppose it's the least we can do. Contact my assistant when you're ready. Until then, have a good trip."

Then I looked at SAIC Hanson. "I do have one other favor to ask, if it's not too much trouble. My smart phone. Shipley took it from me and put it in his upper-right desk drawer. It has all my contacts in it, as well as an app that holds some sensitive passwords. Do you think I could get it back?"

"Not a problem," he replied, and opened his phone yet again to pass along the request.

Once back on the ground at Reagan National, we were met by an agent who handed me my phone while offering us a ride as far as the FBI office with the others. Amber and I exchanged looks, and thanked him, but instead got a ride only as far as the main terminal. From there we rented a car and headed out on our own, free at last to pursue our own path.

Moments after leaving the airport I received a call from Sen. Wyecroft's aide and confirmed a meeting at the Senator's office on Thursday at ten. Then I placed a call to Deputy Director Emerson's office and requested a meeting on Thursday afternoon. He wasn't available until three, but that was okay with me. My vacation was shot anyway.

"Will you be going in to the office tomorrow?" I asked Amber.

"I really should. I've only left a couple of messages for my manager this week, so I'm probably in a bit of trouble already. She's pretty good, though.

When I tell her what has been happening she'll just take the time off my vacation accrual."

"How much time do you have accrued?"

"Oh, another week and several days at least. There's no problem. Summer is actually a slow time for us anyway, and with Borgman gone and his team out of action there will be even less. Why?"

"Well, if things work out the way I predict, I might ask you to play tour guide for a few days next week."

"You can stay longer? Roger, that's wonderful!"

"Not exactly 'stay' longer. We'll have to see what tomorrow brings, but I may be flying home tomorrow night and returning here in a couple of days."

"Flying home? Why?"

"There is a staffing issue I need to take care of, and I have another matter to discuss with my COO. But if I do fly back, I know I'd be here again by Monday morning at the latest. Does that work for you?"

"You're certain you'll be back?"

"Could you put me up for a few days?"

With that she leaned over to me and put her head on my good shoulder. She stayed like that most of the way to her apartment, quiet, not entirely comfortable with my cryptic plans but thoroughly trusting my intent.

By ten o'clock the next morning I had arrived at the Russell Senate Office Building, a relatively plain structure standing across the street from the US Capitol and connected to it by a short subway line. I was sitting in Senator Wyecroft's outer office, thankful that I had packed a sport coat against the possibility of a theater ticket or nicer restaurant, but still feeling underdressed for the venue. The office was live with activity, driven both by the recent reelection news and by the bill he was still sponsoring. He had arrived well before me, and I could hear him through the open office door, fielding congratulatory phone calls as I waited. He didn't keep me waiting long, however.

"Dr. Morgan," the senator greeted me as he came through the door, "I am very grateful you could come help us out. I understand you are also a constituent, is that correct?" The senator had checked me out before the meeting.

"Yes, I am. And a supporter."

"Thank you. Please, step into my office. How's that arm?"

I told him it was a minor wound as I followed him into the inner sanctum, noting that the space available in this older building was more cramped than a man of his stature would command elsewhere. After he indicated a chair for me to occupy and let me help myself from a carafe of coffee, he wasted no more time in getting to the heart of the matter.

"I understand you have become something of an expert in this executive investment club, the Replete Group. I'd like to hear more about how it works. First, though, I would appreciate a short explanation of the work you do—I understand it is somehow related to recent events. I've asked a couple of my staff to join us; I hope you don't mind."

I didn't mind at all, of course, although I had to be mindful of the confidentiality of the FBI's case. I began by describing emergent systems, using the common flock-of-birds example and drawing a logical line from understanding that system to understanding larger, human-based systems such as the recently completed highway project. I didn't want to consume too much time, but I did want the senator to understand my credentials and Replete's desire for them.

Soon the office was relaxed and conversational. I stood and opened the cabinet doors concealing a small white board, and then I began a more detailed explanation of Replete. I started with the structure of the group, both the membership rolls and the companies in which they operated, although no specific names were given. Next I showed how Shipley—who I referred to only as the 'organizer'—would use the Replete network to benefit or punish a given member. I explained how one company's performance could be impacted by the actions of other companies in the group, and how those actions would cause ripples that then required more directives. I emphasized the way a number of fairly simple elements had combined to form a highly complex system, the very definition of emergence, and then showed how only a very diligent person could manage that complexity and explained how a computer program using emergent system simulation would simplify the job. Finally, I described the critical role played by the executive compensation agreement, how it made the group work and how Replete made sure each executive used very similar contractual terms. I didn't have to explain the market risk of exposing Replete publicly; they saw it with frightening clarity.

Throughout my explanations, Wyecroft and his staff asked surprisingly insightful questions. I realized that, prior to my arrival at their office, his staff had researched emergent systems and briefed him on the basics, most likely a standard procedure in preparation for any meeting with the senator. Standard or not, they had achieved substantial depth on the subject in only a few hours, depth that was reflected in the intricacy of their questions. By the time the flow of questions began to slow, we had talked through a working lunch.

As junior staffers carted away the remains of our meal, the senator took a few moments to describe his bill, the boardroom accountability and transparency bill for which he had become known nationwide in the past year. The premise was straightforward enough, with the intent of lifting the veil of secrecy on corporate actions that impacted the investor without compromising competitive information. Its implementation, however, was the cause of much debate. Clearly neither side was interested in creating yet another layer of mindless regulation; still, both sides seemed willing to use the specter of such regulation as a fear factor in their debates. The bill was noble enough in purpose, I supposed, but at risk of floundering without agreement on how to accomplish that purpose.

At that point the senator stopped his narrative and surprised me by asking my opinion, as if I held sway as an expert in his field.

"What do you think of this bill, Dr. Morgan?"

I had to pause a moment before I could form a reasonable response.

"I support the intent, of course, but I also share some of the concerns I've seen discussed in the media. Nobody wants Big Brother in the boardroom, and requiring corporations to produce a lot of large reports is expensive—for the government as well as corporate America. But there are a few things that could be done that would have prevented something like Replete from ever happening, or at least made it a lot more difficult."

"Please explain."

"It would take more than a moment's thought to be complete, Senator, but I can suggest a few things worth considering. First, board-level decisions that have inherent conflict of interest, such as compensation plans, should be made by a referendum of shareholders. Second, to accomplish that, shareholders need to know how well the executives are performing. There's a metric for that, by the way, called the 'market value added' or MVA that shows how well a management team increases shareholder equity. That kind of information needs to be created independently and regularly given to the investors. Third, if you're going to have transparency, shareholders need the ability to communicate with each other."

"Why?"

"Because communication—at least mutual awareness— is a prerequisite for the emergence of a system, in this case an investor community. Without it nothing happens. For example, we have done simulations of what happens to that flock of birds when you suddenly make them all blind. The flock fails. Just knowing the MVA or a proposed executive salary doesn't help because the individual investor can do nothing about it, but an investor *community* could."

"I understand, Dr. Morgan, but implementation is still the key constraint. How would that be addressed?"

"Without time to design the solution, I would envision an online voting system for the referendums, and for communication an online bulletin board for shareholders of record as of the day of any action. It would take some thought to make it practical and secure, but we have people on staff who do that sort of thing."

The senator excused himself, taking his staffers into the outer office for a moment, then returned with a request.

"This Replete Group is a prime example of how important our bill is. What we need, though, is an authoritative report that explains how Replete operates—stated hypothetically, of course—and what features the bill must have to prevent such abuse. Now, my committee has some discretionary funds that could pay for a modest study. Do you think your Institute would allow you to take it on?"

Opportunity had skipped past knocking and seemed to be breaking down my door.

"I am certain there will be interest. I will be in my office tomorrow; can I get you a proposal early next week?"

The senator smiled. By the time we shook hands at his door I was already making plans, plans that went far beyond the senator's bill. Looking at my watch, though, had me scurrying out the building. We had talked into early afternoon and I was due at the FBI in a half hour.

A taxi was much faster than walking the several blocks between buildings, and a lot faster than driving and trying to find another parking spot. Still, I walked into the Deputy Director's outer office with just a minute to spare. As I would have expected from a man with Emerson's discipline, he stepped out to greet me at exactly three. When we were seated in his private office he looked at me squarely and asked, "What's on your mind?" in a no-nonsense tone, then sat forward to listen to what I had to say.

"I understand the Bureau had used Leonard Borgman and his team at the IAR on occasion, as had other government agencies. I don't know if you're aware, but without Dr. Borgman, the team has been disbanded. It is an esoteric field, as you know, and I'm curious as to your plans for filling future needs."

The deputy director hadn't considered this question before that moment, and I wasn't certain from his reaction if he felt it had any priority for him. I watched him sit back and think for a moment, then he addressed me again.

"Are you looking for a job, Dr. Morgan?"

Close, I thought. The man was astute, but I had other ideas. We discussed them for several minutes, and, when Emerson saw that I was merely gathering information, he became a fount of knowledge. In under a half hour I had the basic information and the contact names to continue my quest. More importantly, I had his support.

Before I left I asked Emerson what he expected would happen with the Replete Group members.

"Expedience, Dr. Morgan. It's not a complete solution, but it will work for a while. Now that the members don't have those group directives, we expect operations to return to business as usual in each of those companies. That should buy us time, if nothing else. But I must tell you, this is very, very big. I can't overemphasize the need for your discretion."

I thought carefully about my conversation with the senator and his staffers, and was confident nothing had compromised my confidentiality agreement. In another minute our conversation wrapped up, and I thanked him for his time and support.

I walked the blocks back to my car near the Senate office building, pulling my phone out to call Amber on the way. The oppressive heat of the past weekend had broken, being replaced by air that was much drier as well as cooler. It was as if the weather itself had reacted to news that Shipley was gone. I told Amber I'd be picking her up at her office in a short time, then looked at the deep queue of messages I had received.

Between text messages and voicemail I found that I had achieved a few minutes of fame back home, and looked up the news feed to get the details. The news media, rarely willing to accept a story as thin as the one concerning my shooting, had found that:

"...while the identities of the two gunmen had not been disclosed, the man injured in that exchange was Dr. Roger Morgan, a principal researcher for the Institute for Emergent Systems Analysis. It is still not known if Dr. Morgan was a bystander or if he was the target in the shooting..."

No wonder there were so many messages. I decided to call the office before the rumor mill had me dead and buried.

"Nicki, it's Roger," I said, then I had to stop walking for a moment so I could listen to the outpouring on the other end. I dearly loved and respected Nicki as my closest ally at the office, but given her perfunctory style and a bun behind her head so tight I swear she could hear a dog whistle, I overlooked how sensitive a person she was. It actually took me a moment to assure her I was alive, and another full minute before I could change the topic.

"Nicki, listen. I'm going to be in the office tomorrow morning. Seven-thirty sharp. I'll tell you more about this when I get there, okay?"

"Of course."

"Great. Now, I need you to do a couple things for me. First, let people know you've spoken with me and everything is fine. Second, get me a printout of all outbound phone calls from the building after five o'clock last Friday."

"The night of the break-in?"

"Yes, the night of the break-in. And can you please transfer me to Ariel's office?"

I continued walking until Ariel Ming, our COO, was on the line. There was a near-repeat of the conversation with Nicki before I could get a word in about anything else.

"I thought you were in DC, Roger. What were you doing at the convention?"

"I'm going to be in the office tomorrow, Ariel. I'll explain it then. A lot has happened, and I need to talk to you right away at eight. Can you clear your schedule?"

"Let me…yes, I can clear it. Until ten o'clock be okay?"

"Better clear all morning just in case. Sorry."

"I'm bumping a new client for you, Roger."

"It will be worth it, Ariel. I promise."

In a half hour I had Amber in the car with me, and a half hour after that we were in the drop-off zone at Reagan National.

"You'd better be back Monday at the latest, Roger, or I'm selling your rental car," she warned with a smile, and gave me the lustiest send-off kiss whe could without drawing undue attention. I would definitely be back.

Having been spoiled by the FBI I had upgraded to a first-class seat for the ride home. Of course, I also was trying to avoid rubbing my tender shoulder against some person seated next to me in the back of the plane. Besides, I wanted to get what sleep I could on the flight, or, barring sleep, work on a proposal I intended to make. As it turned out, I was able to do a little of both, working for the first half of the flight and then asleep until we were well into our descent.

My apartment was much as I left it, except it had been cleaned to within an inch of its life. The service I used was thorough, and I left another note for them thanking them for their attention to detail and advising that I'd be out another week at least. That done, I stripped to my skivvies and sat in front of my computer for another hour or so, completing the log I had started and then working on my proposal and dealing with email. Nicki had sent me the phone records I had requested, and it only took a few minutes to see what I expected to see. After that I sent out reassuring emails to those who had heard about the shooting, and after that I called Amber. There was no news to tell her since we parted, and she had nothing new for me, but it was a high priority call nonetheless.

Having traveled between time zones so often in the past several days, my body failed to benefit from the extra time before six o'clock local. Instead, I awoke groggy, and took a prolonged shower to clear my head. The painkillers they had given me certainly didn't help with the head fog, and while I had enough for another two days, I decided to forgo them in favor of clarity at the office.

At seven-thirty sharp I walked into my office, dressed to partially conceal my sling so I'd be less of a spectacle. It didn't help. Nicki was there waiting for me, and a half-dozen others crammed in to hear the tale almost before I could sit down. I shooed them out after a brief and, I'm sure, unsatisfying statement, and then closed the door so I could talk to Nicki alone. I told her as much as I could in fifteen minutes, then promised to give more detail after my meeting with Ariel. That's all the time I would have had with her anyway, as my friend Jerry knocked on my door and walked with me to Ariel's office rather than letting me off with the short form of my story.

"Okay, Roger, who is she?" Jerry asked. "A story like this, there *has* to be a girl."

"Ha! Well, as a matter of fact, I did meet a woman or two in DC, but I was on vacation, remember?" A little bit of mystery was a good thing, as it fueled his imagination enough to tide him over until we had more time to talk. "By the way, are you free this weekend?"

"What's up?"

"I need your help on a real short-fused proposal if you can. Oh, and I'll be gone next week again."

"Okay, then, sure. I'm available by executive fiat, I guess." He grinned at me when he said that; I would never need to pull rank on him. "Call me later with the plan, okay, Buddy?"

"We'll have a kick-off meeting when I'm done in here," I said, and walked into Ariel's office at precisely eight.

"Roger! You look great, considering how the stories had you so close to death." Ariel wasn't one to gush, but this was an extreme case. "Now, what the hell is this all about? I'm completely lost."

"Thank you. I'm fine, actually, just a nick on my shoulder. I'll tell you all about it in a little bit. Then, I need to discuss a business proposal with you. It's big, Ariel, and you're going to like it. First, though, we have a personnel matter we need to handle this morning. Can you get Marc in here?" Marcus Ritter was our Director of Human Resources. "We'll need Cynthia Holt, too."

When the four of us were assembled around Ariel's conference table I launched into an abridged description of the Replete Group, John Carstairs (the name they knew Shipley by) and Special Agent Larry Scanlon. All I needed to explain at that point is that Carstairs desperately wanted information he thought I might have, and had co-opted Scanlon to find it.

"Cynthia, when we saw each other last Thursday night you were very interested in Leonard Borgman and in my DC itinerary. Why was that?"

Her eyes shifted around the table before answering. "It was just social conversation, Roger, you know that."

"And you met with Carstairs on Friday morning?"

"Yes, I did, but what of it? Ariel met with him also."

"What happened Friday night?"

"I went home, Roger. Alone, if that's what you are asking."

"It's not. I'm more interested in when you left and what you did before that."

"I left around five or five-thirty, Roger. What could you possibly be getting at?"

I looked into Cynthia's eyes and mentally pleaded with her to be honest with me, but she didn't flinch.

"I'm sorry, Cynthia, but I know you didn't leave until much later." I looked at the others, confirming I had their full attention before continuing. Then I showed her my cell phone call history.

"Here is a call you made to me after I landed in DC that night. I didn't notice then, but the call came from your office phone. Here it is on the office phone record."

They all took a look at the item above my fingertip.

"There's more, though. About forty-five minutes later you made another call. Right here. This one was to the FBI in Washington, DC, the office of Agent Larry Scanlon, to be precise."

Cynthia was still now, the wheels behind her eyes working at light speed on how she could talk her way out of this. Then I addressed Ariel and Marc.

"Here's what happened. John Carstairs wanted to know if information he was looking for was in my office. He got Cynthia to fake the break-in, making sure to compromise the confidential files so Ariel would have to call in the FBI. When she was done she called Scanlon, a rogue agent who was on Carstairs's payroll. Scanlon worked with the local FBI office to tell them what to look for and gather up the results. All very neat, except for the phone records."

All eyes turned to Cynthia.

"I don't suppose you knew they might try to kill me when you told them where I was on Monday, did you?" I didn't believe she did, but I was applying full pressure and it worked. Cynthia was suddenly anxious to confess to lesser transgressions.

"Roger, I swear I had no idea what this was all about! Carstairs was a new prospect, that's all I knew. He said he was trying to get you to work with him, and would pay me to help him. He needed to get your office searched, and later he asked me to help him find you. That's all I did, honest! You have to believe me!"

I looked at Ariel, and she gave me a knowing look and a nod of agreement. Then I looked at Marcus, giving him a tacit heads-up before turning back to Cynthia.

"I'm sorry, Cynthia, but you're done here at the Institute. I don't know about filing false reports with the FBI or whatever else you may have done, but the Institute won't abide a breach of trust." Then to Marcus, "We'll want the full separation agreement, with non-compete, in exchange for two months' salary."

Marcus walked a stunned Cynthia out of Ariel's office, our eyes following them in silence until they were out of earshot. Ariel was a bit stunned by it herself, I suppose, but I knew what she inwardly thought of Cynthia, and I knew the news of Cynthia's scheming came as no surprise. I, on the other hand, had other inward thoughts at that moment. Sad ones. Cynthia and I had been close, after a fashion.

"Two months, Roger?"

"I know. Standard severance would be a lot more, but this is termination for cause. Could just as easily have said zero severance, but I wanted to give her enough reason to sign the separation agreement."

Ariel looked at me with approval. As COO this sort of thing was technically in her court, but I held *de facto* sway over the technical staff. I had never flaunted her authority, though, so we got along very well at the office.

"Okay," she said. "There will be ripples to this one, as I'm sure you know, but we'll make it through the day. I'll make an announcement on Monday. Before then I'll need your input on reassignments to cover her projects. Deal? Now, tell me what has happened to you!"

"I was honestly just trying to take a vacation, Ariel, when I guess I stumbled into a mess that an old friend had gotten into." With that opening I spent a full half-hour describing the events of the past several days, avoiding anything the FBI might consider delicate. When I was done, Ariel had a look on her face like she had been chased and beaten and shot at herself. It was one of those stories that was big enough without having to grow in the telling, and I found myself actually downplaying parts to maintain full credibility. When it was done, though, I was able to segue nicely into the topic that held the most interest for me.

"There is a big opportunity for us right now, Ariel. The IAR has decided to disband Borgie's group, believing it would be impractical to replace him. That is going to force various government agencies to outsource their needs, if possible, and, as we know, the Institute is the best alternative out there. Others do exist, though, and if one of them should get the inside track on a number of government jobs, they could build up enough momentum to eclipse us. I mean, the amount of potential work there is really that large."

"So what do you propose we do?"

I spent the next two hours explaining my plan, debating various points with her until each was clear. Ariel didn't oppose me at all, but she knew she needed to be able to defend my proposal with the CEO and the Board of Directors. I wasn't worried, though. They might make Ariel jump through the hoops of due diligence, but I knew what I was asking for was reasonable and highly profitable. Besides, they were highly motivated to keep me happy.

"One last thing," I said. "I've been asked by Senator Wyecroft to propose a small study related to a bill he has before Congress. It needs very fast turnaround. If you don't object, I'd like to pull a team together for the weekend—an overtime project."

"You met with Senator Wyecroft?" Ariel couldn't hide the surprise in her voice. "This has been some vacation, Roger! Yes, certainly, pull a team together."

"Thanks. By the way, I'll be delivering the proposal to him on Monday in DC. I should be gone most of the week, I expect."

"Keep in touch this time, will you? You're not on vacation anymore."

I smiled, and she gave me a look of genuine concern and support before I left her office. From there I walked back to my office to find Nicki, fielding any number of questions and best wishes along the way.

"Nick, I'm going to need your help."

She grabbed her ever-present writing pad and asked what I needed.

"First, I need a proposal team." I listed several names for her, and asked her to have them in the conference room for me in a half hour. "Then I need tickets to DC for late Sunday, returning...well, make it for Wednesday evening and we'll change it if we need to."

While she tracked down the others I placed a call to Dale Crest, our VP of Business Development. After the expected discussion about my week I explained the Wyecroft opportunity and invited him to the *ad hoc* proposal meeting in a half hour. Dale's immediate reaction was to show me just a bit of frustration, telling me he should have been brought into it earlier. I ignored his angst, opting instead to dangle a carrot.

"We have some big opportunities out there, Dale. We've done very little in that area, compared to what we could be doing, and this is our foot in the door. I'm hoping you'll join us."

"I'll be at the kick-off meeting, but I'm not sure about the weekend. I'm pretty booked…"

Frankly—sadly—I had expected that from him. Dale was one of those guys that had been so successful in his work, sales in his case, that he had been promoted above his level of competence. He could schmooze customers and was good at chatting and picking up a restaurant tab, but since he'd made VP others always did the work. The opportunities in DC had been there a long time, even though Borgie was there, yet Dale hadn't worked many of them in spite of having a large staff. In my long-term plan, his role was going to be diminished.

My proposal meeting began on time, the staff fully aware of how the Institute felt about one late person causing the loss of several man-hours. Seated at the table were Dale, Jerry for program management, three systems analysts and Nicki. Except for Dale, all were fully committed to getting a final proposal completed for delivery on Monday afternoon. I was to review it on the plane Sunday night, and we scheduled a teleconference for early Monday, local time, in the event of changes. In a transparent show of participation, Dale asked Nicki to send him a copy of the draft proposal for his review when it was ready on Sunday.

I have to admit my mind wandered while we worked on the proposal. It was a foot-in-the-door opportunity we were working on, yet I felt I was both present in the war room we had set up and somewhere else, as if observing myself on hidden camera. I would be focused on the task in front of me one moment, then find myself reliving my DC experiences, then mentally list candidates to replace Cynthia on her active programs, then my proposal to Ariel and finally back to real time issues. Overlaid on all that was Amber, a study in poise and inner beauty augmented with a sharp mind and keen eye. Most of all, she was enthusiasm—in all the right subjects. I was home again, in my most natural and familiar surroundings, and yet I knew my little vacation had precipitated permanent change. Whether that change would be permanent or not was completely up to me to decide.

The remainder of Friday and Friday night were spent on developing the concept of our proposal, the actual services we offered and their expected results. That effort required me to tell the team quite a bit about the Replete Group, and in what became a mental diversion from the proposal pressure we spent a good half-hour debating the ethics of the very rich. I stayed out of it for a while, interested in hearing their thoughts without my unintended influence. Then I began asking some simple questions. Is it wrong to be successful? Is it unethical to accept a higher salary? Should an executive do what is best for the company, or best for his bonus plan? Shouldn't a board of directors define what is best for the company and use that as the basis for a bonus plan? Ethics was indeed a complex topic, and corporate ethics even more so.

Outside of that and maybe a few more mental breaks, the team showed surprising focus. Once we had the services defined, we spent Saturday estimating the amount of work each would require. Sunday we estimated the costs of that work, reviewed and polished the write-up, and iterated as much as time would permit. By the time I was running for the airport, I had a draft that I was confident in. The team had performed very well.

My shoulder was feeling much better by that time, and I had been able to avoid the use of my pain meds for nearly the whole weekend. One of the two exceptions to that was as I waited to board my flight. Towing my luggage and carrying a computer bag, along with the extended hours we had put in over the weekend, took a toll that manifested itself in a dull, throbbing pain, and I finally decided to take a pill. I slept the entire flight without glancing at the proposal.

When Amber picked me up at the airport I had to fight the temptation to blurt out all my plans. I had decided to wait, though. I wanted to be sure our proposal to Wyecroft was well received before I told her. Better that I would be telling her about a "gonna do" than a "hope to do," I thought. Instead I sat on the passenger side of my rental car and watched her smoothly navigate the light evening traffic. She was aware I was watching her, and she certainly seemed to enjoy the attention.

I hadn't been inside Amber's apartment until that night. It was larger than Lisa's—I suppose that's why Lisa had planned to move there instead of the other way around—and my first impression was similar to the one I had in Lisa's home. Of course, Amber knew I was coming, but still there was a casual neatness to it, not the freshly scrubbed look of a place hurriedly prepared for visitors. There were no vacuum cleaner marks on the carpet, no fanned magazines on the coffee table or other signs that gave that "don't touch, I just cleaned that" impression. Instead it had an inviting look, one that spoke to Amber's caring nature.

She showed me that caring nature after we had shared a bottle of wine and a light snack. Any grogginess from that pain pill was gone after my in-flight nap, but the residual effects of that extra rest contributed to, well, to a strong showing that night. It was clear that Amber had intended to focus on my enjoyment, but in the end she appeared equally pleased. I was many miles from my home, yet this had felt like a true homecoming.

In time even Amber's enthusiasm had to give way to sleep. Between my earlier sleep and the time zone difference I remained awake for a while, lying next to her, feeling her warmth radiating onto my skin while I once again reviewed my plans. The steps I was considering were considerable, but I wasn't questioning them. I was instead refining them, ensuring each step I was about to take was moving me to an appropriate goal. There were no guarantees, but I was confident nonetheless.

Monday morning came early, it seemed, but that was okay. It gave me time to complete the proposal review I had failed to accomplish on the plane. Amber took the subway to work as she typically did, leaving me in her apartment to work and, in a few hours, to hold the teleconference with my proposal team. I was alone in her place, and I sat quietly for a few minutes, looking around the room and asking myself how I could have become so involved so very quickly. In a few moments, though, I knew the speed didn't matter. Regardless of pace, the involvement was there.

My review of the proposal produced only a handful of edits, mostly in the pricing area. I didn't think the Institute needed to low-ball the price—it wasn't a competitive situation, after all—but we were breaking new ground, establishing a foothold in a new market. I wanted the price to reflect our long-term business intent. I didn't expect the senator to have more projects, of course, but I did hope he would be a willing reference for future business in the area. I chose a target price in my head, then went through the pricing computation to see how we could make it work.

At the appointed time I turned on my computer and set up a video link through the Institute's server. The team was assembled at the other end, with Jerry acting as point man. Dale was present, having positioned himself in the center of the group, but unsurprisingly, he had little to contribute. The system analysts considered my idea for reducing their time estimates, meeting me halfway to my pricing goal. The rest had to come from tightening the reins on the overhead computation and the corporate margin. I was okay with it; on a small contract like this one there weren't that many dollars at stake. Dale, on the other hand, decided to flex his muscles and debate the point until he felt like he had done his part for the cause, then he simply acquiesced. Nicki took careful notes of it all, and promised to have the updated proposal in my email within a half hour.

While I waited for Nicki's email, my phone rang. It was Jerry.

"Roger, you dog!" Something had stirred his prurient interests, not that that would take much.

"What? Shouldn't you be giving the final numbers to Nicki right now?"

"Yeah, right. She already has them. Now quit teasing. I saw your video feed. Where are you? That was no hotel room."

Oh. Jerry had seen Amber's living room over my shoulder. "Yeah…um…I'm at a friend's place."

"Ha! Tell your friend he decorates like a woman. You're a dog, Roger! You can't do this without at least letting me live vicariously on your exploits."

"Yeah, well, all in good time. Did you call for a reason, or did you just want to give me a hard time?"

"Okay. Yeah, there's a reason. There's a loud buzz around the office today about Cynthia. What the hell happened, Roger? Some people are saying you two had a big fight and you canned her."

"You know better than that, Jerry. Look, Ariel will be making an announcement in another hour or so. There was nothing personal about it. Cynthia broke the rules and had to go; that's it."

I hated this. Office gossip was always quick to conjure up the worst explanation for any management action, and once a manager got painted the wrong color it was hard to change it.

"Do me a favor, will you? I'll tell you some of what happened if you'll help set the story straight with the troops, okay?"

"Sure. So what's up?"

"Cynthia allowed herself to be taken in by a prospective client who wanted some sensitive information. She ended up trying to get it for him and got caught. Nothing personal, Jerry, but she had to go. You know how the Institute feels about trust."

"No details for me?"

"Better not."

"Okay. Well, people know what she was like. Nobody will be surprised to hear this."

"Sad but true. But keep it all on the down-low, okay? The official word from Ariel will be a benign 'pursuing other career options' type of statement."

"Sure thing. And Roger? You don't really have to worry. People know you a lot better than that. You're still the office hero; they just want to know your armor is still shiny."

"Thanks, buddy."

"Okay, I'll let you go. Tell her 'Hi' for me…!"

"Yeah, yeah."

As soon as Jerry's call ended I received the proposal from Nicki and took it to a print shop to be reproduced. It looked good, and I made a mental note to thank the team and to let Nicki know she had done a great layout job once again. From there I stopped for a quick lunch, and then left for the senator's office to deliver our proposal.

I was flying high as I drove to the Russell building. The fact was, this proposal was probably just a formality. I was pretty sure Senator Wyecroft was going to give us this small study contract, as long as it fit in the discretionary funds he had mentioned. Given the contract, the hole left behind when the IAR decided not to replace Borgie, and the information I had gotten from Deputy FBI Director Emerson, I was highly confident my long term plan would be in process very shortly. And Amber, I knew, would be pleased.

I didn't get to see the senator in his office. He was there, but occupied in his inner office. His aide greeted me, though, and asked me to wait while he took a copy of the proposal in to show the senator. Then he took another copy to his desk and flipped through it, marking several pages as he went along. I hadn't expected that; typically a proposal would be reviewed by a team over a period of days or weeks, but he seemed to be doing it all right then in real time. At length he stood and went into the senator's office again. After a few minutes he returned and told me there was one issue—the schedule. The work had to be completed in four weeks. I gulped a little, realizing I'd have to bump another project back home to accomplish that, but in the end it was a no-brainer. That other project was with a low-key client and wasn't at all time-critical. Besides, this was the start of something big, and I knew Ariel and the program manager for the other effort would support the decision. A phone call confirmed that.

After penciling in the schedule change on the contract, the aide went back into Wyecroft's office and came out with the Senator's go-ahead. An hour later the senate's procurement office signed the contract, which must have been some sort of Capitol Hill record. Wyecroft knew we would come through for him and had greased the skids before I ever got there.

I left the Russell building elated, my grand plan having been given a rousing start. When I got to my car I called Nicki, and ten minutes later was holding a conference call with the team, sitting in the shade of the parking ramp so I could focus on the call.

"Everyone there?" Dale was missing and one of the systems analysts was out of the office for the afternoon. We had a quorum. "Okay, I have good news and bad news. Good news is we have a contract. You guys did an outstanding job this weekend."

"Already?" It was Jerry's voice. "That's impossible!"

"Wyecroft's stock is at an all time high this week, it seems. He got it pushed through with initials and a phone call. But here's the other thing. Schedule is all-important. We have four weeks."

It took a moment for that to sink in.

"That's a drop-everything deal, Roger. Any wiggle room on that?"

"None. Get started today. Jerry, you're the PM. As soon as you get things rolling there you'll need to fly out here so I can introduce you to your contact here. Now, everyone needs to understand this: the results of our work will be used to support Senator

Wyecroft's bill, and that bill is a cornerstone of his campaign. This is Washington, DC, okay? It's politics over substance around here, and the politics says it has to be done in four weeks. Got it?"

They did.

"Okay. Congratulations, everyone. This is the start of something huge. Get to it; Jerry, I'll see you Wednesday at the latest, right?"

"See you then."

I started up the engine, feeling the kind of excitement one rarely gets in that kind of business. Everything was going like clockwork, allowing me to think once again about my personal agenda. I had a lot to tell Amber that night, and I wanted to do it with style. With a couple of hours to go before I was to meet her at her office, I decided to research the area a bit and select an appropriate venue for our talk. I didn't want formal—neither of us would be dressed for it anyway—but I wanted it to be special, and it had to be someplace quiet enough to converse. As a stranger to the area, I was just starting to feel at a loss when I got a text message.

Meet me at my place.

It was from Amber. She must have gotten off early and taken the subway home. I quickly got my bearings and steered toward her place, picking up speed as I got closer. When I got to the driveway into her complex I pulled up to a visitor spot and spring out of the car. I hadn't really noticed the tradesman van that pulled up near me, but the side door opened at the same time I stood up, and a moment later all was dark.

My eyes opened to the inside of a moving van, sitting uncomfortably on the floor with duct tape around my feet and wrists. There was another person in the back with me, eyes wide with a mix of apprehension and relief at my regaining consciousness. Amber had been taken as well, and had been sweltering in that van since her lunch break. Judging by the signs that flew by the one window I could see through, we were about halfway to Baltimore.

My head was throbbing, and they had laid me on my sore shoulder, but it wasn't a good time to let Amber see my discomfort. "Are you all right?" I whispered to her, drawing a glare from the man in the passenger seat. It was the man we had referred to as "Amber's ex"; the man we had seen at her office a week earlier and again in Hanover's hotel. I cursed aloud. We'd thought this was over—but we were wrong.

"I'm okay," Amber whispered urgently, "but look who's driving."

I could only see the back of his head, but it was enough for me to guess who it was. A long shock of hair had blown off his head and hung from just above his left ear, revealing a sizable bald spot. I hadn't seen him before, but from Amber's earlier "comb over" description I knew it was former FBI agent Larry Scanlon.

A whispered exchange with Amber confirmed my guess. It also confirmed that she knew no more than I did about our destination. Then I remembered something. Shipley had planned to have Amber taken to someplace in Baltimore back when I was being kept in his “cellar,” only at that time they were intending to hold her there until they got what they wanted from me. I had a feeling this time would be a more temporary visit. The only question I had was “Why?” Shipley was gone. Did he have a partner?

Twenty minutes later we pulled up to a building in Baltimore. Scanlon and his man climbed into the back of the van, unbound our feet and put hoods on our heads, a precaution that seemed unnecessary given their apparent intent. They half-walked, half-dragged us into a building. I couldn’t see it, but judging by my other senses the building was not an open warehouse. It was more of a musty old office building, at least partly abandoned, from the sound of things, and possessing a short hallway to a door though which we were unceremoniously shoved. On the other side was fresher, cooler air and an even more chilling presence, one I felt even though we had yet to hear or see it.

“We are back,” Scanlon announced. “No problems. Nobody saw us.”

Then to us Scanlon said, “Take those hoods off so I can introduce you to the boss.”

“Senator,” I said, addressing him just before I tugged on my hood.

The man seated before me gave a momentary look before asking the obvious question.

“So you did know about me then.” It was State Senator Ron Hanover.

Even Amber, when her hood was removed, looked at me in surprise.

"I actually know very little, except that you are the real founder of the Replete Group. What I don't understand, though, is why we are here."

"Why? You have a lot of nerve, Dr. Morgan. And you have been more than a problem for us ever since John decided to involve you. Do you know what you've done? You have cost me the entire Replete membership and a fortune in dues, and you are responsible for the death of my half-brother. Yes, John Foster Shipley. My mother's son.

"We had the perfect setup. John wanted to run corporate America, and I wanted to become a senator. Maybe even more. And we were building the wealth and power that comes with all that. Together we would have controlled a major portion of the US, no, the *world*, economy. You have no idea, Morgan! You can't possibly understand what it is like to be a king! Another two years and we would have been unstoppable. But now…now I have to start over without John. But first I need to deal with you."

"What can you possibly need from us?"

"I need to know what you know. How did you discover the Replete Group? How did you know about me? How many others know? Damn it, tell me now or watch your girlfriend suffer for your stubborness!"

"Actually I only guessed about you," I said, truthfully. I couldn't call it deduction when so much had been speculative. Still, the odds had been in my favor, I thought. Hanover had ties to Shipley, the man now holding a gun on me had been seen in his hotel, and he was the man with the most to gain from getting Wyecroft out of the race. I also strongly suspected that the reason the FBI wanted us in Hanover's hotel lobby that past Tuesday before I was shot was to let him see us. The FBI, I thought, must have already had questions about Ron Hanover.

"Wrong answer, Doctor," and, with a nod to his man, I received a powerful fist to my stomach.

The punch caught me by surprise and penetrated deep. I fell forward into my assailant, causing him to grab me with his arms under mine, almost in a hug, with his gun pointing out from behind me. In a swift move, Amber, who had been held by one shoulder in front of Scanlon, threw her foot up behind her and caught the rogue agent in the groin. It was my only opportunity. I squeezed my arms down to trap his and lurched to the side, taking the man and his gun to the floor. In concert with my move, Amber thrust herself backward, throwing Scanlon against a cabinet. Scanlon's gun went loose on the floor, and Amber, closer and faster than either Scanlon or Hanover, was able to retrieve it. By the time I had knocked the gun out of the other man's hand, we had control of the room.

Twenty-some very tense minutes passed before the first cops responded to our 9-1-1 call, and another fifteen before an FBI team arrived from the Baltimore office. By the time Hanover and the others were about to be taken away, SAIC Hanson and Agents Dorrow and Wright arrived. During all that time Hanover refused to speak, but Scanlon was just the opposite. He screamed at Hanover, lamenting the career he had been lured out of to serve Replete. He promised to tell the FBI everything he knew, from bribery to manipulation to murder, in hopes of lighter treatment.

As his tirade progressed I realized the motivation behind it: a dirty FBI agent had a short life expectancy in prison. Scanlon was in a panicked fight for survival.

"This one is going to be much messier than last week, I'm afraid," Hanson told me as we stood outside and out of the way of the arresting officers.

"Why?" Amber asked. "It seems like we've finally gotten to the root of the problem. It's finally over, isn't it?"

"For the two of us, yes," I reassured her, "but there's still a problem. Hanover's alive. All the things that nobody wanted to make public are now going to come out. Shipley's prediction of a Pyrrhic victory could come true. This could be a real disaster for our economy."

"And there's no way to stop it?" she asked.

"Nothing easy," Hanson told her. "Nothing easy."

After completing our statements at the scene, our FBI friends gave us a ride back to Amber's apartment. On the way we described the nerve-wracking moment when Amber kicked Scanlon and took his gun.

"He's an old guy who worked white-collar cases from a desk," she said. "I guess I thought I could take him."

Hanson and company laughed out loud at that, while I looked at her with yet another degree of respect. I had better be nice to this girl!

Then I asked Hanson about my earlier assumptions, the ones that led me to believe it was Hanover the whole time.

"Were we put in the lobby at Hanover's hotel to see if he would recognize us?"

Hanson was evasive at first, then apparently decided to be straight with us. "We had been watching him on a campaign fraud case that started about two years ago. Something wasn't right, and we wanted to see how deeply he was mixed up in this Replete thing with Shipley. You weren't being used as bait. The rest of that day was completely unexpected."

I believed him, maybe just because I wanted to.

It wasn't long before we had left Baltimore and were back in Amber's apartment. In spite of the day we'd had, we still needed to eat and I still had an agenda to fulfill. It took no convincing to get Amber interested in going out, and we ended up at a comfortable local Italian restaurant only five miles from her place. By the time we were seated and had our first glasses of wine on the table, the day's ordeal was enough of a memory that we could discuss it without all the emotion we had felt that afternoon. It started with the basics.

"Are we really safe this time, Roger?"

"I think so. We may be called in as witnesses from time to time, but that should be all that's left for us. It's in the FBI's hands now."

"I see," she said. She had become quieter, more pensive, and I had a pretty good idea what was on her mind. "So where do we go from here?"

"I've been thinking about that. You know, I can't stay on vacation forever, and I don't think you would want me in your apartment indefinitely anyway. But there is some good news. The proposal I delivered today. Wyecroft accepted it already."

"That's great, Roger, and you know I'm happy for you, but it doesn't really solve the whole problem, does it?"

"Hmm. Yes, I suppose you're right. But there is more to the story, if you're interested."

Amber looked up again to meet my eyes. "Of course I'm interested. Don't tease, Roger. This is important."

We had been through hell. We had been chased and kidnapped and shot at and kidnapped again and threatened with death, several others actually were dead and we had stopped a scheme that was draining billions from the US economy every year, yet this is what Amber felt was important. And I agreed with her priorities.

"Well, it's really much more than the one contract. When I was home I met with my COO, and I guess I gave something of an ultimatum. You see, the Institute has always had opportunities here, but we didn't have the presence to capitalize on them. Now that the IAR shuttered Borgie's operation and we have Wyecroft's endorsement, we have some great opportunities. Anyway, I pointed all that out to Ariel, my COO, and told her I intended to spend quite a bit of my time developing this market. The market here is big, Amber. It's going to take some time to get our arms around it. There will even be a lot of interesting technical work to go along with it."

The look she gave me was somewhere between damp-eyed relief and wide-eyed excitement. "Roger! This is huge! Will you be moving here?"

"I was hoping you'd help me find a nice place. I'm planning to be here about sixty percent of the time starting, well, now I guess."

"You mean like three days a week?"

"No set schedule. I'll need to keep a presence in the home office—I'm a resource for a lot of projects there—but I want to focus here. That will change in the long term, of course, but I'm sure I'll have options."

Amber thought about that, and then she beamed at me. We ended up eating our pasta quickly so we could have a more private celebration, as if carbo-loading for an evening marathon. Amber was happy, and I found that a happy Amber was a very energetic Amber.

The next morning we saw a news report about an incident in Baltimore that involved State Senator Ron Hanover. Although details were scarce, Hanover had apparently been providing information to local FBI authorities regarding a large-scale investment scam when violence broke out. Another man, a former FBI agent accused of collaboration with unspecified criminal elements, had somehow grabbed a makeshift knife and stabbed Hanover before applying that knife to his own throat.

The few facts in the report were true, the result of a carefully crafted news release, and a very large bullet to our economy was dodged.

9

CHANGED

We tend to think of time as a linear flow of events, with each second or hour or day having the same duration as the one before it. Yet, when I think of the period between that Department of Transportation presentation and the fateful news of Hanover and Scanlon, those days seem very long compared to the rapidly spinning clock of the ensuing months.

Jerry flew to DC as planned, deftly handling our new contract with Wyecroft's staff and soon thereafter becoming the Director of Program Management for the DC region. Of course, that meant he spent some social time with me and Amber, who admittedly needed a few exposures before understanding that Jerry's constant wishful thinking was, in fact, just that. They even became good friends.

The Wyecroft contract was a hallmark of success for us to use in new business pursuits, which, thanks to contacts made through the senator and through the Deputy Director of the FBI, were plentiful. We even made inroads with the Canadian government. I soon had to make proposal assignments on a rotation basis to avoid pulling our employees from their primary roles for too long. Of course, with Nicki's help, I also began building a local capability for our bid and proposal work. It didn't take long for me to convince

Ariel that we needed to move Dale's office to the DC area, but given his roots and his wife's thriving legal practice, he decided instead to leave the Institute. That was old school, maybe, but we got the desired result.

When I wasn't pursuing new business or working directly on the resulting projects, I kept a curious eye on the Replete Group membership. I knew better than to ask the FBI what was happening, but there were clear signs that change was in process. Quarterly financial reports from many of the Replete companies showed dramatic reductions in bonus plan payouts. At the same time, several board members and even top executives found it was time to step down to pursue other opportunities or simply retire. These people were not going to starve—in spite of their complicities they would remain materially replete, the price we paid for a graceful exit from this mess, I supposed.

In parallel with that, Senator Wyecroft, who was re-elected in a landslide, had used our study to bolster his strong case for boardroom transparency and accountability. Thanks to our work, he had created a viable means inter-stockholder communication. Already active investor communities had begun to emerge in certain companies. Those corporations, each of which had been in Replete (through no small coincidence, I was sure), embraced the idea of shareholder communications well ahead of the bill's passage. I often suspected Wyecroft's office had convinced them to act as test cases, providing live proof of concept in a kind of restitution for their involvement in Replete.

I did not have much time to continue my pet project on ethics and the economy, but I never dropped it. Replete had been a case in point, showing how insidious bad ethics can be and how incredibly pervasive the effects. Replete's mode of operation allowed each member to rationalize bad behavior while, inwardly, they knew their actions were for personal benefit. The problem was that, having seen how easily it had been done, I knew there would be more. Wyecroft's bill was just an opening volley in an ongoing war.

Eventually, out of curiosity, I suppose, Amber and I tried to get back in contact with Chuck, the Wealth Gap Monitor guy we had met at the Einstein memorial. We wanted to tell him that he had been right, after a fashion, that the Replete Group had been real and that his Wealth Gap Monitor website had provided the initial clues to help stop it in its tracks. When he didn't respond to our messages, though, we knew it was just as well. There was actually little we could have told him without breaking our confidentiality agreement with the FBI. Besides, as a dedicated conspiracy theorist, he already knew he was right.

I didn't know what the future held for me and Amber—we would discover that as time unfolded—but it looked very promising. And she did have immediate impact: even though I was averaging around fifty hours per week, not including travel, I was working less than I had in the past. For the first time my work was only my living, and life was outside the office.

I had emerged.

D. T. Hopmann

If you enjoyed Replete:

Endo

by D. T. Hopmann

Kevin is planning his future, a new career filled with promise and opportunity as a talented technologist. But that future is still uncertain, and Kevin is already feeling pangs of separation from his friends and from the only life he has known for year.

Then a chance discovery changes everything. Endo. A few common laboratory parts, put together just so, generate clean, renewable energy out of thin air. It is a Holy Grail, a game changer with endless commercial applications. But when Kevin and his team start to develop the technology, they make a second discovery: someone else wants Endo, and will do anything to get it.

Now the race is on to make Endo theirs before someone gets hurt. Or worse. Pushed far beyond his roots, Kevin must learn leadership, business, and more if he is to succeed.

But first he must learn to survive.

Printed in Great Britain
by Amazon